Behold Ellowee

By T.L. Harty

Behold Ellowee

Front cover art: Cover Quill

Printed in the United States of America First

Printing, 2017

ISBN 978-0-9982854-0-5

This book is dedicated to my father and grandmother.

They taught me more in a childhood than I could have learned in a lifetime, if left to my own meanderings.

I miss you both daily.

Chapter 1 The Junction

Waking up in the country seems like it should be a picturesque experience. A passing breeze lightly tickles your face as it caresses you out of your slumber. Only the far-away song of a bird can be heard through the rustling leaves.

My experience, however, started with a vacuum cleaner running through the bedroom. It was my grandmother's not-so-subtle way of letting me know I was wasting my life with sleep.

I had learned a couple of tricks in my years of visiting Grammy and Gramps over the summers. Placing a pillow over my head helped to muffle the sound. It worked for a couple of summers until she counter-attacked with the banging technique (continually slamming the vacuum against the bed until I got up). Effective, yes, but *so* annoying!

"Grammy," I shouted, "can I just sleep for a couple more minutes?!"

To this, she would look at me like I was speaking Japanese and point to her ears to let me know she couldn't hear me. This was confirmation of just how irritating some of my family members could be. Scratch that…most of my family members.

There comes a point where it is useless to do battle with the vacuum and just get out of bed. I dragged my body toward the bathroom. But, because I was still groggy when I turned to sit on the toilet, there were miscalculations and my free fall started way too early. *BANG*! I then mumble something under my breath that has no business coming out of a thirteen-year-old mouth.

To add to this very unpleasant beginning to the morning is the ice-cold toilet seat. The only positive is that the bathroom is so small; it makes it possible to lean over while on the toilet to turn the shower on. It feels like a real timesaver. I spy the radio and get excited until remembering that, out in the country, I will have to settle for whatever stations have decent reception. Flipping through the channels, I hear mostly country music and that will never do. The best radio offering this morning is a lighter rock station.

As "Hot Blooded" by Foreigner plays on the radio, I get my clothes off and hop in the shower. Ah, this is paradise. So much can be accomplished in the privacy of a shower. Yes, there is the standard washing and cleaning business, but the freedom to do whatever, be whoever- awesome!

"Hot blooded, check it and see. I got a temperature a hundred and three…I'm hot-blooded, hot-bloooooooded!" I sound awesome. Just ask the rubber ducky over there near the shampoo, he'll tell you.

Holding a fake microphone, I switch to my roving reporter skills. "Hello Mr. Ducky," I smile while extending my hand to the little plastic dude. "What do you think of the performance you have been witnessing?" I bring the microphone back to me. "You say you love it and you've never heard such a beautiful voice? Well, Dave," I turn to face the imaginary cameras, "back to you in the studio. You heard it here first, straight from the ducky's mouth."

Suddenly, I became dizzy and unable to stand very well. I leaned on the side of the shower with my forehead on the wall, barely aware of the water hitting my back or the cold tiles touching my skin. I tried to shake my head a little to relieve the dizziness. Opening my eyes, there was a stage before me. A play was going on. It must be a Shakespearean play because it had a lot of words that were close to English, but not quite. I had studied this one in school, but struggled to remember what it was called. I realized at that moment I spend way too much time checking out Garrett in English class and not enough time listening to the teacher.

The play continued when the oddest thing happened. Someone, looking a lot like me, came on the stage and they were calling her Helena. I remember this play because, when we read it, the teacher had me read the role of the Amazon Queen because of my height. This is frustrating. Wait! Those are fairies and the name has the word dream in it because the fairies mess with people while they are dreaming. "A

Midsummer Night's Dream" is the name of this play and, if memory serves me right, it's almost over.

There was no taking my eyes off Helena when she was on stage. The resemblance to me was uncanny. When the play was over, everyone took their bows and curtain calls. When Helena came out she looked right in my direction when she bowed. She thought she was too good for such a small production and wondered if she would get the best reviews in the morning paper.

Bang! Bang! Bang! My Grammy pounded on the bathroom door. "Ms. Muriel, you are using all the hot water," she announced.

Her voice seemed muffled and I couldn't hear her that well. I was still staring at the stage and watching the audience stand to exit. Then the stage seemed to move farther away. When I reached my hand out, there was only cold tile.

"Did you hear me, young lady?" she persisted.

I could hear her, but responding was not coming easily. I pushed myself off the tiles and shook my head trying to clear away the fog before answering, "Uh, I'll be out in a minute."

She must have sensed something in my voice and asked, "Are you O.K.?"

"Of course I'm O.K. I've taken a shower before Grammy!" I joked.

"Can you answer a question without being sarcastic?" she prodded.

"Apparently not" was the response that ran through my head, but I opted to keep my mouth shut and stay out of trouble. I also wanted to figure out what just happened. My hands searched the tile for some clue. I smelled the shampoo, checked my head to see if it was injured and stood there with a dozen questions, but no answers.

Maybe a meal had disagreed with me and this was the result. Gramps told me about mushrooms in the area that caused hallucinations. The Indians used them in rituals a long time ago. My Gramps is a firm believer in using what the land has to offer. He and I had taken many scavenger hunts for watercress, wild mustard, mushrooms, etc. Maybe he misidentified a mushroom the last time he went out. He was getting older, but it was hard to believe he could make a mistake like that. He's sharp as a tack.

While drying off, I tried to remember what we had for dinner the night before. The harder I tried to remember, the more irritated I became. I threw on the clothes Grammy had laid out and brushed the matted nest of hair my careless drying off had produced.

My pajamas were a few days old and this was laundry day. They either got washed today or it had to wait another three days. I opened the bathroom door with the pajamas in hand to walk to the hallway hamper. Opening the hamper, I spotted my outfit from yesterday. That was odd, because Grammy usually liked us to wear an outfit more than once. Upon closer inspection, I saw that my shirt had red sauce all over it. We had spaghetti for dinner last night! Being a slob actually does have its advantages. I threw my pajamas in and skipped to the kitchen.

"Good morning, Gramps," I sang, as I kissed the top of his head. He still had a full head of hair and it was so soft that it tickled my nose. I asked, "Did you put mushrooms in last night's spaghetti sauce?"

"Oh sure, always do," he answered.

My Grandpa Wayne is a person who conserves his words and rarely wastes his breath. He will answer your questions and greet you politely. But, he had to be prompted for extra communication. I wasn't sure if he had always been like that or if he thought Grammy used enough words for both of them.

"Were they the mushrooms we find in the fields?" I asked.

"No," he finished. Taking a sip of his coffee, he looked up at me from his seat and smiled.

"Oh, then I give up. I thought maybe they were the hallucination-type mushrooms you have shown me. There was this theater in the shower and some woman that looked like me on stage," I explained.

He stared at me with a seriously confused look on his face.

"I know! It's crazy," I concluded. "Forget it."

Grammy was preparing breakfast for me and accidentally dropped the spatula on the floor. She started mumbling to herself and left the room. I got up to make myself some toast because my stomach was grumbling. "Is Grammy O.K.?" I inquired. Gramps just shrugged. I shrugged back.

"Gramps, where's the jam?" I tempted him to speak. He pointed to it on the table. I noticed his hands. They were leathery from years of use, dotted with age spots of different sizes and hues.

While putting jam on my toast, Grammy came back in the kitchen to continue making my breakfast. She was extra noisy and seemed a little agitated, but Gramps and I knew it was too early in the morning for one of us to have made her mad already. She walked over to the table and put eggs and fruit in front of me.

"Thank you Grammy! It looks yummy," I complimented.

"You're welcome, Muriel," she said. "Why don't you ever seem as happy to see me in the morning as you do your grandfather?"

"Well, Grammy," I explained, "there's this wild woman who wields a vacuum in the wee hours of the morning and a sweet woman who makes me breakfast. Sometimes, the trick lies in telling the difference." I chuckled, "Is that why you seem upset?" I stood up and kissed her on the forehead, "Good morning, Grammy."

She went back to flitting around the kitchen. I would swear there were tears as she worked. It broke my heart to see her cry, but I didn't understand what I had done. She tried to hide her face from us as best she could. Even the dogs seemed to sense all was not quite right. Grammy opened the kitchen door to shoo the dogs outside. I turned my attention towards Gramps in hopes of cajoling more words out of him.

"So, Gramps, what is on your agenda today?" I questioned.

"The usual," he said.

"Could you be a little more specific and maybe try a complete sentence?" I sighed.

He looked put out, but he did share his grand plans for the day. "Well," he started out slowly, "I need to tend to the garden, check the gopher traps…putter around here and there. Part of the fence has been bent for a while, so I might fix that." He saved the best for last when he added, "I plan on going to town to get my hair cut." He finished speaking just as slowly as he had started out.

"You're going to town? You mean where the people outnumber the animals? That thing called civilization? I'm going with you!" I announced. "I'll walk around and look at the shops while you get your hair cut."

"All right," he agreed.

Going to town was not "the usual" for my Gramps. If he could stay on his two acres of property for months on end, he would. The only things that get him to venture forth are a bi-monthly haircut and hunting season. For hunting season, he travels five miles to another piece of his property to hunt, so I am not sure if that should even count.

The word "town" is exciting because I crave a change of scenery when I'm out here in the country. I miss the hustle and bustle of people and activity. Town is only eleven miles and fifteen minutes away, but it's like another world. There are stores, restaurants, parks and people my own age.

Grammy spoke up. "You are not going anywhere. I need your help right here today," she told me. Pointing at Gramps, she commanded, "Go in to town by yourself today, Wayne."

"Oh come on, Grammy. It's not like the trip into town is that long. We won't be gone more than an hour or two," I pleaded. "Look at Gramps' hair!" I whined, pointing to his head. "There is no way his haircut takes more than five minutes…maybe ten, tops."

It was obvious this argument would not be won by me today. Whenever there was a chance of getting my way, Grammy would banter back and forth. Today, she said no and turned away. So that was the end of it.

"Fine," I huffed.

I finished my breakfast and washed my dish in the sink. After the dishes were placed in the drying rack, I went outside feeling dejected, hoping the dogs would offer me solace. Surely, they would understand my predicament. I flopped down by one dog to explain my disappointment. He humored me by setting his head on my lap and would have probably sat there all day listening to my tale of woe, as long as he received a few scratches.

Gramps moseyed out of the house. Every now and again, I could see him come around the house or a shed corner busy with his chores. He knew this property so well. There were times I'd test him by moving a big rock or flower pot and the next day it was right back where it belonged. The yard never looked organized, but Gramps had his own system. I was angry with Gramps that I couldn't go to town. It wasn't his fault, but I suppose the jealousy of knowing he would be going was enough for me to stew on.

Pouting was my next order of business and I found myself to be quite good at it. Every time I thought about the missed opportunity to go to town, I became upset all over again. It would probably be wise to think of something else, but I wanted to be angry. I threw rocks, then twirled the flyswatter on my finger and paced back and forth. Killing flies would be therapeutic. When the sun rose higher in the sky, they'd be everywhere. Grammy yelled for me to get inside, so I put my weapon down on the brick steps. The murderous rampage would have to wait.

I didn't dare speak first upon entering the house. Looking at her, I raised my eyebrows and gave her the "I'm here against my will" look. She walked to the back of the house without saying a word. This was the strangest day ever! My Grammy has never had a problem expressing her thoughts. As a matter of fact, many of us in the family wished she wasn't quite so proficient at it.

Confused, I tapped the table. Her solitaire game was in the works so I sat down to finish it. Surely, this would elicit a response from her when she saw what I was doing. No one was allowed to touch her precious solitaire games. However, a few minutes later, she walked in barely looking in my direction.

"O.K., Grammy, I give up. I don't know what I've done to make you mad, but would you just yell at me and get it over with?" I conceded. "Then, I can help you with whatever you need to get done *and* go to town with Gramps."

"I need your help when your grandfather leaves," she said.

"Is this some sort of wicked scheme? I won't do anything to his garden or his workshop," I protested.

"This has nothing to do with your grandfather," she snapped.

"Oh. Well, that's good," I said relieved. "Do you remember the last time we went into his workshop? That's why he keeps it locked now."

We both tried not to smile as we remembered Gramps' reaction to us reorganizing his workshop. I really thought we were doing something good, but it was Grammy's way of getting rid of a lot of Gramps' little treasures.

Suddenly, Grammy realized what I was doing. "Are you playing my solitaire game?" she questioned.

"A little," I said sheepishly and grinned.

"Get away from there and go do the vacuuming in the living room," she barked. "Don't let me catch you at this table with my cards. There are other decks in the cabinet if you want to play!"

That was very direct and loud communication. Maybe she is O.K. after all.

"You were on a roll with the vacuum this morning," I pointed out. "Maybe you should have just continued into the living room." I rushed out of the room and considered myself lucky when she didn't come yelling after me.

The vacuum was in a small hall closet. I retrieved it and unplugged a lamp to plug the vacuum in. It was hard not to giggle at the groovy, reddish shag carpet. I wondered when they were going to change it, but neither grandparent was that concerned with upgrades or improvements. They figured if what they had worked- why change it?

After vacuuming, I dusted. The T.V. was like a mere decoration in the living room because, unless the planets were aligned just so, you weren't going to get a decent picture. Although, around 2 p.m., the Phil Donahue show came in pretty well. This was extremely unfortunate for me, but it delighted Grammy to no end.

I continued making my way around the room halfheartedly dusting. When the clock was my next task, I frowned. The little hand was on the eight and the big hand was on the six. It was only 8:30 a.m. and there was no doubt in my mind that this day was going to be a long one!

After the dusting was completed, there really wasn't much else to do. Thankfully, the house was very small: only five rooms in all- two bedrooms, one bathroom, a living room and the kitchen. My Grammy wasn't a neat freak, but she liked things picked up. It was early and I was still holding out hope that she would allow me to go into town with Gramps. However, she would have to be the one to bring it up. If I suggested it, the answer would be no for sure.

Other than keeping out of Grammy's way, I had no plans for the rest of my morning. There were a lot of books, magazines and catalogs in the living room so I grabbed a variety of reading material and took a seat. "Smithsonian Magazine" was full of exotic places. I decided that one day I'd love to see Barcelona. It looked so beautiful, and the people were always smiling in the pictures. They're either a happy people or they know a camera is pointed at them. I would have to find out when I traveled there.

I used the department store catalogs to pick out a new wardrobe. It was an imaginary shopping spree because there wasn't a lot of money to spend on clothes, but pretend shopping was fun. When I had completed my wardrobe, it was time for a little poetry. Emily Dickinson was my favorite. The poem about her hearing a fly buzz when she died was so intriguing. Of all the things that could have gone through her mind when she was dying, she concentrated on a fly in the room. Yes, it was slightly morbid, but it never bored me.

The art books were the most confusing. Some of the "art" in them was just awful, but the challenge was to look at the paintings and try to see the appeal. No matter how long I studied a couple of the paintings, I found no redeeming qualities. You couldn't pay me what the painting was worth to hang it in my room and have to look at it every day!

As this cultural enrichment time came to a close, something caught my attention outside. I shoved all my reading material off of me to look out the window. Grammy was hanging the wash on the line. I rolled my eyes. There was a perfectly good dryer on the back porch, but it was rarely used unless it was raining or really cold. "The Middle Ages," I commented to myself.

I started putting the books and magazines back on shelves or in the baskets. The time had flown by as it was almost eleven. That meant that the temperature was rising outside and Gramps was going to come in soon to eat his lunch and go into town. He never wore a watch, but he knew exactly what time it was by where the sun sat in the sky.

Like clockwork, they both came inside. Grammy started to make lunch while Gramps cleaned up and sat at the table with his newspaper. You knew by watching them that they had done this dance for years. In my head, I was holding up judging cards...8.5 for execution...10 for consistency and zero for originality.

It was sandwich day today. The only surprise for lunch would be what kind of sandwich we'd eat. The excitement was underwhelming. Upon delivery, it was discovered that it would be a ham day. I've never liked ham, but complaining would only ensure that we'd be served ham more frequently. I bowed my head and sarcastically said something about being thankful I wasn't here to listen to the gross sound the ham makes when it comes out of the metal can. That earned me a little smack to the back of the head. Luckily, Grammy cut up fresh vegetables from the garden and they were delicious. The veggies got most of my attention. I ate enough to fill me up, so I only had to eat half of the sandwich. Gramps finished his sandwich then pushed himself away from the table.

"Well," he announced, "I'm going into town now."

He looked around the table to see if any new decisions had been made. I looked at Grammy with the best "please can I go" look known to man. She didn't look at me and started to clear the table. Gramps wouldn't dare go against her wishes. He shrugged his shoulders, patted me on the head, gave Grammy a kiss on the cheek and left.

I didn't try to suppress my anger. It was quite possibly the noisiest table-clearing effort of my life. The forks were dropped a foot above the stainless steel sink. The garbage can lid was spun around and around. Cabinets were slammed and re-slammed just for effect. In the middle of my little rant, I didn't even notice that my grandmother was standing in the middle of the kitchen watching me carry on.

We locked eyes. I wasn't going to speak first. That would be like raising a white flag or throwing in the towel. Too much anger was involved to retreat or give in. We just stared at each other until I was able to see what was really going on. Grammy didn't look mad at all. As a matter of fact, those pesky tears from earlier were tracing her cheeks.

"Muriel," she said with urgency, "I need you to tell me everything you remember about the vision you had in the shower. I heard you telling your grandfather about it."

"Yeah, I don't know what that was about," I said, waving it off. "The smell of the shampoo might have been too strong or I got up too fast after washing my legs," I reasoned.

She didn't take her eyes off of me. "Tell me what you saw," she repeated.

I blew out a sigh and felt ridiculous, but did as I was told. "Well, there was this Shakespearean play," I said.

"Yes," Grammy acknowledged, as she moved closer to me with an eager look on her face.

"Uh, and I thought one of the actors was looking straight at me," I went on, stepping back because Grammy was invading my personal space.

"Was the actor a man or woman?" Grammy asked.

"She was a woman. She actually looked a little like me," I said, feeling ridiculous. "Maybe it was a vision of my future and I am going to be a conceited actress," I laughed at the thought.

"Why do you say a *conceited* actress?" Grammy inquired.

"Because I heard what she was thinking. She believed she was too good for the production and hoped she would get good reviews despite the poor performances of the other actors," I explained, not quite sure how I had known all that insider information.

At this, my Grammy got a worried look on her face, reached her arm out to grab mine and let her head fall. I'm not sure if we stood like that for seconds or minutes. She let go of my arm. Grammy walked to the window and looked out. She wanted to make sure that Gramps was already on his way to town and didn't get distracted by a neighbor or a gopher trap. She pulled out a chair and motioned for me to have a seat. I sat.

"Muriel," she sighed in her most serious tone as she took a seat beside me, "it's time that you and I have a talk."

Chapter 2 Labor Pains

"C'mon, Muriel, push!" Rick bellowed at me.

I was pushing so hard that I thought my eyes might come out of their sockets. Just then, a glorious reprieve from pain arrived which helped me to catch my breath.

"O.K., you can relax for a minute," explained the doctor, "but I am going to need you to push even harder the next time."

Rick stroked my ankle and smiled at me, "You are doing a wonderful job, honey."

I really wanted my Grammy in the delivery room, but Rick had been reassuring me what a great coach he was going to be. In my lifetime, I had a wide array of coaches and they all had experience with the subject matter they were coaching. To my knowledge, Rick had never had a baby. This fact made me want to kick him in the face.

Luckily, I was warned about violent thoughts toward my husband during labor. I nervously smiled at Rick and kept my foot in the stirrup because I knew he was only trying to help. He was excited to meet our son.

"Aaaaaaaah," I screamed as the pain returned.

"Alright," said the doctor, "this needs to be the final push. Muriel, the baby's heart rate is dropping and if we don't get him out now, we will have to…"

The doctor didn't even finish his sentence before I heard the baby cry. I kept lifting my head up to see our beautiful son, but the 22 hours of labor had exhausted me and my neck wasn't cooperating.

"Would you like to cut the umbilical cord, Rick?" the doctor asked, handing him the surgical scissors.

"I would love to," Rick smiled as he took the scissors, and snipped the cord where the doctor indicated.

"Can I see him?" I asked excitedly, still trying to lift my head up for more than a few seconds.

Rick walked up to the head of the bed bending down to kiss my cheek. "We have a little surprise we weren't expecting," he whispered in my ear.

"If you tell me we are having twins, I will never forgive you," I said, curious to know the actual surprise.

"Let me raise you up a little," Rick said as he used the button on the bed control to raise me to a slight incline.

The nurse finished cleaning the baby, wrapped him in a blanket and laid him in my arms. There is no way to explain the feeling when your child is laid in your arms for the first time. Two little eyes trying to focus, with the innocence only newness can possess. I didn't check for ten fingers or toes because he was all wrapped up. I assumed they were all there.

Tearing up, I looked at Rick, "He is so handsome," I sniffled.

"No, *she* is incredibly beautiful," he corrected me.

"What?" I snapped. "No Rick, we were supposed to have a boy." I was shaking my head no and pulling the blanket open for a full inspection now.

Rick put his hand over the baby's blanket to stop me from uncovering the baby. It was obvious that he was a little embarrassed by my reaction. "I know the difference between girl and boy parts, Muriel. I assure you it is a girl," he whispered.

I bit my lip trying to hold back tears. My joy was gone and the disappointment settled in quickly. Rick could sense that I was unhappy about the announcement, but he was understandably confused. He scooped the baby up in his arms and turned away.

It was only 10 a.m. and the rest of the day was a flurry of activity. I nodded off between feedings and visitors. Everyone gushed over the baby's beauty and her unusually dark hair. She was rocked and kissed for the majority of the day and barely made a peep.

The phone rang around 1 p.m. Rick answered it and handed it to me with a big smile, "You'll want to take this."

"Hello," I said, which sounded more like a question.

"How are my beautiful granddaughter and my new great-grandson?" Grammy asked on the other end of the line.

"Oh, Grammy," I cried as soon as I heard her voice. "We had a girl. We had a girl," I repeated as I bawled. We both cried. This was supposed to be one of the happiest days of my life, but my Grammy and I knew better, so we shared in the sorrow.

"See you later, alligator," she whimpered.

"In a while, crocodile," I finished the rhyme and hung up the phone.

The nurse kept coming into the room to ask if we had a name picked out for our little girl yet, but we couldn't decide. We asked if we could sleep on the decision and let her know in the morning. She said that was fine, but that the law required a name before we could be discharged. We shamelessly mocked her when she left even though she was just doing her job.

Rick took on a serious tone now, "You know we are going to have to pick out a name for our little girl. I don't think Gregory would be a good fit anymore."

"No, I suppose not," I smiled in agreement. "You would think with all the improvements in technology that mixing up the baby's sex would be a difficult error to make," I complained. Rick didn't acknowledge my comment.

A name was something that would require thought and time. We had the name Gregory picked out, but that had taken months to decide. Rick sat in the corner of the room with our baby and rattled off names while he held her as though she was going to speak up and agree to her favorite.

I remembered an old family name that went back generations, so I asked Rick if he liked the name Deidra. I only threw it out there because I was running out of ideas and fully expected it to join the many names we had decided against.

"Who was named Deidra in your family?" he asked.

"The name goes back generations. It's an old Gaelic name. Long ago every woman in the clan had it as a middle name if not a first name," I explained. "We don't have to use that name, but they won't let us go home until we put something down on paper. I don't know about you, but I'd like to go home tomorrow."

"I don't know," Rick cooed to the baby. He rocked her back and forth and asked her, "What do you think baby-waby? Do you like the name Deidra, little one?"

Just as Rick finished the question, our newborn let out the biggest burp I have ever heard from someone so tiny. Rick was convinced that was affirmation that she liked the name. That would seem to be a reason not to name her Deidra, but bodily functions have a different allure to men. He quickly called the night nurse in to let her know we had decided on a name. She arrived with clipboard in hand ready to take down all the information.

"Great, so you have a name picked out for your daughter?" the nurse asked poised to write down our decision.

This name would be her identity to the world. Such an important decision was nerve-racking. It was all going too quickly.

"Her name is Deidra," Rick said before I could slow everything down. She wrote the information on the chart and it was done. Her name, for better or worse, was now Deidra.

"And the middle name?" she asked.

Rick and I looked at each other and she surmised we were completely unprepared for that question.

"I'll let you sleep on it," she said, while plastering on a fake grin. "You can give the middle name to the day nurse. A middle name is not necessary, but children usually like to have them," she finished and whirled around, almost hitting the dining cart being wheeled in with our dinner.

The meals were placed on our tray tables and the server quietly left us to our dinner. He was now my favorite employee in the hospital. Had he hit the nurse with the cart, I'd have written a glowing letter to the hospital administration about his incredible job performance.

"You need to think of a middle name, Rick, right now!" I half yelled. "If that nurse has to come in here one more time and we're not…" I trailed off and tossed my head back on the pillow, frustrated.

"I'll give you four choices of a middle name and you pick one," he finalized.

"Ugh! Fine, but this is just your way of putting it back on me," I glared at him trying not to let him see me smiling. Rick was the only person I knew who could both annoy and amuse me at the same time. "I'm waiting," I informed him.

Rick gently put Deidra in her rolling plastic hospital crib and faced me. He looked more handsome than ever after seeing him care for our child.

"Here they are in no particular order- drumroll please," he announced. Picking up the knife and spoon from my tray, Rick started banging the silverware on the table. It was his version of a drumroll. "First, we have May. Second, let's hear it for Lyn and following in position number three is Joan. Last, but not least, can I hear your applause for Gail?" he finished.

When he was done and the banging silverware was silenced, I stared at him aghast. "Are you kidding me right now?" I unleashed. "Those are all one-syllable names. Our child will sound like she's from the Deep South. Deidra May? Deidra Lyn? And wasn't Gail the name of an old girlfriend? Forget it. I'd rather she doesn't have a middle name if those are my only choices."

"That's fine, but when she asks why she wasn't special enough for a middle name- I'll be sure to tell her that it was Mommy's fault," he smirked.

His mistake was leaving the fork on my tray. It went flying across the room intended for any part of his body. Lucky for Rick, my aim was a little off.

"Now, violence is never the answer," he giggled. "I tell you what," he said as he bent down to kiss my forehead, "why don't we use your name for her middle name? You have a beautiful name and you can share it with her."

The only thing that I had kept all these years from my mother was the name she had given me. I considered changing it many times, but I conceded that my name was not a piece of my mother, but my beloved Grammy.

"Rick, I am tired and that is fine. After I finish my dinner, I am going to try and get some sleep. Can you get new ammunition...I mean clean utensils for my meal?" I giggled.

When he returned, we enjoyed our dinner together and settled in for the night. I have a feeling my comfort level was a bit higher than Rick's, who had to fashion the chair next to me into a sleeping area.

As exhausted as I was, sleep did not come easily. Visions flooded my mind. I sensed flashes of disappointment from past generations of women as they held their little girls. Some women wept, while others chose to give their children up or leave before their daughters became of age. One woman was so overwhelmed with grief that she handed her daughter to her husband and walked off a cliff.

My head fell forward and a woman came into view. Her clothing style suggested this scene was from long ago. Her eyes filled with tears while she stood pleading with her grown daughter to understand. It was rare for a mother to raise a daughter with such love and devotion, but the years flooded my senses to show a dutiful and loving mother. The daughter walked away, sensing that her mother was going to hurt herself. The daughter continued to walk on.

I must have been moaning because Rick grabbed my arm. "Are you O.K., sweetheart? Should I get the doctor?" he asked.

"No, no, I'm fine," feeling relieved to be fully present again. "I'm just tired from all the day's events and it seems our Deidra is too," I said as I looked into the crib where she was still sleeping.

The next thing I knew, the sun was streaming through our window and Deidra was fussing to be fed.

"Nothing like a restful three hours of sleep," Rick said sarcastically, as he rose from his makeshift bed.

I just moaned and reached for Deidra so I could feed her. It was an automatic response now after only one day. She was training me well. The nurse came in to wish us a good morning. She was far too chipper which annoyed me immediately. It was the same nurse that was rude to us the day before.

"So, this is Deidra," the nurse said. "It's a pretty name. Did you have a middle name for her?"

"Yes," I answered. "It's my first name, Muriel. Can you just copy it off of my medical records? People tend to misspell it."

"Will do!" she practically sung. The nurse left while I continued to nurse Deidra.

"Rick," I pleaded, "can you go to the nurse's station to see how soon we can bust out of here? I want to go home."

"Sure," he answered and off he went.

I loved him for visiting the nurse's station every hour after his first attempt. Success finally came around 2 p.m. We signed the papers and Rick scooped up our little girl. The nurse insisted I take a wheelchair ride to leave. So I slowly settled into the chair and Rick gave me Deidra for the trip to the car. We maneuvered through the hospital at what seemed a snail's pace.

Riding home, I stared out the window, but gave Rick a half-smile every now and then in hopes it would be a sufficient replacement for conversation. It seemed to do the trick. My mind was whirling and reality was sinking in. How could this happen? I was supposed to have a boy! A girl was not what I had envisioned when my husband wanted to start a family. When we originally got married, neither of us wanted to start a family. We were too young and had so many plans for our future. The fact that Rick didn't want kids was a huge part of my attraction to him. Not having children would be the easy route. No chance for a female birth.

But, it didn't take long for Rick to change his mind about wanting children. He even mentioned looking forward to parenthood shortly after our wedding. This change of heart left me feeling slightly betrayed and I expressed that I had no intention of ever getting pregnant, but Deidra managed to surprise us both.

The first three months of pregnancy would find me a nervous wreck. But, at the three-month checkup, the ultrasound technician told us the baby was a boy. I was relieved and could enjoy the rest of the pregnancy. At the six-month checkup the baby was again confirmed to be a boy. Yet, here I am with a little girl in the back seat…so much for my faith in modern technology.

I was grasping the overhead handle in the car so tightly that my hand started to cramp. I have to stop this train of thought right now! There could be no more dwelling on the fact that she was not a boy because one day she would know my thoughts. She would feel my disappointment at her birth. That harm had already been done. From this moment on, great care needed to be taken. When Deidra grows up, it will be her choice to forgive me.

We pulled up into the driveway and Rick looked at me and grabbed my sweaty hand. "Are you alright?" he asked. "You haven't said a word since we left the hospital."

"You know, just tired. I'm not sure if you're aware, but I gave birth recently," I chuckled. I took back my hand and wiped it on my pants trying to erase all signs of stress. This was supposed to be a joyful time.

He smiled while looking at Deidra in the back seat and then at me, "Well, here we go. It's the first day for our family at home. I wonder if it will be this exciting when we bring home baby number two."

To that I said nothing because, if I had my way, there would be no baby number two. I smiled and opened the car door to escape any further conversation about the future, fictitious baby.

We brought our sleeping Deidra up to the all-blue nursery and gently placed her in the crib. She didn't even stir.

"We might have to do something about the décor in here," Rick said, pointing to the truck and airplane wallpaper. "Maybe put up some flowers or rainbows. I'm not sure. What do you think?"

"We don't have to worry about it right now. Would you make me some tea? The doctor said warm fluids would help with the cramping," I tried to change the subject.

Sure. Any particular type of tea?" he asked.

"Surprise me," I challenged him.

Rick left the room to start the tea, leaving Deidra and me alone for the first time since she was born. Looking down at her, I took the time to soak all of her in and trace her features with my hand. She was a beautiful baby. I pulled up the blue rocker and threw the dinosaur pillow that was on it across the room. Once seated, I held on to the crib bars and leaned my head against them never taking my eyes off of her.

"Hi, I'm your mom," I whispered. "Daddy is downstairs making some tea so I thought this would be a good time to chat. In a dozen years or so, when you come of age, you will come upon a time our kind calls the junction," I was getting choked up. "It is very confusing, but I will be here to help. You have been born into a long line of women with a unique curse. I've heard it called a gift, but that's ridiculous. It hasn't been a "gift" to any of us. You are an Oris, Deidra. Our origins go back a couple thousand years to a beautiful coastline in Ireland."

"My grandmother took me there once. Maybe we could go together one day. Your middle name is from your great-grandma who was born on that coast and it's my first name," I paused. "You'll probably call me mom, but most people refer to me as Muriel. It's an older name that means "bright as the sea". If you grow up and decide you don't like it, we can blame your father. He kind of dropped the ball when I asked him to pick your middle name."

"It won't be easy," I continued. "The curse might be entertaining at first, but eventually, you will be hurt and angry by what you witness." A sigh escaped my body.

"Here's your tea, honey," announced Rick as he entered the room.

"Oh, thank you. It smells delicious," I commented, as I took the tea from him.

Sitting back in the chair, I slowly rocked and sipped the tea.

"Well, honey," Rick announced, "I'm going to try and get some sleep. Who knows what this evening will hold."

"I'll be there in a minute," I smiled. "Deidra and I are having our first serious conversation."

Rick looked into the crib and smiled when he saw that Deidra was fast asleep. He gently touched her cheek and slipped quietly out of the room. I watched Rick walk down the hall and through our bedroom doorway.

My attention returned to Deidra, "So, kiddo, you better rest up," I explained. "There will come a time when your sleep is not very peaceful." Arising from the chair and running my hand along the crib, I made my way to the fire truck light switch. After turning the lights out, a decision was made there in the darkness. My child will always be loved. Deidra will be an exception to the Oris line. I just know it.

I stood there for a while thinking about how much I wanted her to live separate from our history and realizing her name itself encompasses our story. She never needs to know what the name Deidra means.

I laughed out loud realizing my foolishness. Someday, she will see me standing there, looking over her crib and planning to withhold the meaning of her name. She will know it all: everything I've witnessed, my hopes and dreams, my darkest thoughts and actions…everything.

Walking down the hall toward my bedroom, I had to lean against a wall. A vision of the woman from the old country returned. It was the same woman I saw in the hospital after giving birth to Deidra. The woman was speaking to her baby daughter and sharing similar hopes and dreams for her life that I had just shared with Deidra.

The scene changed and her daughter was a grown woman of twenty or so, walking away from the mother. I felt a deep pain and found myself hovering above the mother as she took her final breath, with a self-inflicted knife wound to her chest.

It was a chilling reminder that there are no exceptions.

Chapter 3 The Talk

I sat in the chair while I watched Grammy pace back and forth. It seemed like she wanted to get this little talk just right.

"You," she started and stopped just as suddenly, shaking her head. I watched her as she looked around trying to organize her thoughts. Then, she just blurted something out. "The woman you saw in the shower this morning was your mother," she announced.

I sat there and blinked not sure what was going on. It was only clear that whatever this chat was about, it would never compare to a trip into town.

"What are you talking about?" I questioned.

"Listen," she went on, "I know what I'm about to tell you will be very difficult to believe, but you must pay attention and have an open mind. I always hoped you would get passed over."

I just sat there having no idea what she was going on about, watching as she wrung her hands and nervously began speaking again.

"Muriel, you are an Oris," she said. "It means that you will see things. More accurately, you will have visions about your mother's life. It is sometimes helpful because you will be able to learn from some of her mistakes, but you will also see her dark human nature," Grammy explained as agitated as ever.

I got up out of the chair and stopped her pacing by gently grasping her hands.

"Grammy, you need to sit down. This story you are telling me is upsetting you so let's just calm down and have a seat together," I said. "We will figure everything out."

Her hands were trembling and she resisted me leading her to a chair, but she sat down. I laid my hands on her shoulders and kissed the top of her head. I plopped down in my chair and sat directly across from her while looking her in the eyes. My Grammy was not one to get easily flustered which made this situation a little unnerving. She looked heartbroken, and it seemed her heart was breaking for me. There was only one thing to do: inject humor.

"So Grammy, exactly when did you start drinking today?" I teasingly asked.

"Very funny, young lady," she glanced away. "You know, I'm not going to be around forever and you would be wise to glean some knowledge and information from me while I am here."

"Really Grammy, you are playing the death card?" I sighed. "O.K., I will listen to your little fairy tale. I'm an artist or something?"

"Would you pay attention Muriel? You are an *Oris*!" she exclaimed.

"O.K., O.K. I am an Oris. What does that even mean?" I questioned, not understanding the importance of the information.

"That was the first question I asked my Grandmother," she mused. "Now that I think of it, I thought she was a bit off-her-rocker when we had our little talk," she confessed. "The word Oris is a combination of two words: the Greek word gnosis and the Latin word *oratio*. The word *gnosis* means knowledge and the word *oratio* means to speak. It makes sense because we eventually have all knowledge of our mother's life and whether we want to accept it or not, her life speaks into ours."

"I don't even remember my mother. She left when I was three and the only thing she has ever spoken into my life is that I wasn't important enough for her to stay," I huffed.

I sat there blinking and was confident that any minute now Grammy's vacuum cleaner would soon be banging into my bed. The only explanation for this craziness is that this was all a supremely strange dream. I folded my arms and pinched my side. The sooner I wake up the better.

"You have the most beautiful eyes," Grammy said. I blushed a little at the abrupt change of subject.

Grammy cupped one of my cheeks in her hand. "Looking into those big, green eyes reminds me of home," she observed. She dropped her hand. "There is more to tell you, but I don't want to overwhelm you with loads of information. You will have many questions as your junction continues," she stated.

"My junction…" I wondered. "What is that?"

"Your junction has started now. That vision in the shower this morning was the first bit of insight into your mother," she explained. "The visions will become more frequent and you will begin to learn all the good and bad things that make her who she is. Our people usually start their junctions around twelve or thirteen years of age. A junction is just the crossing over of innocence to knowledge."

"Well, why that vision? What does it mean?" I rambled, not stopping for answers, "And we have people? Where are they? Who is our leader?"

"Slow down, Muriel," she insisted. "I said you would have questions. Unfortunately, I don't have all of the answers. There is no way to know why you had that vision or what it may mean. I only know it was a part of your mother's history. I remember being at that play you witnessed in your vision," she paused. "Once you go through your junction, you will be able to pick up greater details from your visions and be aware of the complete scene. It will all be a little fuzzy in the beginning."

Rising from the chair, I was the one pacing now while trying to gather my thoughts. I would glance at Grammy every now and again. "Please," I looked at her eagerly, "tell me this is all a joke. I won't be mad. We can laugh about it. You should have seen how serious you were when you told me," I giggled nervously.

Grammy couldn't even look at me. She dropped her head and stared at her lap. "This is no joke, sweetheart," she said, lifting her head. "This is who you are. This is who I am. You will get used to it because you have no other choice," she finished.

"Why is all this happening now, Grammy? What is special about today?" I wondered.

"Well, usually the onset of the junction comes from increased hormone levels. Most Oris start getting visions around the time they start menstruating," she explained.

"Well, isn't that just wonderful!" I practically yelled, "As if adolescence isn't awkward and wretched enough! This is so incredibly unfair. I don't want to be one of these Oris people. Can I call someone to have my membership revoked? Is there a way to stop any of this from happening?!"

"No," Grammy simply answered.

At this point, I was too tired and emotional to continue the conversation. Somehow I knew the answer to my own question was no, but hearing it from her lips was devastating. I suddenly felt claustrophobic and needed to escape outside. After fumbling with the door knob, I ran into the yard. It was hot already and the sun felt like it was shining right through me.

There was a large stone ledge to the left of the back door, and the overgrown lilac would shelter me from the sun. I took my shoes off and put my feet in the kiddie pool. When I was younger, I'd splash and play in this little pool for hours. It seemed a lot bigger then. Leaving my feet to soak, I laid back and watched the cloudless blue of the sky. Closing my eyes, I started muttering to myself.

"This can't be real. My mother has been out of my life for so long. I don't want to know about her thoughts! How can I learn from someone I loathe?" I paused and sighed, "What a crappy day!"

One of the dogs decided to lick my face which startled me and sent me tumbling out of the chair. Landing on the hard concrete was enough to bring tears to my eyes, but the tears did not come from the concrete. They came from all the information whirling around in my head. In a rage, I punched at the water in the kiddie pool and then sprung to my feet. I was wrestling with the pool now, straining to lift it up and finally flipping it over.

My chest was heaving up and down as I watched the last of the water trickle off the concrete surface. It took a while to calm my breathing. My knuckles were bleeding and I was soaked through, so I threw the pool down and made my way to the lone bathroom of the house.

After slamming the bathroom door shut, I removed all my wet clothes and rinsed off my knuckles so I could stop the bleeding. I averted my eyes from the mirror directly in front of me. There was a fear that the reflection would be that of a stranger.

The hydrogen peroxide didn't even burn or sting when it poured over my knuckles. The adrenaline was probably still rushing through my body. Eventually, the bleeding stopped and I was able to apply some bandages. And after a few minutes, the pain in my butt from the fall became apparent just as I needed to pee. Timing is everything.

I gingerly sat down on the toilet and grimaced when my butt made contact. I held the toilet paper by the very tips of my fingers when I wiped so the bandages wouldn't get messed up. When I saw blood in the toilet, I figured my knuckles were still bleeding. When I inspected the bandages, they were white, with no sign of blood. I wiped again. The blood was not from my knuckles at all. Glancing in the mirror, I said, "Nice to meet you. Today you have apparently become a woman and an Oris." And then, I sarcastically added, "Let the good times roll."

I grabbed my grandmother's robe, wrapped it around myself and hopped right back into bed. A few minutes later, there was a quiet rapping at the door. I didn't respond. The door slowly creaked open and my Grammy inched around it and into the room. She sat on the side of the bed and stroked my hair. I smiled, feeling as though I had nothing to smile about, but doing it anyway.

"So, today has been kind of a big day for you," she stated. She had lived in this country most of her life, but today I could hear the slightest Irish accent in her voice.

"I am not sure if big is the right word. Shitty, painful, confusing- those may be more accurate adjectives," I answered. "I just don't understand any of it. What does Gramps think of the whole thing?"

Grammy got a concerned look on her face. "This is a woman's affliction and you can never discuss it with men. Even the women don't fully understand it," she explained. "How exactly does one explain something you don't comprehend yourself?" she questioned. "Some women have tried to explain it to their husbands, but it can end badly."

"What do you mean by that?" I wondered.

She tucked the covers up under my chin and smoothed them out. An uncomfortable grin came across her lips and she merely said, "It's just not a good idea. People won't understand." She quietly arose and made her way out.

The clock read 2:30 p.m. and I wondered how long or *if* I would sleep, but slumber came and rescued me quickly and stayed with me until morning.

There were three things that happened that day that would never happen again: I went to bed before my grandparents, I swore in front of my Grammy without being scolded and the vacuum cleaner would forever be silent in the wee hours of the morning.

Chapter 4 Daddy's Little Girl

Being a father looked good on Rick. He doted on Deidra whenever he got a chance. She was becoming a very smart, sassy young lady and her father encouraged both traits. Rick enjoyed all the responsibilities of being a father, except punishing her. That chore was mostly left to me, which was fine with him. It guaranteed he would not lose his status as favorite parent.

When Deidra was almost four, Rick and I packed up for a day at the beach. It was such a joy to watch Deidra getting older and see the wonder in her eyes as she experienced new things, but the beach was my favorite reaction.

Rick and I were both holding her little hands the first time she put her feet in the sand. She lifted her legs up right away and looked at the two of us as though she wasn't sure her feet should be on such a surface. Rick and I reassured her and once she familiarized herself with this new sensation of sand, there was no stopping her.

We unpacked the car, which became tricky as Rick and I had to split our time between trips to the car and running after Deidra. As much as we encouraged her to help us unpack, she wasn't the least bit interested. Only when lunch was unpacked did Deidra come up the beach and away from the water. We sat down to eat.

"Oh no, Deidra!" I teased, looking in the cooler, "We didn't bring enough food for you!"

"It's O.K., Mommy. I'll just eat Daddy's food," she confidently announced.

We all shared an unusually quiet lunch together while staring at the water. The breeze blew Deidra's dark curls around her face. Rick must have noticed the beautiful scene too, because we glanced at each other and smiled.

After lunch, Deidra laid out her towel underneath an umbrella. With a sippy cup in hand, she fell fast asleep. I don't think I have ever been more jealous of anyone than I was of Deidra at that moment. Not only because I couldn't remember the last time I had a good nap, but because she had no fear and could merely fall asleep while the waves crashed on the beach.

"The water is just beautiful, isn't it Rick?" I asked and glanced in his direction.

He had been staring at me, "It is, but it doesn't hold a candle to you, Muriel."

"Stop, you will make be blush," I smiled.

"There it is," he said, "that irresistible smile that had all the boys on campus mesmerized. I still don't know how I got so lucky."

"I'm the lucky one. It is a blessing to still be a part of this family," I whispered.

"What do you mean?" he asked.

"Well, my own mother left my family when I was three," I explained. "I am related to her, which made me afraid that leaving could be hereditary."

"You are nothing like your mother," he said, knowing there was no bigger compliment.

"I wish that were true, but we share a history and her blood runs through my veins. It only makes sense that there are some similarities. As much as I try to deny it, there are things we have in common," I pondered as I stared out to sea. "The trick is making different choices…" I trailed off.

After a few minutes of silence, I peeked over at Rick. The fresh air had overcome Rick and he was fast asleep, too. "Oh, I see how it is," I giggled.

An all-too-familiar vision came to me. It was my mother and father on a beach making love. As if that wasn't bad enough and something that would send me to therapy for life, I also knew what my mother was thinking. She didn't even love him. Sure, she liked the thought of being in love and being wanted by a man, but that was just to fill a need in her. She didn't care about what he wanted or needed. The vision left just as suddenly.

The vision reminded me of when I was sixteen and my father and I were packing to move to a new home. There was an old blanket stored in my dad's closet. It was ratty, so I put it in the pile we were going to throw out. My dad saw it in the throw-away pile and retrieved it. The blanket was faded and worn, but it was the one my parents were on at the beach. It was easy to remember that blanket because I kept trying to avert my eyes to it while having my vision.

"Dad, that's a pretty ragged, old blanket. Don't you think we should throw it out?" I asked.

"I'm sure it doesn't look like much to you," he said as he refolded it, "but, it is where you began."

I knew exactly what he was talking about. I was conceived on that blanket. The only proper thing to do at this time was to freeze or play dead, but that would look a little suspicious. So, I kept packing. My dad walked over and lifted my chin to his face.

"I know your mother isn't here and that cannot be easy for you, but I want you to know that whatever may come in the future, you were brought into this world because two people loved each other very much. You were conceived in love," he finished, believing every word he just spoke.

I smiled and muttered a thank you, but I knew the truth. At the end of the vision, my father hugged my mom. He told her he was glad his first time was with someone that he loved. My mom hugged him back, while rolling her eyes. That is the snapshot I have of my conception.

The breeze continued to dance around our spot on the beach. Looking at Deidra, I wondered what she would see if she was as unfortunate as I to see where her life began. Was I caring with Rick? My eyes weren't rolling, but did the thought of another man cross my mind, even for a second? Would she know I was trying to do everything in my power to avoid a pregnancy? She would know I didn't want her.

The waves crashed loudly on the beach, stopping my destructive train of thought. I quickly busied myself so there would be no thinking about the what-ifs. I started folding blankets and packing up the things that weren't needed. The car was loaded with everything except for the towels and umbrellas where my sleeping beauties were laying.

Slowly, Deidra began to rustle. It took her a while to realize where she was but, when she saw the waves, she was up and running. Rick awoke when he heard her screaming as she ran toward the water. I followed behind her and let the waves lap at her knees. She looked up at me and smiled. I was convinced that smile could bring world peace, calm the raging seas or even better- she would be passed over in the Oris line. It rarely happened, but I was still holding out hope. How could a mother *not* have hopes for her child?

"Deidra, it's time to go home now, sweetheart," I told her, knowing the news would not be received well.

"No," she immediately replied.

In the sweetest voice I could muster, I explained that her stuffed animals really missed her and we needed to get back. Deidra seemed conflicted when she received this bit of information, but quickly came to a conclusion.

"No, Mommy. The beach and the water-crash need me," she proclaimed.

I sighed. "Well, kiddo," I said as I picked her up, "the beach will be here when we come back, O.K.?"

We began making our way back toward the towels. You would have thought the way she squirmed and fussed that I had told her it was bedtime. When we got up to the towels, I put her down and started drying her off.

"Hey, honey," I asked Rick, "can you keep an eye on our little daredevil for a couple of minutes? I need to use the restroom before we go."

"Sure. I think I can manage," he answered with a wink. He said that with a super hero stance, which slowly disappeared once he realized Deidra had once again gone bolting toward the waves.

Her battle-cry was "water-crash" which would seem a more difficult term to use than waves, but there was no changing her vocabulary when she had decided on a name for something. So, for the umpteenth time today, Rick went to save her from the clutches of the water-crash.

Even when we were building sandcastles or burying Daddy in the sand, Deidra would keep an eye on the waves as though they were calling her home. She had a love of water since she was a baby. Bath time was never an issue. The only issue was when the bath was over. Deidra's fingers would be pruned and the water had gone cold, but she was still mad when we dried her off. The bath wasn't technically over until we watched the last bit of water go down the drain.

Coming out of the beach's restroom, I stopped and watched Rick and Deidra playing. She was holding up her arms to get spun around. Rick grabbed her arms and twirled her as she squealed with delight.

I haven't had many opportunities to witness Deidra from afar. The busyness of taking care of a child rarely allows for moments of reflection. They were so beautiful together. It was apparent how much they adored one another. They would need that in the years to come as I would become a disappointment. I closed my eyes to listen to Deidra's laughter and ached.

"C'mon, you hooligans," I yelled. "We need to get home before dark."

Rick and Deidra ran up the beach laughing. Before they got off the sand, Deidra turned around. She looked at her Daddy, motioning him to follow suit. They both faced the water and Rick waited for instruction.

"Goodbye," Deidra yelled towards the waves.

Rick saluted. He looked down at Deidra to make sure his gesture was acceptable. Deidra looked at her father and nodded her head, letting him know she was pleased with the salute.

She did the same thing with her bathwater after the last drop had gone down. She would whisper goodbye.

We all climbed in the car for the ride home, making sure we had our water and snacks at the ready. As we pulled out of the parking lot, Deidra kept her eyes on the waves until they were out of sight.

I quietly cried the whole way home.

Chapter 5 The Morning After

There was a far off ticking sound. It was constant and seemed to be getting louder. It took a long time for me to realize that the sound was my Grammy's wind-up alarm clock. There is something to be said for that time of day: the groggy, clueless, well-rested bliss of morning.

Ever so slowly, reality seeped in. My backside was sore. I wiped the drool off my face and scratched myself with the bandages on my knuckles. My stomach wasn't quite right either, cramping and uncomfortable. Ah, yes, I'm remembering yesterday now.

It seemed odd that the vacuum cleaner hadn't made an appearance. It must be very early. Then it occurred to me that not only could I hear Grammy's clock, but I could see it too. I moved the shade that was near my head and the early morning light made me squint. Focusing my eyes on the clock, I saw that it was after 8 a.m. My heart fell to my stomach and I thought that something must be wrong with Grammy. I threw the covers off and ran to the kitchen in a panic.

There was an audible thud when I slammed into the doorway of the kitchen for my not-so-elegant stop. Grammy was sitting at the dining room table calmly sipping coffee and reading the newspaper.

"Good morning, Muriel," she said without lifting her head out of the paper. "How did you sleep?"

Ignoring her question, a sigh escaped me because I was so relieved to see her immersed in her daily routine.

"What gives, woman?" I asked in need of a more respectful tone and flailing my arms around dramatically. "Where was the vacuum? Why didn't you wake me up ridiculously early?"

She lowered the paper. "Yesterday was a stressful day and I wanted you to get your rest," she explained. "We need to go into town to get some stuff for your monthly visitor, so go shower and get ready. I'll make some toast and fruit for your breakfast. Go on," she actually shooed me with her hand.

I mumbled to myself as I followed her instructions. "Stressful? Muriel you are an Oris. And you became a woman. What could possibly be stressful about that?" I sarcastically interjected, "Of course you have questions Muriel, but no one has all the answers." By this time, I was at the bathroom mirror pretending to laugh at the whole predicament even though nothing about it struck me as humorous. I stripped down to get in the shower where my rant continued, "My monthly visitor," I sneered and rolled my eyes. "Who calls it that? More like monthly, murderous mess. Ugh."

After I got myself together and ate what Grammy had prepared, we walked out to the car for our trek into town. The garage looked like an old barn and was quite a distance off from the house. Their property was on a foothill that gently descended downward to the garage.

There were always a bunch of birds that were pecking at the dry grass on a little mound between the house and the garage. They waited until just the last second before we got to them before rising up into the trees so we could walk by. They wouldn't wait long to return to their spots after we passed. I didn't look back to watch them land today. It seemed a childish habit and I was no longer a child.

We got into the car where Grammy said the same thing she always said, "We are off like a herd of turtles." That was her way of telling me I took way too long to get ready. She chuckled, patted me three times on my knee and backed out of the garage. Grandpa waved from the yard as we embarked, while the dogs waited patiently for his next move.

I laid my head back on the headrest, looked at the speedometer and then out the window. "You know Grammy you better at least go the speed limit so I don't bleed all over your seat."

"Muriel, we don't talk like that!" she snapped.

"You are so old-fashioned," I giggled. "What should I say? My monthly visitor is going to take a trip on your car seat. Is that better?"

"Muriel, you vex me," she said, annoyed.

The seat belt was across my chest so I kept moving it under my armpit. I tried to do it without my grandmother noticing, but she noticed everything.

"Put that seat belt on correctly, young lady," she demanded.

"Well, I'm not supposed to talk about such things, but my mammaries are kind of sore and this seatbelt is really uncomfortable," I explained. "Why do we have to go into town anyway Grammy? Can't I just borrow some of your stuff?"

"Ha!" she exclaimed.

I was clueless what that outburst was all about, so I looked at her, waiting for an explanation.

Grammy looked at me and then to the road a couple of times. "Muriel, I don't have my period anymore," she laughed. "You cannot be serious." When she realized I was serious, her tone became concerned and she asked, "Hasn't anyone explained to you how a woman's body works?"

"Not really," I shrugged. "I mean, we learn stuff in school, but mostly how our bodies develop. We haven't talked about our bodies as they get older. The teacher explained our parts, how they work, how people do sex, but that's about it. Oh! And all the bad things that happen from sex like disease, unwanted pregnancies, bad reputations…stuff like that. It's kind of scary," I sighed.

"Do sex," she giggled. "That is an interesting verb choice. Well, just so you know, when women get older, usually around 50ish, they go through menopause and stop menstruating. No more periods."

"Fifty!" I said in disbelief and looked out the window. "That is a long time from now. Can Gramps just shoot me when we get home and put me out of my misery?" I asked, unsure if I was joking.

"We'll call him when we get into town and ask him to load his gun," she grinned.

"And you wonder why *I'm* sassy," I rolled my eyes.

The trip into town takes about fifteen minutes. It was a two-way highway. One lane went into town and one lane drove out of town. We passed one car, and I don't mean that we actually passed a car in our same lane. There could be a tractor or an animal transport in front of us going ten miles per hour, but Gramps or Grammy wouldn't pass another vehicle. They must have known how to do it because they saw people passing them regularly. It made me crazy.

The lone car we saw was coming from the other direction. Both Grammy and the other driver waved.

"Do you even know that person?" I inquired, almost annoyed.

"That was Trent. He does my hair and just about everyone else's hair that lives here," she told me. "Besides, I would wave even if I didn't know for sure who the person was. That's what you do in a small town. Doesn't your Dad ever wave at people in the city?" she wondered.

"Yes, but his hand gesture requires only one finger- not all five," I glanced at her, giggling. Her pursed lips meant she understood exactly what I was talking about.

There was no more conversation until we reached the drugstore. When we arrived at the drugstore, I didn't want to get out of the car. My Grammy knew everyone in town and news traveled fast. There was a fear that the front page headline of the town's *Gazette* would read: "Muriel Chamberlain's Granddaughter and Namesake Becomes a Woman." Imagining this made me slink down in the car seat even more.

Grammy had already made it to the door of the drugstore before she realized I wasn't behind her. She walked back to the car, opened the door and said, "C'mon, let's go!"

We went into the drugstore and found the correct aisle which was labeled "female products." I think the labeling was more of a safety precaution for men, so they didn't accidentally wander through the horror.

"Well, what do you think, Muriel?" she asked way too loudly. "Which product would you prefer?"

"I don't know," I answered very quietly. "Give me a second."

"Barbara, can you help me and my granddaughter with something?" Grammy seemed to be speaking into the air. But, a sales clerk rounded the corner heading straight for us.

"Hello," Barbara said as she walked towards us with the warmest smile. "What can I help you two ladies with today?"

"Do we need help?" I nervously asked Grammy under my breath.

"Barbara, this is my granddaughter," she explained as she hugged Barbara. "I am not sure if you remember her. I've been bringing her to the hospital for years during my nursing shifts. You may have met her when you were a candy striper."

"Well, it is very nice to see you again, Muriel. Although, you were so small back then that I wouldn't have recognized you. What a beautiful young lady you've become," she complimented. She stood there smiling. Grammy nudged me out of my frozen state.

"Um, thank you," I feebly replied. I looked at Grammy and apparently my response was not adequate, so I also smiled. It was the most fake, uncomfortable smile I could muster, but I didn't have a real one in me.

"Well," Barbara said giddily, "let me show you some options and explain them to you." She walked over to a small table and pulled a tablecloth off a pile of products and picked up a box. "Now these are just your standard pads. There are different thicknesses for daytime and nighttime. These can be worn in addition to tampons or on their own," she continued to spout off information quickly and it seemed she didn't need to breathe.

"Now, if you wear tampons, it is always a good idea to wear panty-liners. Panty-liners are very thin pads that protect your underwear from seepage. They can also be worn on days when your bleeding is very light. Your period will not be very heavy right at the beginning of your period or at the end. What do you think you would be most comfortable using?" she smiled waiting for my response.

"I don't know," I picked up a box of tampons and looked at the directions. "These things actually go inside of you?" I asked with a look of disgust.

"Most women prefer them," Barbara explained. "I tell you what, why don't we send you home with a little of each product so you can experiment and see what you want to use." She looked at Grammy to make sure that was O.K. and received an approving nod.

"What is this?" I inquired, picking up a box.

"That is acne medication," Barbara replied. "Your complexion is flawless so you won't be needing any of that. How strange that you don't have one blemish. Be thankful," she instructed. "That is very unusual."

Barbara gathered a few of the boxes up and hummed her way to the counter. Under different circumstances her sweetness would be appreciated, but today was a bit rough.

There were no other customers in the drugstore that morning which was a relief. Mostly, just little kids running in and out to buy penny candy. There was a park nearby and they would run between the park and the drugstore. The only other exciting place for kids was the frosty shop, but that was more of a hangout for the high school kids. Purchases there required more than pennies.

"Let's say we put this stuff in the car and walk across the street for lunch," Grammy suggested as we were leaving the drugstore.

"Sure, Grammy, but I'm not very hungry. Maybe a half sandwich would be O.K.," I reasoned. "Let me get something out of one of these bags so I can use the bathroom in the restaurant." I reached into a bag I was carrying to open a box of the pads. It didn't matter what kind of pad I grabbed, only that it was retrieved quickly and in a stealthy manner. As I pulled the box toward me, the corner of the box cut the plastic bag and all the contents fell out onto the parking lot pavement.

I quickly bent over to pick up my drug store purchases. My heart seemed to be loudly beating. As bad luck would have it, it wasn't my heart, but the sound of a basketball being bounced by a very attractive boy. He kindly stopped to help me fumble the miscellaneous female supplies back into my bag. By this time, I was turning the color of a beet, but he didn't seem fazed at all.

"Thanks," I muttered.

"No problem," he said noticing my current shade of red. "I have three older sisters. This is nothing." He smiled. He started to bounce his basketball again and off he went up the street.

I retrieved from the bag what was needed and looked at my Grammy, who was not doing a very good job at suppressing her laughter. I snatched the car keys she was holding, opened the trunk and threw the bags in. Slamming the trunk was just what I needed to make me feel a little better.

"O.K. Grammy, let's go across the street," I said turning toward her. "You have some explaining to do."

"For what?" she asked incredulous.

I tucked her arm under my own as we started toward the restaurant. "Funny thing, your friend Barbara had a whole table of products ready to show us," I said waving my hand over an imaginary table. "You or I never actually said what it was we needed help with. Very curious, don't you think?"

"Well," she blustered, "maybe she just assumed given your age…" she peeked at me over her glasses to see if I was buying any of her rubbish.

We stopped in front of the sandwich shop. I looked at her and raised my eyebrows. "Grammy, you are a role model for me. What kind of example are you being if you lie?" I asked with a smooth tone. I raised my voice, "You called her ahead of time to tell her we were coming, didn't you?!"

She smiled. That was all the answer I needed.

I opened the door to the restaurant for her. She was relieved when she saw someone waiting and quickly said, "Can we please have a table for two, miss? Do you have something toward the back?"

We were escorted to a cute little table in the back of the sandwich shop where we both put down our belongings. Grammy took a seat. "I will be right back. I'm going to use the restroom," I declared.

"I'll just leave your menu on the table," the waitress told me as I left.

My trip to the bathroom didn't take long. My walk to the table, however, was uncomfortable and when I sat down the pad made a noise that I was certain everyone in the restaurant must have heard. "What looks good, Mrs. Chamberlain," I asked Grammy as I flipped through the menu.

"I think I will get the special," she answered. "It is any half sandwich with a side. The coleslaw is really good here so I just need to decide between that or the fries."

"That sounds good. I didn't eat that long ago so a half sandwich will be perfect," I decided. "Why don't I get the fries, you get the coleslaw and we can share?"

Just as we made up our minds, the waitress returned to take our order. Grammy got a half turkey with cheddar on wheat and I opted for the salami and provolone on sourdough. We both ordered the iced tea because that was a specialty of the sandwich shop. The cool tea would be a nice complement to the warm day outside.

Once we got our tea, Grammy took a sip then looked at me like she was waiting for something to be said.

"What?" I blinked.

"I was expecting more questions or conversation about what I told you yesterday," she hinted.

"It's still hard to wrap my mind around it, Grammy. An Oris," I said in disbelief. "It can't be real."

"Muriel, it is very real and you must have some questions," she reached across the table for my hand. "It's best to talk about it."

"Yeah, but you said you don't have all the answers anyway," I frowned.

"I have some answers and that is better than nothing. Believe me. You do not want to go through this without any information," she told me as she shook her head and pulled her hand away to drink some more tea.

"There is something you said yesterday that I am curious about," I started. "Yesterday you said that you had hoped I got passed over. What does that mean?"

"It doesn't happen very often, but some women in our line don't become an Oris. They live normal lives without any visions and have regular relationships with their mothers or daughters," she explained. "We call it being 'passed over'."

"How does someone get so lucky?" I wondered.

"No one knows for sure, but many of our female ancestors blame the men," she snickered. "It did seem logical though, given what happened."

I stared transfixed, waiting for the explanation. Grammy started digging around in her purse. She pulled out these little pink packets of fake sugar for her tea. She told me that some of the restaurants in town don't have fake sugar, but that she takes a couple of extra packets from the ones that do so she can sweeten a drink if it needs it.

"Not interested in your sugar issues, Grammy," I told her as impatient as ever. "Why did our ancestors blame the men?" I pressed.

"Keep your voice down, Muriel. We are sitting at a table in the back for a reason," she growled. She lowered her voice and continued, "They blamed the men because in the beginning of the late Middle Ages, there was this stunning young girl from a neighboring village of our ancestors. When word started spreading in regard to her beauty, she was only thirteen and not of marrying age. Back then, thirteen was a perfectly acceptable age to marry everywhere else in the world. However, Oris women argued for a marrying age of fifteen so a young woman wouldn't have to deal with their junction and marriage all at the same time. Folklore tells us that anyone who saw this young maiden was immediately smitten. Men on trade routes through Ireland would stop in the village just to see her. It didn't take long for her name to be on the lips of royalty all over Europe: *Enya*."

Grammy stopped to take another sip of tea and smooth out the napkin on her lap. "They all vied for her hand. A prince from Germany ended up marrying her when Enya turned fifteen. It was an elaborate affair and the girl's family didn't attend. They were paid a king's ransom for their daughter, but not allowed to see her after that," she paused. "The prince's parents wanted people to think she was of noble blood."

"Wow!" I said outraged. "She was purchased! Did she even have a choice in the matter or was it completely up to the parents?"

I saw the waitress coming toward our table with what looked like our order. I sat up straight, not even realizing I was bent so far over the table. Grammy noticed my loss of eye contact and change in posture, so she didn't answer the question.

"Here are your sandwiches, ladies," the waitress said as she placed them on the table. "Is there anything else I can get for you?"

I quickly scanned the table and saw that the mustard was already on our table. "Nope, I think we're good, thanks," I said trying to get her to go as quickly and kindly as possible.

Grammy pointed at her half-empty glass of tea. "Can I please get some more iced tea?" she asked. My *ugh* was audible and Grammy glared at me. She then smiled at the waitress and said thank you.

"Be a little more polite, child," she frowned.

Thankfully, there was a pitcher of tea close by so the waitress was able to fill Grammy's glass almost instantaneously. I didn't touch my sandwich in fear that the sound of my chewing might hinder hearing more of Grammy's explanation.

"Can we eat our lunch while we continue this conversation, or can you only do one thing at a time?" She pointed at my sandwich, "It looks delicious. Eat."

I made pretty quick work of my half sandwich and so did Grammy. We were nibbling on fries and having coleslaw when I asked again, "So, do you think Enya had a choice when marrying that German dude or was it up to her parents?"

"That German dude was Prince Stoffel. In English, his name would have been Christopher and I can't recall exactly where in Germany he was from," she paused and I could tell she was trying to remember. "Anyway, there were a few princes in Germany at that time from different regions of the country. This was an exciting time in history. The European population had risen and the economy was strong, which brought about many political and social changes."

"Stop with all the history! You are sending me to Yawn Ville. Just explain what happened that made the women blame the men for the Oris line," I pleaded.

"Let me go use the restroom and I will finish when I get back," she raced off.

The only thing left in her iced tea glass was a wedge of lemon and some ice so it only made sense she had to use the restroom. I've heard the term "can't hold her liquor," but Grammy said she was at a point in her life where she couldn't hold much of anything.

Just as Grammy emerged from the bathroom, I heard someone screech in excitement, "Muriel, is that you?!"

I turn to see my Grammy smiling at the woman approaching her. "How are you, Ruth?" Grammy asked as they hugged.

I paid no attention to the rest of the conversation. They laughed and talked. I threw my napkin up on the table in an act of surrender. How appropriate that it was white. The merriment only lasted a few minutes which, in teenager time, equated to an eternity. At least there was no interaction required on my part, and I ate the rest of the fries.

Grammy returned to the table and sat, "Ah, she is such a sweetheart and the best cook in this whole town."

Before I had the chance to express how very little I cared, the waitress came to our table and asked, "What kind of pie would you two like today? We have berry or lemon meringue."

"Pie…did my grandmother call ahead here to make sure we got some period pie?" I was getting angry. I pretended to hold a phone to my ear, my voice getting loud, "Please give the poor girl a dessert because she will now be bleeding monthly." I looked at the waitress,

"No thank you, miss. Pie does not sound good to me today. Tell me, did she talk to you personally or was this all discussed at the town meeting?" I questioned her and waited for a reply.

The girl stood there and didn't seem sure how to answer me. "Um, no, a piece of pie comes with your meal," she explained, and moved out of my line of vision, while pointing at the billboard closer to the front. It read in big, bold lettering: Pie with any combo today – a slice is nice.

Not sure how I missed that. Embarrassment, it seemed, was the only thing on the menu for me today. I apologized to the waitress, stood up and made my way out of the restaurant. There was no need to glance at Grammy as she was either embarrassed or angry. I sat on the stairs out front to ponder what an ass I had just made of myself while Grammy paid the bill and probably did some apologizing on my behalf.

"Rough day?" someone asked.

Turning to look behind me, I saw that it was the cute boy that helped me at the drug store. He had the basketball under one arm and must have been walking back from the courts. He stood there with a beautiful smile on his face.

"You can say that," I answered.

"Anything I can help with?" he asked, continuing to smile. Feeling uncomfortable because of the lengthy eye contact, I looked away.

"You know," he said as he took a seat next to me, "whatever you are dealing with can't be that bad."

"Oh, really…and you know this how, stranger-with-ball," I said a bit perturbed.

"We're not strangers. I met you an hour ago," he grinned.

I pointed at the door behind me and explained, "Any minute now, my Grammy is going to come out of that restaurant behind us." Looking in his eyes again, I continued, "She is going to be mad. What's worse is that I deserve whatever punishment befalls me. I was an idiot." I shook my head in disbelief of my behavior.

"Sounds rough," he said turning to see if the door was opening. "What do you think she might do? Maybe have you spend your summer in a small country town where you rarely see anyone your age? She could take away your radio and TV privileges. No country music or Family Feud for you, young lady," he mocked as he wagged his finger at me.

We smiled at one another and then laughed realizing we were both acquainted with the same bleak summer existence.

"You're here for the whole summer, too?" I wondered.

"Oh yes. This is my eighth summer here. I'm about three blocks away," he pointed. "Where are you staying?" he asked.

"About 15 minutes by car that way," I looked down the road and sighed.

"Sorry. That has to be even tougher," he leaned over and picked a long stem daisy from one of the flower pots beside the walkway. "Here, maybe this will brighten up your day. Well, I better go. I was supposed to be back 15 minutes ago," he explained as he stood up and dusted himself off. "My grandma gets a little concerned when I'm late because I told her if a stranger offered me candy, I would get in his van if it meant escaping this place," he laughed. "What's your name?"

"You can call me Enya, but that's not my name," I smiled back at him.

Just then Grammy emerged from the restaurant, "Douglas, you are getting so big. Tell your grandma that Muriel said hello. I haven't seen her in a few months."

"Yes ma'am," Douglas answered.

He smiled at me one more time as he turned to go. I watched him walk for a bit with my nose in the daisy until my Grammy figured out it may not have been the most innocent of stares. I stood up and Grammy grabbed my arm so we could get across the street.

"He is too old for you so just get that out of your head right now," she demanded.

"How old is he?" I asked.

"He has to be around 15 or so," she guessed.

"Well, I'm a woman now and I can determine if that's too old for me," I joked. "On the way home, will you finish your story about Enya, Grammy?"

"Sure, sweetheart," she answered. "We'll stop at the crossing and dip our feet in the water."

Chapter 6 Kindergarten

"Muriel, where did we put Deidra's lunch box?" Rick yelled from downstairs.

"I think it is already in her backpack, honey," I yelled back, trying to shove Deidra's feet into her new shoes. "These shoes fit you last week. Your feet couldn't have grown that fast, could they?" I giggled.

Deidra giggled, too, as I moved her foot left and right trying to stuff them in her shoes. She turned her hands up and shrugged her shoulders to let me know she had no idea. Her beautiful dark brown eyes were keeping my full attention. The room went silent and I could almost hear her eyelashes as they blinked. It was a slow motion moment where I could enjoy her smiling mouth and eyes. It hurt how much I loved her.

The shoes finally on, I picked her up and hugged her. Closing my eyes and hearing her heart beat as if it were inside my own eardrums. She wiggled out of my arms and ran to show Daddy that we got her shoes on. Everything was a big accomplishment today because it was all in anticipation of her first day of Kindergarten.

I was excited for Deidra, but not thrilled about my plans after we dropped her off. Rick wanted to go out for breakfast and have a talk. He took the day off for Deidra's first day. Kindergarten was only half of the day, but that still meant a possibility for a 3-hour discussion. Rick had been seriously talking about wanting more kids and was now even willing to go to a doctor and try to figure out if we could fix or change our current routine. It seemed as though having more kids was going to be the topic of yet another one of our talks and just the thought of it was exhausting.

Rick walked in with Deidra in his arms and announced, "She wants to wear her yellow socks and not these pink ones anymore. Can we change them?"

“She is wearing the pink ones because we are running out of time and I am not wrestling her shoes on again,” I said in a decisive way, so there would be no arguments.

Deidra started crying because she wasn’t getting her way. “You don’t want my first day to be perfect!” She yelled at me through tears.

“There is no such thing as perfect sweetheart. That is the best lesson you will learn today, and any day for that matter,” I informed her.

Rick looked at me and back at his daughter who was in tears. I could tell he couldn’t believe I wouldn’t change her socks. He didn’t understand that all my days were spent attending to her every need. She got her way 90% of the time. There were times I needed to put my foot down just so she knew who was in control.

I walked past the two of them to get some coffee downstairs before we left for Central Elementary. Deidra would be attending there for the next six years. I gathered her lunch, school supplies and stuffed animal. Then, I yelled up the stairs for Rick and Deidra to come down so we could go. They walked hand in hand down the stairs and we all smiled at each other.

“This is your big day,” I announced excitedly.

“It’s gonna be the bestest day ever, Mommy!” she proclaimed loudly.

We took a few pictures before heading out and then we were on our way. It seemed silly to drive there instead of walk. We were only a few blocks away, but Rick wanted to head out to breakfast right after we dropped off Deidra. We parked the car and got her situated in the correct line and took more pictures.

All the kids were lined up and you could tell how excited they were as the line started moving. They would soon be escorted into their new classrooms. Deidra was grinning ear to ear and waving much like all the kids. I looked her up and down because I wanted to remember this moment. That’s when I saw them: yellow socks. I was waving and smiling, but I suddenly had an urge to ball up my hand and punch Rick right in the gut. I thought better of it as that may not be the best first impression of our family at Deidra's new school. One thing was for sure- this morning's breakfast talk would not go well.

Once all the kids were in and the doors were shut, the waving stopped. We made our way back to the car in silence. It would have been nice to let my mind think on Deidra's first day, the new friends she was going to meet and the new experiences she was about to embark on. It wasn't happening. All that was running through my head were visions of those yellow socks, which made me see red.

When we were in the car and on our way to breakfast, I turned on the radio to avoid starting a conversation too early. Rick turned it off.

"I want us to talk this morning," he said.

"We can talk when we get to the restaurant, Rick. Let me just relax for a second," I reached to turn the radio back on.

"Fine," he conceded, and pulled into the parking lot of the restaurant that was closest to the school. "We're here."

"This is where you wanted to eat?" I asked.

"No, but I want to make sure we both have a chance to discuss everything on our minds and it would probably be a good idea to be close to the school just in case Deidra's first day doesn't go well," he reasoned.

We walked to the restaurant door. Rick opened the door for me, which I still appreciated. He was always a gentleman. I thanked him as I walked in then asked the hostess for a table for two. We were seated and given our menus. The smells of the restaurant reminded me that I hadn't eaten yet this morning and just how hungry I had become. The waitress filled our coffee cups and took our order. We both sipped the coffee and looked at each other and around the restaurant.

"Well, is there anything you would like to discuss, Muriel?" Rick asked.

It was difficult to tell if he really wanted to hear my issues. It seemed as though he just wanted to clear the path for his topic of interest, but that would have to wait because I was still irritated.

"Since you asked, would you like to explain how our daughter went to school this morning in yellow socks? That might be a fun discussion," I questioned, with sarcasm evident in my tone.

"Was it that big of a deal?" he asked.

"No," I answered flatly.

"Then why is it bothering you?" he asked in sincere disbelief. "So she wore yellow socks to school instead of pink ones. This is really what you want to talk about? I took a day off of work to squabble about the pros and cons of yellow vs. pink," he finished.

The fact that he didn't even know why something like that would bother me just upset me that much more. The added quip about the "pros and cons of yellow vs. pink" sent me over the edge. I was seething.

My tone went low, my words were carefully articulated and I bent over the table so only he could hear me, "You asked me in front of Deidra about changing her socks and I said no. You then changed her socks for her anyway. Thus, teaching her that if she doesn't like the answer Mommy gives her that Daddy will let her get her way. Next time either keep your stupid questions to yourself and decide the ridiculous sock debate on your own or respect my answer," I finished and sat back up in the booth.

He didn't really know what to say. Rick had always been a processor. He needed time to think about what was just said, and I barely had the patience to allow him that luxury. These were not the makings of the best conversations, but we worked with what we had.

"I'm sorry," he whispered. "I don't think of all the angles like you do."

My anger left me. Once he apologized for something, I had to let it go because I knew he was genuinely sorry. Earlier in our marriage, I used to get mad that he would apologize. It would diffuse my anger and anger was one of the few things I was good at. How he loved this hot-head was a mystery.

"It's O.K.," I succumbed. "What do *you* want to talk about?"

He didn't waste any time getting to the point, "Well, Deidra is in school now and I figure if we are going to try and have more children, we should probably really focus our efforts."

"Stop with all the romance. Nothing is hotter than 'focused efforts'," I giggled.

"Muriel, I want this to be a serious conversation. I know we were never certain we even wanted children, but now that we have Deidra, I can't imagine our lives without her," he gushed.

What Rick didn't understand is that I had to imagine my life without Deidra all the time. Someday, the odds were good that I would be without her. Deidra would make a choice to turn away from me like so many other females do to their mothers in the Oris lineage. The possibility of having another girl was enough to make me not want to have any more children, and I was taking precautions so a pregnancy would be avoided. Being dishonest with Rick was painful, but there seemed no other way.

"I think that if we can't have a child naturally, maybe it just wasn't meant to be. Can't Deidra be enough?" I questioned.

He grabbed my hands and looked into my eyes. He was being intense now and making it difficult to avert my eyes without being disrespectful.

"I want to have more children, Muriel. We are good parents and we have so much to offer a child," Rick was practically pleading now.

At that moment, I wanted to tell him everything about my lineage- let all the information just pour out of me in one big, run-on sentence. It didn't matter if he didn't believe me or thought I was crazy. It would finally be out there.

Rick's face spun around and became a different man. This was not uncommon and I recognized this was a vision. There was a beautiful forest landscape behind the young man. He looked puzzled and agitated. He spoke to me as though I was someone else.

"Matilde, what are you speakin' of darlin'?" he looked straight at me and sneered. "I've never heard of an Oris. What kind of nonsense is this? I can't be marryin' a damn fool or crazy person," he shook his head and walked away.

This particular vision came to me as a warning. It was meant to protect me from myself by not telling Rick the truth about my history. In reality, I should have known better for even contemplating that path. Even though the Oris line was where I came from, it still puzzled and confused me. And trying to tell Rick now after all these years was a ridiculous notion.

"Muriel," Rick said loudly, "this is not a good time for you to zone out on me. We have to come to some conclusions."

"Fine," I said sadly. "I don't want to have any more children and you do. That is pretty conclusive. What are we supposed to do," I questioned, "flip a coin?" I leaned over the table and practically begged, "Please stop asking me about this. These discussions are not going to change my mind. When we got married, neither of us wanted children. I wouldn't trade Deidra for the world, but I don't want another child."

"You are so damn selfish!" Rick blurted out in frustration.

I recoiled, "What?!"

"Maybe Deidra would like a brother or sister," he started. "Maybe your husband would like another child to love. You are a great mother, Muriel. Why don't you want to have another child with me? It breaks my heart."

Every time this topic came up, his longing for a child made me feel two things: deep love for him because Deidra inspired him to be a father to more children and intense loathing because he would not consider how I felt.

"Rick, another child may mean a lot of tests and procedures that we don't want to go through. What if the outcome is that we can't have children anyway?" I countered.

He slid a brochure across the table, it read: *Willows Fertility Clinic.*

Pointing at the brochure he said, "This is the best place around and they have different levels of fertility care, from basic counseling to medical procedures," he was smiling now, thinking his argument was won. "We can set up an appointment and go from there. At least take a look at it, honey."

My arms stayed crossed to assure no accidental touching of the brochure. "I understand how strongly you feel about having another child, but I feel just as strongly that we don't have another baby," I explained. I pointed at the brochure. "I won't be looking at that and I hope you can let this go. Having the same conversation every year is getting a little tiring. This debate will erode our marriage after time. Is that what you want to happen? Can we please be content with our lives just as they are and move forward?" I asked rhetorically.

The look on Rick's face said it all. No words needed to be spoken. He was crushed. "I'm not hungry anymore," he slid the car keys across the table. "I need some fresh air so I am going to take a walk. I'll see you at home."

"What about Deidra?" I wondered. "Are we going to pick her up together after school?"

"No. I'm going to take a long walk, Muriel. I'm sorry," he apologized and then he was gone.

The waitress came to deliver our food to the table. I ate my meal looking at the empty seat and full plate of food across from me. Stabbing a bite of egg it occurred to me that I was a little jealous of Rick. Deidra would never know that her Dad did not want to go pick her up from her first day of school.

A vision was coming on which I tried desperately to fight. I was not in the mood for more insight, but a woman kept coming in and out of my line of vision.

"Matilde, you should not have said anything," a woman scolded in a hushed tone. "You know the men don't understand this ailment. It's not somethin' that should be spoken of 'cept between the women. What were ya thinkin'?" she asked with a worried expression.

This was not a question for me to answer. I knew from previous visions that I was merely witnessing history. If I were to answer the question out loud, everyone in the restaurant would hear my response and the person in my vision would not. So I waited for "Matilde" to answer and continue the vision until it ran its course.

"I am so sorry darlin', but they have made their decision," the woman said averting her eyes. "Be strong Matilde. This moment in time will mentor future generations of our kind," she said as she kissed my cheek with tears in her eyes. That scene changed into a forest area. There was noise in the distance.

These visions could be like nightmares in that I did not want to go toward the noise, but I was not in control. As I approached what looked like a town square, all the noise was quieted. There was only the crackling of a bonfire that broke the silence. Perhaps there was some sort of celebration taking place. I stared in horror because this was no celebration…Matilde was being burnt at the stake.

"Is there something wrong with your breakfast?" the waitress interrupted. "You were groaning a bit."

It would always take me a while to recover from a vision. Rick said I was "zoning out on him" when it happened. Thankfully, it wasn't a common occurrence. I didn't hear what the waitress had said. Judging by her concern, I used the standard response.

"I'm fine. Thanks for asking," I smiled. "I just get a little cramp in my leg sometimes," I lied.

She cleared the plates. "Can I get you anything else?" she asked.

"Nope, just the check," I replied, trying to sound cheery.

I didn't feel like waiting, so I put more than enough money down to cover the check and tip. A car ride to clear my head would be good, so I grabbed Rick's keys. The tears came before the restaurant door even shut behind me. The sobbing was uncontrollable once inside the car.

The weight of my secret, at times, could be suffocating. I think of the flames that engulfed Matilde and wonder if she was one of the lucky ones. She died speaking the truth, having never known the devastation of bearing a child who would hate her.

Rest in peace brave Matilde.

Chapter 7 The Crossing

The crossing was no more than a mile away from Grammy and Gramp's house and we would often walk the dogs there. It got its name because it was an area where livestock often crossed to find different grazing land. The stream was also a popular watering hole for animals. It was common to see cattle knee-deep in the cool water.

When we arrived, there didn't seem to be any cattle or sheep in the area. The water looked refreshing, so Grammy and I found a rock by a shade tree. We slipped off our shoes and dipped our feet in.

"Wow!" I said startled. "How can this water be so cold when it's sweltering outside?"

"Let's just enjoy it," Grammy smiled. "This tree will give us shade from that hot afternoon sun," she explained pointing to the tree not far from us.

"So, tell me more about Enya," I encouraged.

"You mean Anna," she started. "When Prince Stoffel brought her back to Germany, they changed her name to something less exotic. It was a name the German people could easily relate to."

I interrupted, "Enya is a pretty name!"

"Oh, child, calm down. Things happened like that all the time back then," she explained. "It is just the opposite of what is happening today. Now, people want to change their name to something unique so they stand out," she frowned. "Shall I continue or have you had enough of this story for today?"

She knew very well that I was bursting at the seams with curiosity and wanted her to go on, but she had no patience for any more of my interruptions.

"I'll be quiet," I surrendered.

"Well, won't that be unusual," she laughed. I glared at her, but didn't say anything.

"Now, I know history is not your favorite topic, but it is important to this story," she stopped to see if I was rolling my eyes or going to say something.

I wasn't moving. I could suffer through some history for answers.

"Enya," she shook her head, "I mean Anna traveled to Germany in March of 1315 to prepare for her wedding and be introduced to the German people. In the spring of 1315, the rains and cool temperatures came to her village and did not stop. The villagers took this to mean that they should not have sent their jewel away. The rains were also all over Europe, but they were not aware of that. Those rains and cool temperatures made farming impossible and food became scarce. Livestock died." She picked up a rock and threw it in the stream. Grammy continued, "People were foraging for food in the woods, eating bugs, tree bark, whatever they needed to do to survive."

My hand shot up into the air. Grammy shook her head and laughed, "Yes, Muriel?"

"How long did that last?" I asked.

"The first good harvest was in 1317, but people were eating everything they could get their hands on, including the seeds for future crops so harvests didn't return to normal until 1325 or so. It was known as the Great Famine," she explained.

I was impressed. "You really know your stuff Grammy," I said.

"It's your stuff, too, Muriel. History belongs to everyone," she commented, while splashing her feet. "Once our ancestors survived famine, they contended with an even bigger threat called the Black Death. I am sure you learned about that in school already," she assumed, as she looked at me.

I nodded. We had learned about that in school last year or the year before. I only remembered that a lot of people got sick and died.

"Well," she elaborated, "our people thought the Black Death could be avoided if they just stayed on the Emerald Isle and didn't let anyone on their soil. I've had visions of our ancestors from that time frame and they are horrifying."

She took a moment to recover from the images. "Unfortunately," Grammy went on, "there were people who fled to Ireland with the same notion and must have carried the Black Death with them. Although no one really knows, it could have very well come on a breeze."

"Come on a breeze," I scoffed. "That can't be possible." I saw Grammy's expression, changed my tone and asked, "Can it?"

"Of course it could," she insisted. "You can see parts of Scotland from the northern coast of Ireland and parts of Wales from the south. The shortest distance between Great Britain and Ireland is less than 15 miles. Can you imagine how frightening that must have been when war was being waged and you would watch your enemy cross the channel coming for you? The bravery and fear wrestling inside the soldiers must have been their first battle before they even met the enemy."

It was then that I realized the school system had failed me.

None of this stuff was ringing any bells. The way Grammy was sharing this information, a.k.a. history, was interesting…even riveting.

"The Black Death came to Ireland in 1350," she explained. "The records at that time are not exact, but they suggest that around 50% of the population died in Europe during the plague."

"Why is this history important to the story about Anna?" I asked.

"Well, Germany was struck by the plague in 1349 and Anna had survived," she smiled. "After the plague went through Ireland, Anna decided to make the journey to see her village where she grew up and visit any family that may have survived all the hardship. It was 1351."

I was attempting to do math in my head, "So, that would make Anna…"

"Fifty-one," Grammy interrupted, "which was highly unusual. It was rare to live that long back then, but we are from a strong stock of people."

"What do you mean?" I asked.

"There is some disagreement as to the original inhabitants of the land of Eire," her accent was a little stronger when she said Eire. "We do know that at different times, Viking warriors and Roman centurions attempted to invade parts of the country. Many of these men had children who make up quite a bit of our ancestry. Some children were born into healthy relationships, but most were probably the product of rape."

The word "rape" jolted me with an uncomfortable feeling so I just waited until Grammy continued.

There was only a short pause and then she went on, "Anna visited her home village that neighbored our ancestors' village. Even with all the famine and sickness that swept through the country, she was able to find some men and women who were related to her," Grammy paused to take her feet out of the water and put her shoes back on. "As with all returning relations or favored guests, there was a celebration planned for Anna. The surrounding villages were invited and the festivities were planned. Parties like this would begin a week after she arrived." Grammy peeked over at me to see if I was still paying attention. "This gave everyone time to prepare food, but it gave Anna time to gather the women together and reveal why she had really returned," she shared.

"Dun…dun…dun," I said in suspense of what was to come.

Grammy smiled at my enthusiasm and went on, "Anna asked that all the women age thirteen and up from the villages get together a day before the celebration at noon. Anna said that in Germany the women would pray over the farmland each year before planting the crops. This was a lie," Grammy winced, "but Anna wanted the women to be able to speak freely. There was no better place than in the middle of a field. The middle of the day was also when the men were done with most of their chores. They would typically be eating or napping around then."

"When the day arrived and the women were gathered," Grammy stood up and cleared her throat, "Anna spoke to the women: We are not here to pray. My name is Enya Lorrah and I was born and raised in the village of Gilfin until the age of fifteen. My mother sold me to a Prince in Germany. I had three daughters, two sons, many grandchildren and a happy life. I lost one daughter, one son and many grandchildren to the Great Pestilence. I lost one daughter to illness before the pestilence came."

"What is that Grammy…the Great Pestilence?" I interrupted without being able to help myself.

Grammy seemed perturbed as she was taken out of character. "It's the same thing as the Black Death," she answered. "People from that time period called it the Great Pestilence."

"Where was I?" she searched. "Oh, yes," she got back into character and began speaking like she was Enya again. "Let me be direct. I am an Oris. I realize that word is spoken in hushed tones if at all, but I am too along in years to dance around the subject. I have had visions of my mother that started at my junction. Visions of all kinds still haunt me from my mother's history. Hear this: none of my daughters continued in the Oris line. They have never seen visions of me or asked me questions. They were passed over and I believe it is because my husband was a foreigner with no ties to this land. There could be no other explanation," Grammy bowed, while I clapped in appreciation of the performance.

I had a ton of questions, but asked the one that made me sound like a two-year-old, "And then what happened?"

"They probably went to the celebration and had a wonderful time," she answered matter-of-factly.

"That's it?" I asked.

"Well one of the women recorded what Enya had shared in the Book of Deidra," Grammy put her hand up to stop my next question. "The Book of Deidra is a place where women from our region have recorded much of our Oris history. The book is named after an ancient Irish woman. Legend has it that Deidra was the daughter of a royal storyteller under King Conchobar. One of King Conchobar's druids prophesied that this baby would be a girl and would be more beautiful than any other woman in the land. The price of that beauty, however, would be bloodshed and wars like none the region had seen before. The king was advised to kill the baby as soon as she was born, but he took her away from her family and had her raised in secret. He planned to marry her when she came of age and keep her for himself."

A warm exhale of air from over my shoulder blew hair across my face. I carefully and slowly turned around to find that I was practically nose-to-nose with a bull. If it were a regular cow or a sheep, there would be nothing to worry about, but bulls could be temperamental.

"Um, Grammy," I whispered not moving my nose away from the bulls', "a little help."

Out of the corner of my eye, I could see Grammy look over and jump at the sight of the bull.

"Okay," she said, "stay very calm and make no sudden movements. I am going to slowly back away and see if I can't get the bull to move." Grammy backed away and I could no longer see her. Then the faint call of "here bully, bully" rang through the air. It took everything in me not to bust out laughing. The hot air of the bull once again exhaling on me helped to curb my sense of humor. I slowly stood up. The bull's eyes were beautiful and kind. I wondered how I could ever be scared of such a sweet-looking beast, but my view widened to his horns and it all came back to me.

The bull didn't seem angry. Nor, could he have known he was blocking my path to the car. This was the bull's house and he had no reason to fret.

It took a while to realize, but the ticket to my escape had been with me all along. The long-stemmed daisy that Douglas had given me was still in my hand. No grazing animal worth its salt could resist such a delicacy. When I lifted it to his nose, he gave it a couple of sniffs before deeming it edible, then gently took it from me. His snack took a while to chew, giving me ample time to grab my shoes and side-step his immensity.

I looked ridiculous walking toward the car. It was slow and painful because my shoes were in hand instead of on my feet. Every rock or pebble on the path to the car was causing a tormented look on my face.

Grammy was near the car, silently motioning me toward her. It was best not to look at her because, by the expression on her face, you would have thought I was going to die at any moment.

But, after getting safely into the car, I saw that the bull hadn't moved a bit. He may have turned slightly to watch me awkwardly walking or witness Grammy's expression. Either way, this didn't seem like his first rodeo with silly humans.

I exhaled, not realizing I was holding my breath on the way to the car. "How did an animal that big sneak up on us?" I asked in disbelief.

Grammy was just shaking her head, still a little rattled by the events. "I have no idea," she concluded.

"Well, the flower that Douglas gave me could very well have saved our lives," I smiled at Grammy. "My hero."

Grammy rolled her eyes.

"Oh, I'm sorry," I giggled, "here bully, bully was a very solid plan. Hard to believe that didn't work. What were you thinking!?"

She was still flustered, "I didn't know *what* to do. That was the first thing that came to mind."

We both looked at each other and had a great laugh. The kind of laugh where the tears are escaping your eyes and your belly hurts from it all.

"Grammy," I said after getting the laughter under control, "I really need to pee. Can you hurry home?"

"Of course, honey," she answered. "Maybe I should call Douglas' grandma and tell her how much we appreciated the flower. Although, I don't know if she'd believe it."

"Well, if you do, I told him my name was Enya," I admitted, a little embarrassed. "I just wanted to feel like the beautiful girl from your story."

She patted my leg three times like always, and said, "Oh, sweetheart, you are only going to get more and more beautiful. I just hope you are responsible with that kind of power."

We drove away from the crossing and the car kicked up a cloud of dust as we left. I looked back to see the bull watching us go. He didn't seem the least bit menacing but lonely for company.

He must have been enjoying Grammy's history lesson, too.

Chapter 8 Lies Beget Lies

The movie was getting ready to start. Deidra kept looking back at the door. She was concerned that Rick wouldn't make it back in time to see the movie start. He had gone to get popcorn for all of us, but he was cutting it pretty close.

Just as the lights dimmed and the feature presentation was getting ready to roll, Rick made it to his seat and put the popcorn on Deidra's lap. She sat between us because it was important that the popcorn be easily accessible to all. We smiled at each other in anticipation of the movie.

As soon as the movie started, what I saw on the screen was not what my family was watching. This had happened before while watching T.V. It was best for me to keep my eyes on the screen, and if I did hear muffled sounds of laughter around me, to smile.

My Grammy was arguing with my mother on the phone.

"Linda, you should open a bank account up for your daughter," Grammy pleaded. "Your aunt and uncle left you plenty of money. Bring a little money here and I will even open the account myself." I could tell this conversation was not going how Grammy would have liked. She continued, "You are not being reasonable. Muriel is only six. By the time she becomes an adult that money will have multiplied so it could be used for college. She will see that you did something good for her," she encouraged.

When Grammy got very upset, she would half cry and half yell. I have no idea how she did that, but she was doing it now. "Don't you even want to try?" she yelled. My mother must have hung up on her because Grammy said hello into the receiver a couple of times. She slammed the phone down and threw a notepad across the room. She was screaming through tears.

The vision faded and the people in the theater around me were laughing, so I faked a smile as my heart ached. I watched the rest of the movie while my mind was otherwise occupied.

When we were driving home that night, Rick and Deidra were talking about the movie. Deidra asked, "Mommy, what was your favorite part?"

Rick chimed in, "Yeah, Muriel, what would that have been?" The look on his face spoke volumes. He must have recognized that I was barely paying attention.

Thankfully, Deidra was easier to fool. She was only twelve, but my tricks wouldn't work for much longer.

"There was something about the main character at the end of the movie…" I trailed my sentence off and let Deidra fill in the blanks.

"Do you mean how she did the right thing even though she might lose everything?" Deidra said excitedly.

"Exactly," I added. "That must have been really hard, but it showed what a good person she was."

Not convinced, Rick asked me, "What was her name again?"

"Lilliana, Daddy!" Deidra screamed from the back seat, before there was a chance to respond. "How could you forget that?!"

"Really, Rick, she *was* the main character," I added disappointedly, impressed with my guess of the main character being a she.

Rick peered in my direction, but I pointed at the windshield and said, "Eyes on the road sweetheart." He must have been fuming.

When we got home, we all went in separate directions: Deidra up to her room to reenact the entire movie with her dolls, Rick to the sofa to finish the Sunday paper and I went to the kitchen to start on dinner. Rick came into the kitchen after a few minutes and leaned on the wall.

"Will you even be hungry for dinner?" I asked. "We did eat a lot of popcorn." I was trying to avoid the inevitable conversation that was coming.

"You weren't even paying attention to the movie, Muriel," he accused. "And thanks for making me look like a jerk in the car."

"I have a lot on my mind, Rick," I explained. "Besides, I think you were attempting to make me look like a jerk. Don't expect any sympathy for that backfiring on you."

I looked in the refrigerator, "Shoot, no cheese. I am going to run to the store and get some. I wanted to make a tuna casserole." I grabbed the car keys and said, "I'll be back in a few minutes. If the water starts boiling before I get back, you can just turn it off."

The parking lot was practically deserted at the closest store. Getting the cheese was quickly accomplished.

Rick was still in the kitchen when I got home. He looked at me so strangely. I returned the awkward glance and went to put the cheese away in the fridge.

As I was walking to the fridge, Rick said, "I could really go for some Jell-O tonight. Shall I make it?"

I put the cheese into the deli drawer and couldn't bring myself to turn around. Rick doesn't like Jell-O. He *knew*.

"When the water started boiling," he explained, "I thought I'd boil the noodles for you and get the ingredients together, but you know what a klutz I can be. When reaching for the noodles and the cream soup, a few things in the cabinet fell out. Guess what I found?"

Here we go, I thought. My eyes were shut while I tried to calm my breathing. After the initial shock wore off, I shut the refrigerator door to turn toward Rick. The look on his face was unbearable: a mix of pain and betrayal. The worst part was that it was deserved.

"I know what you found," I tried to prepare myself for the lies to come. "My birth control pills."

"Is this why we couldn't get pregnant all those years?!" he yelled and threw the pills across the kitchen.

"Of course not," I lied. "Those were prescribed to me because cramping during my period has been exceptionally painful lately. They are not used exclusively for preventing a pregnancy, Rick!"

“I see,” he was still infuriated, “and you felt the need to hide them in a big Jell-O box in our cupboard because it was no big deal?”

“I’m not sure why I did that,” I was trying to think of a response that made sense. “You have always wanted another child and I didn’t. I was afraid if you found those pills, you would think I have been taking them all along. Having another child has been a sore subject between us for years.”

Of course, taking them every day is exactly what had been going on during our entire marriage- even when I got pregnant with Deidra. There were a few things that were part of my daily routine and that Jell-O box was one of them.

Rick still didn’t seem convinced. I looked into his eyes and tilted my head because this needed to be convincing. “Honey,” I practically whispered, “it was a stupid idea to put them in the Jell-O box, especially because I forget to take them all the time which doesn’t do much for my cramps every month. If you won’t mind, I will keep them in my bathroom drawer. Would you be okay seeing them?”

“Muriel, the hope of another child was given up long ago.” He added, “I’m not sure why the thought of it has me flying off the handle. There are times you are with us physically, but mentally you are worlds away. I’m mostly upset about that.”

We hugged, which brought tears to my eyes. Rick was the most important person in my life. I loved him dearly, but apparently not enough to be honest with him.

We loosened our embrace. He pushed a wisp of hair off my face. “I can never stay mad at you. Just look at that face,” he said. “I will leave you to the tuna casserole.”

The phone rang in the other room and Rick went to go answer it. When he came back into the kitchen, I could tell something was wrong. “What is it, honey? Who was on the phone?” I asked.

“It was your uncle,” he frowned. “Your grandmother and grandfather have been in a car accident.”

“Are they O.K.?” I asked, more worried than my tone would suggest.

Rick didn't say anything. I waited for an answer. It was obvious he didn't want to speak, which made me nervous.

"Rick! Are they O.K.?" I raised my voice.

"No," Rick shook his head, "they're gone Muriel."

The casserole dish in my hands fell to the tile and shattered- so did I. Never in my life was I overwhelmed more than in that moment. Two of the people I loved most snatched away in an instant. There is no way to explain the agony that followed Rick's announcement because I don't remember much.

Deidra must have heard the crying because she wanted to come into the kitchen. Rick had the sense to stop her as there were bits of the casserole dish everywhere. Rick explained the situation to Deidra, but there was no way for me to hear through my sobs.

Deidra and I had just talked to Grammy on the phone the week before. She always told Deidra "see you later, alligator" to which Deidra was supposed to answer "in a while, crocodile." Grammy and I had always said that to one another, and now it was Deidra's turn. Since Deidra was about four, her response stayed the same: "I am not an alligator. I'm a little girl." It made Grammy laugh. She would tell me I had a stubborn one on my hands.

The two days that followed were a blur. Rick, Deidra and I flew to be with family and friends for the memorial service. The airport was about three hours away from Grammy and Gramps' house where all of us would get together. The drive to the house brought back a flood of memories. Every mile was filled with a story, a special place…a tear.

Deidra had a lot to talk about after being cooped up in the plane, but I had very little patience to deal with her questions or conversation. I just peered out the window while Rick and Deidra interacted without me. There was the thought that she would one day see my indifference to her in that moment. In my grief, I didn't care.

Right before we got to the house, there was the old grey barn. *Landmark!* I yelled in my head. When Rick passed that, the tears were uncontrollable. It took me a while to get myself together before we pulled up the lane. The house looked the same. In my life's history, it had been there all along and would always be in my heart.

Rick unlatched the metal hook on the gate that creaked when opened. My grandfather's voice was practically audible: "A little oil and it will be good as new." The hundreds of yellow daffodils were hibernating because it was fall. It seemed appropriate as they would be an unwanted cheery sight.

There was no need to knock. The front outer door was open and we could see through the screen door that there were people inside. The first person I saw was my mother, who was the last person I wanted to see. She was having makeup applied to her face by someone else. This made me curious, but not enough to engage her in conversation.

Rick and Deidra said hello to everyone and then went outside to play with the dogs and view the cows in the pasture behind the house. I saw my cousin Judy in the kitchen, which was an immediate comfort. Although geography made quality time difficult, she was like an older, dear sister. We hugged and cried.

"I know what Grammy meant to you, Muriel," she said. "I am so sorry."

"Ju-Ju, she was your Grammy too," I looked at her puzzled.

"Yes, but she was like a *mother* to you," Judy explained, "and Grammy really stepped up when your mother left."

"Speaking of the woman who gave birth to me," I glanced in the living room where she was. "What is up with the personal makeup treatment and that bad bruise on her face?" Judy looked concerned. It seemed she was trying to figure out what to say next. "Judy, what's the matter?" I wondered.

"The accident wasn't her fault, Muriel. You need to know that," she said. "The police ruled it to be the other driver's fault."

I had a confused look on my face and shook my head, "I don't think I know what you're talking about, Judy. What do you mean?"

"Your mother was driving the car when Grammy and Gramps died," she announced.

It was too much to take in. Judy led me to a kitchen chair and helped me sit.

"I am so sorry," Judy whispered so only I could hear. "I wanted to tell you before you came, but the rest of the family said it wouldn't be a good idea. You deserve to know now, though."

"And what is the deal with the makeup?" I asked.

"This is not something I knew about," Judy sighed. "Your mother is allowing a news crew to come up and interview her." Judy looked around, "Because Grammy and Gramps were original settlers to this area the station thought it would be a good human interest story."

Judy's hand was on my shoulder and I squeezed it a bit to thank her. I hadn't been this angry in a long time, and I handled it just like the cooped up little kid on a summer visit: I went outside where breathing seemed easier.

I picked up a huge clay pot and threw it against the concrete. Rick came running over to see if there was anything he could do.

"Honey, are you O.K.?" he asked.

"No," I said matter-of-factly, "I am going for a walk." I gave Rick a kiss on the cheek and left.

There was an old schoolhouse that Grammy and I used to walk to on many summer days. It would be a good place to work out the new information rattling around in my head. The path to the schoolhouse started off the main road about a half mile east of the house. Even though I was emotional, it was important to keep my eyes open for snakes. Both Grammy and Gramps had taught me well, and it was ingrained in me to walk with a big stick, just in case.

The schoolhouse was another mile off the main road. This walk wasn't helping me to forget the pain I was feeling at the loss of my grandparents or the thoughts of wanting to strangle my mother. The strides became longer, quicker and the stick was dropped. By the time the schoolhouse was in sight, I was sweating profusely. It wasn't that hot out, but my walk had turned into a run.

I fell on the schoolhouse steps gasping for air. The news crew may have been coming to honor my grandparents' memory, but she would make this about her. She always did. It was the attention she craved and she sought it at every opportunity- even in tragedy. I didn't want to hate her, but she made it so easy.

The time at the schoolhouse that afternoon was important. There were no houses in the area to hear the screaming. No mirrors to see the mess my tears were creating…just a silent God listening to a ranting, broken, devastated little girl.

It would have been so easy to fall asleep on those steps after such an emotional tirade, but I needed to get back to Rick and Deidra. The news crew should have come and gone during my walk. This would be best because my patience, much like my energy level, was low.

The dogs were there to greet me when I opened the gate. They must have been confused as to why their masters haven't returned home. We visited for a while until I was sure that I could walk into the house calmly. There was no need to let everyone see the venom between my mother and me. "If I ever needed a big stick to deal with a snake it would be now, huh, boy?" I asked the dog.

The kitchen was quiet even though that is where the majority of my family sat. Everyone was eating bagels so I decided to get one for myself. Grammy had at least a hundred of them in her patio freezer. She traveled out of town for shopping and always stocked up.

Judging by the fullness of the freezer, she must have gone shopping around a month ago. When she would get home from shopping, she yelled for Gramps to unload the car. He would round a corner somewhere with his red wheelbarrow and start making trips.

In the kitchen, there was a spot between Deidra and Rick at the table, so I sat there to put some cream cheese on my bagel.

"How was your walk, Mom?" Deidra asked.

"It was good," I had decided and smiled at her. I took a bite of the bagel, and that's when the woman everyone called my mother decided to talk.

“Come over here and spend some time with Grammy, angel,” my mother told Deidra in a whiny tone as though she wanted to cry.

Deidra did as she was told. I couldn’t take another bite of my bagel without the chance of being physically ill. For her to call herself Grammy and tell Deidra she was an angel didn’t seem within her rights. She acted like she wanted to spend time with my daughter, but that would imply that she loved Deidra. My mother wasn’t capable of such deep emotions.

“That’s better,” my mother said when Deidra got to her. “Spend some time with me this evening.”

“Yes, Deidra,” I glared at my mother, “your grandmother hasn’t gotten enough attention today.”

“I don’t deserve that, Muriel,” she said in an attempt to defend herself.

“I doubt you will ever get what you truly deserve, but here’s to hoping,” I raised the water bottle on the table, and faked a ridiculous smile.

“C’mon Deidra, maybe there is something on TV we can watch,” she said as they left the room. It was apparent that my mother was angry.

“Do you really think that was necessary?” Rick asked.

“Yes,” I said flatly. I was very satisfied with my yes answer, but Rick looked as though he needed more. “There isn’t a person in this house she hasn’t lied to, stole from or otherwise endangered. She is a bad person with poor judgement who only cares about herself.” I paused for a second and then felt compelled to continue, “Did you notice how she hasn’t even tried to console anyone else today? As though she is the only one that suffered a loss? She isn’t capable of sympathy. And all this attention just gives her a high.”

My uncle Winston spoke up, “We are going to plan for the memorial tomorrow if you guys are up for it. We have picture boards to put together if you would like to help with that.”

I took another bite of the bagel, “Sure, she keeps all of her pictures in the bedroom closet. I mean, she kept…,” the tears interrupted the sentence. Talking about my grandparents in the past tense was too much. I went to the bathroom, shut the door and melted to the floor.

That was the only bathroom in the whole house. Someone would have to use it eventually. I stood up to pull myself together, looking in the same mirror of my youth. The changes that mirror had seen. Walking out of the bathroom, I stroked the hanging towels. Everything was left in the house with the expectancy of Grammy and Gramps return.

In Grammy's bedroom was a small walk-in that I used to play in as a child: trying on clothes, hunting for treasure or hiding from the world. When I opened the door, Grammy's smell enveloped me. I breathed deep and felt as though she was giving me a big hug.

Through the night, the picture board came together. We ordered refreshments for the memorial service, and my aunt had gotten a beautiful guest book in town from one of Grammy's dear friends. Grammy had already made arrangements for both her and Gramps for a burial plot and headstones.

There wasn't much more to do except to pass out from sheer emotional exhaustion. Because I had an inkling my mother would be staying at the house, I made hotel reservations in town before arriving. Deidra, Rick and I said our goodbyes to everyone and traveled the 15 minutes to the hotel where we collapsed into our beds.

Morning light seemed to come far too soon. Deidra wasn't awakened by it, so I snuck into the shower first. The memorial was today, but I had no intention of going. My patience level with my mother was capped and it would be better if I kept my distance. It was important for her to get all the attention she believed was due her while I preferred to shy away from it. Grammy was mine in life- she could have her in death.

After the shower, I came out of the bathroom to the smell of fresh coffee. Rick was reading the newspaper, and there was a cup of coffee on the table for me that he must have purchased at the minimart down the street. The warm beverage would clear my head for the events of the day.

"How was your shower?" Rick asked.

"It was desperately needed," I answered. "It felt good to wash yesterday off of me."

"When did you want to go to the memorial?" he asked. "It starts at 9 a.m. and goes until noon. The burial is at 2 p.m. for family only. He held up the paper, "Look, your grandparents are all over the local newspaper. There will be a lot of people there."

"I'm not going to the memorial. Would you take Deidra with you today?" I asked glancing at her still asleep. "Maybe go around 11 so you don't have to be there for long."

Rick didn't argue or ask why. He knew the decision to stay away from the memorial was an agonizing one for me to make, but that it was done with good reason. I loved that about Rick. He trusted my judgement in so many circumstances.

"Sure. What are you going to do today?" he asked, sounding worried.

"Well, my Grammy used to take me to a little zoo about 40 minutes from here. That's where I want to spend the morning," I nodded and answered his question.

After finishing the coffee, I grabbed the car keys and was on my way to the zoo. Surprisingly, the long drive and time spent at the zoo were a great comfort to me. I was able to escape the tears for a bit.

Around noon, it was time to head back. I decided to be there for the burial but to keep my distance so I couldn't hear anything. There would be no forgiving the pastor or anyone else if the perfect words were not spoken. Driving into the cemetery was surreal. It was vacant save one area where my family was gathered. I stopped the car quite a distance away and couldn't recognize anyone, which was best. "I'm close, Grammy," I whispered.

There was a hill behind me, and climbing it would make for a better vantage point. Almost the entire cemetery was visible midway up the hill, so that's where I sat. Someone was speaking, but the words were impossible to make out.

A car was arriving at the same entrance I had just come into. The driver parked beside my car. When the woman got out, it was a relief that I didn't recognize her. However, that relief quickly turned to dread as she started climbing the hill and coming straight for me. I kept my eyes focused on the one part of the cemetery as she approached, hoping the stranger would sense my lack of desire to chat.

"Hello," she said.

"Hi," I replied, not even looking in her direction.

"I lost someone this week and she was like a mother to me," she shared.

That was a declarative sentence, I thought to myself, which doesn't require a response, so none will be given. This intruder was on my hill after all.

"She is being laid to rest right now," she pointed down to where Grammy was being buried.

That jolted me enough to glance in her direction, but my eyes quickly returned to the burial.

"She was one of the best teachers to walk the Earth," she added.

"She was a nurse, not a teacher," I corrected the intruder, not looking in her direction.

"Did you know her?" she asked.

This time I looked at her with a sneer, "She was my grandmother so I guess you can say that I knew her."

"And she never taught you anything?" she asked.

The thought of Grammy's history lessons softened me a bit. "Actually, she taught me anything worth knowing," I smiled. "She was one smart cookie. So, I understand why you would say that she was a great teacher."

"She was so smart that she knew if your mother was still living when she passed away, that you would not be anywhere near the service. That fact has made you a little difficult to find today," she finished.

This is where my patience quickly evaporated and this woman was now annoying me. "Who are you? Why were you looking for me? How did you know my Grammy?" I peppered her with questions.

"How about we meet for coffee tomorrow morning before you leave, and I can answer all your questions?" she suggested.

"How about you answer my questions, to include how you know that I'm leaving tomorrow," I yelled, while standing up to confront her. "Or I can throw your ass down this hill."

She had the nerve to smile. I grabbed the collar of her jacket fully intending to launch her down the hill. It was a mere 25-30 feet down and there was a slope she would bounce off. If she had any large motor skills, she could easily stop her descent mid-way down. Either way, she'd live.

"Wait!" she yelled. "Muriel, your grandmother asked me to contact you! As of our last meeting, she still hadn't told you," she was speaking quickly. "Please, her death was so unexpected and she planned to tell you soon."

This woman, whoever she was, had the correct amount of fear in her eyes so I released her. If her answers didn't satisfy me, she would tumble. "Tell me what?" I asked suspiciously. "My grandmother and I didn't keep secrets."

She smoothed out her clothes. I hadn't noticed before, but she was beautifully dressed. "I am sorry that I have approached you on a day like today," she started, "but your grandmother was a very secretive person and I had no way to contact you otherwise. Your information was only released after she passed. Did she ever tell you that you are from the L.O.E.?"

"That's it," I said as I started toward my car. "Never heard of such a thing. We're done here."

She followed me down the hill.

"It means that you are from the line of Enya," she sounded desperate. "Please, Muriel, I am also an Oris, and your grandmother was a mentor to many of us."

That stopped me in my tracks. She knew too much, which made me pause for a second. No one but my grandmother had ever said that word to me: Oris. I continued to the car.

"Please meet me for coffee tomorrow morning at the café where she first told you the story of Enya," she pleaded. I didn't stop heading toward the car. She spoke again, "Your grandmother said to tell you to be like a herd of turtles. Um, no, turtles are herding off. Wait! I'll remember," she shouted, struggling to come up with the correct phrase.

I opened the car door and looked half way up the hill to where she was standing. I said, "Off like a herd of turtles. That's the phrase you are butchering…off like a herd of turtles."

"Yes," she happily exclaimed, "that's it!"

I got into the car and drove away not knowing what tomorrow would bring. My heart was full of sorrow, and my head was spinning from this last encounter. Regrets were never very productive, but I couldn't help thinking I should have thrown her down the hill when I had the chance.

Chapter 9 *Late Night Swim*

When Grammy pulled up to the house from our short drive, I grabbed my bags out of the trunk and made a bee-line for the bathroom. The dogs tried to greet me when I came into the yard, but there was no time because the tea was looking for an escape route. Once in the bathroom, I threw the feminine products into the tub and unzipped my pants. All the tea that I drank at lunch found a new home.

My Grammy was waiting for me outside the bathroom when I emerged. "Are you figuring out all your new products, Muriel," she asked.

"Yes, although I have not tried anything complicated yet, just the pads," I explained. "I got a little cocky because the pads seemed self-explanatory…sticky side down, but I think I put it on backwards at the restaurant. I don't know."

She ignored my answer and announced, "Someone from the hospital called while we were out, and they need me to take the swing shift tonight. You can come in with me and go to the pool for a while and then help with the patients after the pool closes."

Water was a love of mine, so swimming always sounded great and hanging out with the patients was an adventure. "That would be fun, but what about swimming with my period?" I wondered.

"You go back into that bathroom," she bossed, "figure out how to use the other products and go swimming- life as usual."

I must have looked unsure about the whole idea. "You can always stay home with Gramps," she offered, smiling. "I think he has a western movie planned for the afternoon." I peeked behind Grammy to see Gramps waving one of the VHS tapes in the air and smiling in our direction.

"O.K., let me get my suit on," I conceded.

"We need to leave in 30 minutes, so hurry," she directed. In reality, we could have left in an hour because Grammy was always early. She would get no argument from me this afternoon, however, because this spontaneous change of plans was exciting.

My swimsuit was in one of three drawers that Grammy emptied for my summer visits. She didn't want me living out of a suitcase all summer, so she kindly made room for my stuff. On the back of the bedroom door was a full-length mirror. The mirror's reflection of me in my swimsuit was different from the year before. Maybe being on my period had swelled my chest a little. I looked down and poked the top of my boobs and then cupped them with my hands. Cleavage…I spy cleavage.

My hips had changed, too. I put a hand on my hip and turned sideways in the mirror to discover a butt had also appeared out of nowhere. This two-piece swimsuit looked a little too good, so I quickly put a t-shirt and pair of shorts over it. Grammy would never let me go to the pool looking like a teenager, and this was the only suit I packed for the summer.

Grammy hadn't noticed any changes on her own or at least, she hadn't said anything. I walk around with this body every day and I had no clue what was going on. If anything, it was a little sad. Gone were the days of throwing on a swimsuit and not worrying about body part containment. Would this mean bras were next? I liked the comfy sports bras, but they were probably the reason I never noticed the boobies coming in.

I grabbed a small tote for a towel and change of clothes. I threw a couple of granola bars in because dinner was a long way off and swimming made me quite hungry. Luckily, the food at Grammy's hospital was good unlike the rumors about typical hospital cuisine. When Grammy finished getting ready, she yelled for us to go.

Driving back into town on the same day was odd. I looked for the bull when we passed the crossing, but he must have moved on. Even though doing something out of the norm was wonderful, I had to ask Grammy, "Why did you retire if you still want to work?"

Grammy smiled, “Retirement is such an odd thing. It’s like someone telling you, ‘thanks, but you are too old now to be of any use to society. Relax and enjoy the rest of the time you have’.”

“What’s wrong with that?” I wondered.

“Absolutely nothing if you are the relaxing sort,” she explained. “But why stop doing something I love when I am perfectly capable? And don’t forget that working gets me…,” then she pointed at me to finish the line I had heard a thousand times.

“…another mile up the Nile,” I finished, less than enthusiastic. It was a reference to her many globe-trotting trips she took every September after I went back to school. She had been using that poem for as long as I can remember.

“So Grammy,” I inquired, “what ever happened to Deidra? Did she end up marrying King Cocobar?”

“His name was King Conchobar,” she corrected. “Deidra did just as the prophesy said and grew up to be the most beautiful woman in the land. However, she had fallen in love with a young warrior in Conchobar’s army and eloped with him.”

“Did she live happily ever after?” I asked.

“Not quite,” Grammy responded. “Deidra and her new husband fled so they would be safe from Conchobar’s wrath. But, when any powerful man saw Deidra’s beauty, he wanted her for himself and attempted to have her husband killed. They were forced to flee to a small island with her husband’s brothers for protection. They were able to live in seclusion for a short time.”

The car slowed down. I had forgotten we were even driving because I was listening to the story so intently. A car was attempting to pass. This flustered Grammy and her response was to brake. After the car passed, we got back up to cruising speed, which was around 45mph. Grammy would then be able to continue the tale.

“King Conchobar found out where they were hiding,” she continued, “and he sent a search party for them. He told the messengers to let them know all had been forgiven and he would welcome them back with open arms.”

"Since they didn't live happily ever after, I'm guessing they never made it back," I concluded.

"They made it back," Grammy told me. "The king just had no intention of forgiving them. Once they arrived, Deidra's husband and two brothers were killed. The king, trying to eliminate witnesses, also murdered one of the messengers. The king regretted that because the messenger was the son of a very powerful man in Conchobar's kingdom. The father started a war against Conchobar for killing his son," she explained, grimacing. She glanced over in my direction and asked, "Do you want to stay until the pool closes tonight?"

"What?" I asked, not focusing on her question. Instead, pictures of swords, lies and death whirled around inside my head. Her question jolted me out of the past and I realized we were already stopped outside the pool. "Grammy, can we finish the story of Deidra?" I begged.

"Sorry, Muriel, but I have to get to work. It will have to be continued later," she decided.

"Fine," I said disappointedly. I looked in the direction of the pool, which by the sound of things was the usual madhouse. "The pool sounds pretty busy, Grammy, so I'll stay until closing and just walk up to the hospital after I change," I informed her.

"See you then," she smiled and off she went.

I paid my entrance fee into the pool. Everyone was required to shower off before entering the pool area, but I wasn't planning on getting into the water until all the little kids were out. The last thing I wanted to deal with was an elbow to the face or the urge to drown a kid who felt the need to splash me. I walked into the pool area dry as a bone and quickly laid out my towel.

According to the clock, it was almost 3 p.m., which meant the younger kids would be leaving in two hours. Anyone under 10 had to leave at 5 p.m. This was by far my favorite rule. The decibel level lowered considerably, making for a more relaxing environment.

At 4:45 p.m. came the lifeguard's announcement. All children 10 and under were to leave the pool area by 5 p.m. The huge wave of disappointed voices, crying and complaining commenced. The music being piped through the speakers changed to a mellower vibe. There wasn't much to do in this town besides go to the pool, which should make me more compassionate, but I remember getting kicked out before I was 10. They would live. There were some adults who never came to the pool until the younger kids had left. These adults even seemed annoyed with the kids 10 and over, but they would also survive.

It was torture to see the water from my towel and not be in it. As soon as the kids vacated, I dipped my toe in by the pool stairs and slowly walked all the way in. The water hugged me and danced around me. I couldn't help but smile. I dunked my head under. It felt like home.

I floated on my back while listening to the music. Had I not been in water, I may have fallen asleep. The clouds above me were puffy, but soon they morphed into different shapes. This was not like the game where you find an elephant in the sky. This was similar to when the tiles in my shower changed to something else. When I reached my hand up, I dipped under the water.

The clouds became puffs of smoke that filled a room. It was difficult to see exactly what was going on, but I could make out that one of them must have been my mother. She was laughing and tossing her hair back as she sniffed a line of white powder off a mirror. It was fascinating to see all of this going on until I was jolted up out of the water.

"Are you O.K.?" a concerned voice asked. "Can you breathe?" The fog of the vision left me. Slowly, I opened my eyes and calmly answered, "I'm fine."

"You were under the water for a long time," the voice said. "She's O.K.," he told those that had stopped to make sure all was well, "you can continue your swimming."

I tried to focus my eyes and see his face, but the way the sun was shining behind him made it difficult. He turned a little, "Douglas, is that you?" I asked.

"Yes," he smiled. "Am I really that forgettable?" he questioned. "It was only a few hours ago. You really know how to hurt a guy."

The vision had really done a number on me. It took a while to get my bearings back, although I did know that whatever just happened brought Douglas to my rescue, so it couldn't have been all bad.

"Put your arms around my neck," he instructed. Douglas was standing in about four feet of water while cradling me in his arms.

"I'm O.K. You can just put me down," I told him.

"I can't," he said. "Protocol says that if I dive in for a save attempt, I have to make sure the swimmer gets to the wall or safely to the steps."

I put my arms around his neck and smiled, "I may just begin to like rules. Why did you jump in to get me anyway?"

"You were under water for a really long time," he answered.

"I can hold my breath for a really long time," I quipped.

"Apparently, you can," he laughed. "Maybe you weren't under that long. I haven't been able to take my eyes off you since you got here. You snuck into the pool area without showering off, bad girl."

Blushing, I responded, "Well, as far as criminal activity goes, that's pretty tame."

"True. I wanted to come tell you that it was required, but it would have just been an excuse to talk to you and I wasn't sure how you'd take it," he explained.

We were looking at each other for a couple of seconds, but it felt like an uncomfortable amount of time. My arms were still wrapped around his neck and he was holding me in the water.

"So, about that 'safely getting me to the wall' part of the rescue," I hinted.

He shook his head, "Oh yeah, I'm sorry."

He walked me to the side of the pool. I grabbed the side of the wall, put my feet on the floor of the pool and jumped off the bottom to spin to a seated position on the edge of the pool.

"Thanks again," I said. "You saved me twice today."

"Twice?" he asked. "You'll have to tell me about that when I get off duty."

"I can't," I said, genuinely disappointed. "I have to walk to the hospital after the pool closes."

"Let me give you a ride there," he offered.

"If it's no trouble, that would be great," I accepted.

"Don't be ridiculous. It's the opposite of trouble," he smiled. "It will be my pleasure."

With that, he swam to the other side of the pool. I watched him lift his body out of the pool before turning to get back on my towel. There were a couple of sneers directed toward me from other girls, but it didn't concern me.

It was 6:30 p.m. and the pool closed at 8 p.m. Much to my surprise, the next hour and a half was filled with impure thoughts about Douglas. These were new ideas that I had never pondered until today. Boys had mostly been an annoyance, but Douglas was different. Or was I different? Had becoming a woman changed me that quickly? Was it possible?

At 7:30 p.m., I got up to go to the locker room to change into fresh clothes. My hair desperately needed to be attended to, but I didn't bring a brush so I just ran my fingers through it. I ate one of the granola bars so my stomach wouldn't growl. The clothes I brought would have been much cuter if I had known Douglas would be driving me to the hospital.

The locker room was deserted after 15 minutes. I decided to wait for Douglas on a bench right across the pool entrance. There was a little park there and he would see me when he came out or drove by. There was a clock in the front of the pool building, but it was a little too far to read from the park bench.

When it felt like I had been waiting for a really long time, I walked over to get a closer look. It was 8:20. Maybe Douglas had changed his mind. Grammy would be furious if I didn't arrive at the hospital by 8:45. Even if I didn't stop swimming until right at closing time, it would take me 15 minutes to change and 30 minutes tops to walk to the hospital.

After weighing the pros and cons of continuing to wait, I decided to head toward the hospital. Making Grammy angry wasn't worth the risk.

I hadn't been walking very long before a car pulled up. "Did you change your mind?" Douglas asked out the car window.

I kept walking. "No, I thought *you* did and I have to be at the hospital by 8:45."

He drove alongside me, "I'm sorry, I should have explained that I have to clean up and put chemicals in the water before I go. I usually don't get out of there until 8:30, but I rushed today. C'mon, get in so I can drive you," he finished.

It took him 3 minutes to get me to the hospital. One good thing about a small town is that there's no traffic. There were plenty of parking spaces, but he chose the one that was furthest away from the building.

"Well, thank you," I said opening up the door, "I really appreciate the ride and you saving my life earlier today," I joked.

He pointed at the clock, "We have almost 15 minutes before you have to go. Am I really that difficult to be around?"

I looked back over my shoulder and smiled at him. He was adorable. I closed the door, "You're bearable." We laughed.

"How old are you?" he asked.

"I'll be fourteen soon." I patted the dashboard of the car and said, "I take it since you can drive, you must be at least sixteen."

"Beauty and brains," he smiled, "that's a deadly combination. I turned sixteen last month. That's also how I can work at the pool. You can't work there unless you're sixteen."

I put my head down and couldn't look at him. He had dark hair and his eyes were a beautiful hazel color, but when he smiled, it was hard to concentrate.

"You are so beautiful," he announced unexpectedly.

My hair was a ratty mess. The clothes I was wearing could easily look just as good on him. My stomach felt bloated and I smelled of chlorine. Beautiful was not an adjective to describe me at that moment.

"Can I see you again? Maybe take you on a real date?" he wondered, waiting for a reply.

I looked at him. This was all very confusing. I had never been on a date. It was humorous to think what Grammy might say if she knew a boy wanted to date me. Of course the answer would be no, but it would be an entertaining topic of conversation.

"That would be nice," I said, "but I don't get to town very often. I'm not sure how this would work."

He shared his plan, "If your grandparents are anything like my grandma, they go to sleep around 7 p.m." I gave an affirming nod. "So," he continued, "I will drive out by you around 8:30 for a picnic. We'll have it close to your grandparents house so we will hear them if they come looking for you. We can watch the stars and talk."

"You're an evil genius," I complimented. "Sounds like a plan, but I really have to go."

"Hold on. A gentleman always gets the car door," he said.

He opened his door, ran around the car and opened my door. He put his hand out for mine, which I gave to him. He raised me out of the car and pressed me against the car looking down into my eyes. We just stared at each other for a bit. I wrapped my hands around his waist. He slid both hands up by my ears and slowly went in for a kiss while never losing eye contact. I closed my eyes and kissed him back.

There were no thoughts going through my head; I was completely present in the moment. I was only aware of him leaning against me, his hands holding my head and his lips touching mine. When he stopped kissing me, he touched his forehead to mine.

"I'm sorry, I should have asked to kiss you," he apologized. "I just had to see if I was right."

"Right about what?" I practically whispered.

"If love at first sight was possible," he explained.

I hugged him before releasing my arms from his waist. We looked at each other and smiled, which was the perfect opportunity for me to run into the hospital. I didn't look back or wave, just ran like someone was trying to kill me. Love at first sight?! So, he was a crazy person. It seemed befitting given the way this summer was going.

By the time I got to Grammy's wing of the hospital, the run had turned into a slow trot. It was still enough to get Grammy going.

"Muriel, we do not run in a hospital!" she scolded. "Did you have a good time at the pool?"

"I'm not sure what happened at the pool today," I responded.

"Well, we can talk about that later. Why don't you go get some dinner at the cafeteria and then come back to help," she suggested.

For dinner, I chose the cheese ravioli and a side salad. It was very good. When I returned to the nurse's station, both Grammy and her co-worker, Doris, were there.

"Grammy, when did you have your first kiss?" I blurted out. Doris raised her eyebrows and looked over at Grammy just as interested as I was in the answer to come.

"When Grandpa and I got married at the ceremony," she answered. "You know, when they say you may now kiss the bride."
I squinted in disbelief while glancing over at Doris.

"I don't believe that either," Doris said, shaking her head. "Not for a second." That comment earned Doris a smack to the shoulder with a patient file.

"I was somewhere around your age, if you must know," Grammy conceded. "I don't remember exactly."

"What was his name and how did you know him?" Doris probed.

"Doris, Mr. Neeley needs his meds now," Grammy said, obviously trying to get rid of her.

"Already done," Doris countered. "If you think I'm going to miss this gem of a conversation, Muriel, forget it," Doris laughed. Grammy didn't want to laugh, but she seemed to understand how

Doris was entertained by it all. A small smile escaped Grammy's lips even though she was trying to resist it.

"Well, if I can't get rid of you, Doris," she announced, "I can certainly get rid of my granddaughter. Go to the art room and read," she instructed, "but be quiet. Some patients are already sleeping."

I did as I was told and wasted away a couple of hours until Grammy got off at 11 p.m. There was so much I wanted to ask her on the way home.

When we got into the car, I started with the questions right away. "Grammy, how come no one ever told me that my mom did drugs?" I asked.

"You are going to find out all about her, Muriel. No one has to tell you anything," she explained, sounding tired.

"Is there any warning when the visions will come? Do they come at any specific time?" I wondered.

"There are no warning signs," she remarked, "but they tend to come more often when an Oris is relaxed. However, there are many women who claim the visions have come about when different emotions were at a heightened state."

"What kind of emotions?" I asked.

"Grief, fear, anger, love…you name it," she said listing off examples. "A lot of this information has been handed down for centuries in the Book of Deidra."

"Speaking of Deidra," I interrupted. "What happened to her? The last thing I remember is that Deidra was back in Ireland and her husband and his brothers were killed."

"That's right. The king had his loyal servant, Egan, kill the men. Deidra was then forced to marry King Conchobar." Grammy took a sip of water and then continued, "Deidra was miserable- grief stricken. She couldn't eat or sleep...wouldn't smile. This went on for a year, and I imagine the king tired of her no matter how beautiful she was. One day, he asked Deidra what she hated most. Her answer was King Conchobar and Egan."

“After everything they put her through, that is understandable,” I sympathized. “What did he do?”

“The king wasn’t very understanding,” Grammy said. “He gave Deidra to Egan to be his wife.”

I gasped, “No! Not the man who killed her husband.”

“Yep,” she nodded. “Conchobar was a real sweetheart. Deidra was riding in a carriage the day after her marriage to Egan and threw herself out. She dashed her head against the rocks and killed herself.”

Tears were coming, but I fought hard to keep them at bay. What a silly girl I was to get emotional over some history. It must be another side effect of my newly-acquired period.

“The name Deidra means broken-hearted, sorrowful and raging,” Grammy went on. It’s a common name in our history.”

“Why? Why would anyone name their child Deidra after hearing that awful story?” I asked, outraged.

“Because the women have lived as Oris and can relate to the heartbreak and sorrow,” Grammy said. “The men in our line knew of Deidra’s beauty and wanted their daughters named after her for that reason.” Grammy held my hand and started squeezing tightly.

“Ouch!” I yipped.

“Landmark!” she yelled out.

We had rounded the corner and were close to home. The grey barn was still visible at almost 11:30 at night because the stars were out in full force. I glared at her feeling tricked. She laughed in victory. That barn was a contest of sorts for the family- our sign that we were nearing home. Everyone wanted to see it first.

Once we got home, we made quick work of brushing our teeth and getting to bed. Deidra’s story was fascinating, but my mind kept creeping back to Douglas as I lay awake in bed. He was gorgeous, sweet, had his license…the list went on. It was only my first kiss, but it was amazing. The only question mark rattling around in my head had to do with the nonsense he said about love at first sight.

Besides, he couldn’t possibly love me. He didn’t even know my real name.

Chapter 10 Lorrah

My body decided to wake up at 5:30 a.m. the day after the memorial. I tried to talk it into going back to sleep, but it was no use. Showering or stirring might wake the others in the room, so I put a long sweater on over my pajamas, grabbed my tennis shoes and slid out the door. My pajama bottoms looked like yoga pants, but it wouldn't have concerned me if they were plaid, flowered or had sleeping animals all over them.

This morning found me feeling hollow, almost void of emotion. The last couple of days were tiring and my brain seemed to shut down almost as a protection mechanism. It was a welcomed state. I slipped my shoes on and off I went. If nothing else, the fresh air was a welcomed change to our room.

Main Street hadn't changed much. It still had the same small-time, comforting feel it always did. My brain slightly reengaged and there was no doubt I would be meeting that woman at the café this morning. It was something Grammy wanted. There was nothing I wouldn't do for her.

The boards on the Main Street walkway creaked. Because it was so early, it seemed incredibly loud. The café where Grammy had shared the story of Enya was now a coffee house. It was hard to believe, but it was already open for business this early. The aroma coming from inside was too much to resist. The sign on the door made me appreciate the simplicity of this town even more: "Coffee: Open 5 a.m. until 3 p.m.". Where we lived, all the shops were trying to use word-play to name their coffee shops. When everyone is doing it, it's no longer special. Dear God, I thought, that sounds just like something my Grammy would say. I choked back tears.

Coming into the shop, I was a little worried that it would evoke painful memories, but it had been completely renovated and looked nothing like the old restaurant. A woman immediately asked what she could get me even though I was still in the doorway. It was apparent caffeine was running through her veins already.

"Um, can I get a medium coffee with cream and a bear claw?" I asked.

"Coming right up," she said.

While she readied the coffee, I perused the menu board and saw the prices. What was I thinking? My purse was in the hotel. "Miss," I said, "I am so sorry, but I forgot my purse in the hotel. I will be right back."

"Don't be silly," she smiled and handed me the coffee and pastry. "Just pay me later."

These were just the kind of actions to be expected in this town. People believed the best of each other. It had been ten long years since my last visit here, which made gestures like that too easy to forget.

"I'll pay for her order," the woman from the cemetery said as she laid money on the counter, "and can I get another large, black coffee?" She glanced in my direction, "This is going to be a long morning."

Immediately annoyed, I addressed her, "A long morning for you? You have some nerve! What happened to meeting here at seven, anyway?" I asked.

"Your grandmother made me promise to stay here all day," she explained, "from the time this place opened to when it closed. There isn't anything I wouldn't do for that lady, so here I am as promised," she raised her arms from her side and let them fall.

"It appears you're chipper in the morning," I said, sarcastically. "I am a lucky woman."

"Here you go," the woman handed the stranger her coffee. You could tell the friction between us was making the woman behind the counter uncomfortable.

The stranger offered some suggestions, "We can talk here, take a drive or go back to my hotel room. Which would you prefer?"

"First, before we go anywhere- what is your name? There are a couple of names I'd like to call you, but they are not very flattering," I smiled.

"My name is Lorrah," she answered.

"Well, Lorrah, I don't care for any of your options. How about we go for a walk?" I suggested. "There is a park not too far from here, and I can guarantee there won't be any children in it at this time in the morning."

"That sounds good. After you," she said as she opened the door for me and we headed out.

"So, tell me," I started, "how exactly do you know my grandmother?"

Lorrah grinned, "Your grandmother saved my life in a manner of speaking. My lot in life was not a very happy one years ago. I didn't understand the visions, and my foster parents thought mental issues were the cause. They wanted to have me committed or medicated. It seemed reasonable to me at the time, too, because I didn't understand what was happening."

"Where had your parents gone?" I asked, feeling a kinship to her.

"Oris women don't always stick around," she explained. "You know something about that. My mother gave me up for adoption five days after I was born. Once she found out that I was female, she started the adoption process. I know nothing about my father," she finished.

I pointed the way up to the park and we turned onto the correct street. We walked for a little while in silence. My animosity for Lorrah melted away after learning she was completely abandoned as a child. When we reached the park, my mind was abuzz with questions. There was a park bench, but I was drawn toward the swings. Movement helped to keep my visions at bay, and I wanted to be fully present for this conversation.

"There are so many questions I want to ask," I broke the silence.

"You are welcome to any information I have," Lorrah smiled as she got on the swing beside me. She must have noticed my softening toward her.

"If you were abandoned, how did you find out that you are an Oris?" I asked while looking around, still feeling uncomfortable saying that word out loud.

"A great aunt came to me and explained everything," she answered. "The older generations are responsible for explanation and they take it very seriously. I thought she was crazy, but she put me in touch with your grandmother."

"What did you mean when you said my grandmother saved your life?" I wondered.

"Well, she helped explain my visions and understand our history. The same thing she did for you," she shared. "I don't know where I would be today without her guidance- probably a psych ward. You were lucky she was there when the visions first started. The story she tells about going into town to get period supplies is hilarious. And "here, bully, bully" at the crossing still makes me laugh. It's surreal being in this town where it all took place."

"She told you about that?" I asked.

Lorrah looked at me surprised, "Most Oris know that story. It is in the Book of Deidra." She searched my face trying to read my reaction. "Remember when I told you that your grandmother was from the line of Enya?"

"Yes," I answered.

"Well, because of that fact, she is the leader of our kind. Sorry, was the leader," she teared up a little. "Talking about her in the past tense still doesn't seem right."

"That's what I don't understand. She told me that Enya was from a neighboring village of our ancestors," I argued. The thought of my Grammy lying about anything didn't seem possible.

"That is true. Your ancestors didn't come from Gilfin. They came from the village of Bray," she swung back and forth. "When Enya was sent away to Germany, it was right around the time the great rains came. The villagers were very superstitious so they thought the rains were punishment for letting Enya go. The tales of Enya's beauty were very well known through all of Europe. The villagers believed men would return to the village of Gilfin in hopes of finding the next beauty."

"I still don't understand what this has to do with my lineage," I interrupted.

Lorrah stopped swinging and explained, "Muriel, Enya had three younger sisters that would also grow up to be just as beautiful. The family realized that the only way to keep them safe was to move. They moved to Bray. In the end, it probably wasn't necessary because the famine and Black Death made travel almost non-existent. You are a descendant of the youngest sister," she concluded.

"Why was I never told any of this until now?" I inquired.

"Your grandmother said you didn't take the news about being an Oris very well. That for quite some time you pushed your identity away. Apparently, you have a bit of a temper and she thought it best not to unload everything on you at once." Lorrah went on, "Your grandmother should have told you years ago, but she wanted to protect you. She promised to fill you in on everything at Christmas this year."

It slipped my mind that Grammy was coming out for Christmas this year. We had been planning the details of her trip for months. "How is it you know so much about my grandmother's plans?" I wondered.

"It was in the newsletter," she said flatly.

The look on my face must have screamed confusion. Lorrah giggled, "The Oris are a pretty organized lot nowadays. We have been able to compile information to help each other get through the challenges of our affliction."

"Affliction," I huffed, "that's an understatement. So, what did my Grammy do exactly? What were her responsibilities as the leader?"

"She hosted meetings all over the world compiling information and deciding what was relevant to be recorded in the Book of Deidra. Your grandmother also shared stories about her summers with you as you aged," she told me. "She would announce any new findings about your visions. And she always took time to speak privately with young Oris who didn't have any support."

This brought a smile to my face. All those trips Grammy went on every year must have been peppered with these meetings. If she could help someone, she never missed the opportunity. I closed my eyes and kicked the swing up again. What a lucky little girl I had been to have her in my life.

Lorrah interrupted my thoughts, "Um, Muriel, what was her name?"

This question jolted me and brought my defenses up again. It made no sense that someone Lorrah claimed to be so close to wouldn't even know my grandmother's name.

"Excuse me! How is it you don't know her name?" I asked, confused. I stood up from the swing giving her a look of disbelief.

"No one knows her real name. We call her 'Ellowee' or 'El' for short. Your grandmother led a very secretive existence," Lorrah seemed concerned that I had no knowledge of this information. "The name comes from a quick pronunciation of the acronym L.O.E. for line of Enya."

I sat back down on the swing. There was a whole history about my grandmother that was unknown to me. It hurt that she had never shared it. Knowing Grammy was coming at Christmas to tell me all of this was a small comfort, but I longed to hear this information from her lips. I needed to look into her eyes while she spoke, because her gaze would help me be secure in the fact that everything would be alright. Even as an adult with my own child, I still needed her.

"No one knew where your grandmother lived." Lorrah went on, "We wagered with each other and most people thought she called Russia home." Lorrah looked around the landscape and raised her arm, "I would have never guessed she lived here. Ellowee could have lived wherever she wanted. She must have preferred the small-town life."

We swung back and forth, looking around at the countryside.

"You know," she added, "a lot of people tried to find this place…tried to find Ellowee. Even though no one knew where she lived, she had many of our addresses and would sometimes write to people. The letters were postmarked from all over the world and rarely the same place twice."

"How did you come to know about her home now?" I wondered.

"Ellowee left a package with her attorney to be delivered after her death," she explained. "She chose me to receive the package." Lorrah had to turn away as she was getting choked up. "I have never been more honored by anything than when I realized your grandmother had faith in me to carry out her wishes," she shared.

A yell of attack came from over the mound above the park. It was three young boys coming to live out their pirate or soldier fantasies bright and early. The parents probably live close by and were not prepared to deal with that level of energy this early in the morning, so they sent their sons to go play in the park. It seemed a bit early for the park to be occupied, but this town stirred earlier than most.

"Do you have the time?" I asked Lorrah.

She raised her sleeve and read the time off her watch as 7:45. The watch she was wearing was beautiful and had to be quite expensive. I was glad for Lorrah. Whatever difficult beginning she had in life, she must have been doing well now.

"It was very nice meeting you, Lorrah. I appreciate you taking the time to talk to me, but I really have to get back," I announced pointing back toward town. "Maybe we can exchange phone numbers or addresses and keep in touch," I suggested. "It would be so nice to know another Oris, not to mention that you also knew my grandmother."

We both got up out of our swings to exchange a hug.

"I am afraid that your grandmother may not have put her faith in the right Oris. This seemed like it would be easier," Lorrah shared as we began to walk back.

"You did wonderfully," I complimented. "I apologize for being so difficult when we first met. You didn't deserve that. This has been a very emotional time for me, and I hope you will forgive my poor manners."

"Of course," she kindly said. "That ring on your finger…" she trailed off, looking at my hand.

I looked down and saw the ring that my grandmother had always worn. My grandparent's last will and testament had been read last night before we left for the hotel. There were a few things they wanted to go to specific relatives. This ring was one of those things. It wasn't particularly high in value by monetary standards, but it meant the world to me.

A vision was coming. The trail we were on began spinning so I found a tree to lean against. It was lucky that a vision hadn't come since the theater back home.

"It's not fair," a teenage girl complained. "It should be Pearl's responsibility, not mine."

"You know that is not the way this works, Muriel! Pearl cannot have children and she will die from her illness," an older woman explained.

This was a vision of my Grammy! She couldn't have been more than sixteen or so. It was obvious she was very upset. The tears flowed and she shook her head. "Maybe I won't be able to have kids!" Grammy screamed. "Pearl is the eldest!"

"Calm down and listen," the woman commanded. "Whether you like it or not, this choice is mine and you will be our next leader. Your cousin Pearl is a wreck who can barely take care of herself let alone our people. You are bright, resourceful and strong. There is no other choice but you."

"It's not fair! What kind of life will this be for me?" Grammy wept.

"The life you want it to be," the woman answered softly. "You will have a life for yourself, but in helping others your life will be complete and have deeper meaning. At sixteen, this is a difficult thing to understand. Be brave, my sweet girl, and give your great-aunt your hand." With tears in her eyes, my Grammy raised her hand. The woman slipped the same ring on her finger that I now wore on mine.

Coming out of this vision was a quick process. Lorrah was pacing back and forth about five feet away from where the tree was holding me up.

"No," I whispered.

"I'm afraid so," Lorrah nodded assuming the vision's basic message. "Your grandmother said you would be the best leader we have ever had."

It only took a second to mourn my old life. As much as the responsibility of taking on this new role frightened me, it became clear it would honor my grandmother. There wasn't a choice to make, because there was only the right thing or the selfish thing to choose between.

Besides, if my Grammy could become Ellowee at sixteen, I could certainly accomplish the task as an adult. How hard could it be? I'd attend a few meetings here and there and decide what to write in the book.

I stood up. "So, what do we do now?" I asked Lorrah. "Where do I start?"

Her face lit up and a sigh of relief escaped her. We continued to walk into town.

"First," she started, "I will offer you a job that requires traveling. This will give you flexibility to travel when it's necessary. Your family should still leave this afternoon, but you need to stay here for a week. We'll tell your husband it's to tie up loose ends here with your grandparents and also to start training for your new position. Your first Oris meeting is in a couple of days about an hour from here. You will be now be known as Ellowee to everyone you meet at these meetings. Your real name is not to be used," Lorrah was rattling on.

"Whoa. Slow down, Lorrah," I suggested. "I said 'where do I start'. Let me tell my husband about staying behind first and go from there. I think a job in marketing would suit me best," I mused. "What do you think?"

"Done," she said.

While we were walking down Main Street, we ran into Rick and Deidra.

"Hi, honey," Rick greeted me. "Deidra and I were going to get some breakfast before heading out to the airport. Would you like to join us?"

"No, thank you, sweetheart, but I would like to introduce you to someone," I said, putting my hand on Lorrah's back. "This is Lorrah. She just interviewed me for a position in the marketing department at her firm." Lorrah was holding up well, having just had this sprung on her. I made the formal introductions, "Lorrah, this is my husband Rick and my daughter Deidra." Rick shook Lorrah's hand and smiled, as did Deidra.

Rick's reaction was that of surprise because I hadn't even spoken to him about returning to work. Once we were alone, he would tell me that going back to work was a rash decision after the trauma of losing my grandparents. He missed his calling as a counselor. "If it's O.K. with you," I addressed Rick, "I would like to stay behind for a week. Finish up some business with my grandparents' estate and start job training about an hour away."

"Whatever you need, honey," he smiled. "I should be able to hold down the fort for a week."

"I'll miss you," Deidra announced as she hugged me. "Are you going to be alright?"

I nodded, "Enjoy your breakfast and I will say goodbye to you at the room a little later."

Lorrah and I walked on toward the hotel. "You don't waste any time, Muriel," Lorrah giggled. She got more serious. "I didn't know you had a daughter. I'm so sorry," she said no longer giggling.

"It seems strange to have someone apologize to me because I have a daughter. But, at the same time, it is refreshing that someone understands the challenge," I explained.

"She is beautiful. The name Deidra suits her," Lorrah observed. I didn't want to think of her beauty or what that could mean.

"What exactly are my responsibilities as Ellowee?" I asked.

Lorrah seemed very concerned about my question. "Didn't you see everything in the vision? You should have a basic understanding from that," she told me.

"I saw my grandmother being given the ring," I said. "She didn't want it, but she took it anyway."

"That's interesting," she said, obviously lying. "You should have seen all that Ellowee has done through the years, to include the responsibilities and dangers of the position."

"Dangers?" I asked. "Why will there be dangers?"

"Um, Muriel, how many visions do you get a day- on average," she inquired.

"Luckily, I don't get visions every day," I told her. "Maybe a short vision once a month or so. I try to avoid them as much as possible. I've learned a couple of tricks." I delivered my answer with a bit of pride, but Lorrah seemed concerned by my response. She even looked a little frightened.

"And this has been the course of things since you started having visions?" she probed.

"In the beginning, there was one or two a day sometimes. But, I was able to get it down to one or two a week," I shared, smiling. "Now, one or two a month is all I have to deal with. Maybe someday, they will disappear altogether. Wouldn't that be lucky?"

"Yes, lucky," Lorrah repeated, in shock. "Muriel, do you have any idea what you are agreeing to by becoming Ellowee?"

"Not really," I confessed. "But, if my Grammy wanted me to do it, I will honor her wishes."

We had reached my room. "How about we meet at the coffee house tomorrow around 8 a.m. and travel to where this meeting will be?" I asked. "We can stay there overnight to prepare. You said the meeting is two days from now?"

“Yes,” she answered. “That sounds good. I am staying at the hotel across the street if you need anything or want to talk more. No Oris except me knows that your grandmother has died,” she informed me. “Your first task as Ellowee is to make that announcement.” Lorrah started across the street.

The dread of that responsibility sunk in.

“Wait,” I yelled out. Lorrah turned around. “I forgot to tell you. Her name was Muriel Elizabeth Chamberlain. I’m named after her. She was an amazing woman.”

“Yes, she was,” Lorrah smiled. “Let’s hope it runs in the family.”

Chapter 11 Happy Birthday to Me

Swimming was reason enough to sleep like the dead, but spending time with Douglas and staying up late was just the combination needed to ensure I woke up in the same position as when I had fallen asleep.

I lifted my arms up over my head while still in bed to facilitate a long, noisy stretch. It was one of those satisfying stretches that made me want to go back to sleep so I could do it again. What a pleasure it is to wake up on my own with no vacuum banging against the bed!

By the smell of things, my birthday cake was already in the oven. Telling Douglas that I would be fourteen soon wasn't a lie. I merely omitted the part about it being the next day. It always seemed like it would be better to have a birthday during the school year with my friends, but mine fell on June 17th. Grammy and Gramps did their best to make it special. Grammy would bake a mandarin orange cake. It wasn't my favorite cake other times of the year, but for my birthday it was perfect- refreshing and light.

Sometimes my mother would call on my birthday. It would be awkward, but the call never lasted longer than five minutes. For someone who rarely spoke to me, you would think she would have more to say. Every birthday, I wished it didn't matter to me if she called or not. Yet, whenever she didn't call, my hopes of something changing between us or having a relationship with her were dashed again. It was a vicious cycle which left me angry that I dared let myself hope again.

My father, on the other hand, would sing to me and I had to listen to his rendition of "Happy Birthday" in its entirety. We would talk for ten or fifteen minutes. The topic of conversation could range from cars to the weather. We would always end up laughing, which made me miss him terribly. The summer was his time to vacation or do things on his own. Being a single dad couldn't be the easiest life, but I sometimes wished we could do things together.

Besides the phone calls, my birthday also meant that I could choose what we were having for dinner. I selected Grammy's zucchini casserole for two reasons: It was pretty much the only meal that she could make well, and I liked it. There would be a couple little gifts and cake, but not a lot of fanfare. Then, the next day would be the eighteenth of June. I tossed the blankets aside and sarcastically said to myself: "Let's get this party started."

It became impossible to get up out of bed. The room started spinning, my head fell back down on the pillow and I stared upward as my eyes began to focus on a scene. It played like a movie. There was a far-off cry at first, but as the scene came into view the crying got much louder. There was a lot of blood, and I found myself hovering over a scene in a hospital. It was the woman from the play- my mother. She had just given birth to me. The sobbing was from her, not her newborn.

She was shaking her head when the nurse tried to hand her the baby that was bundled in blankets. She wouldn't hold the baby. The doctor looked at her chart and asked if she was certain she wanted this next procedure because she would not be able to have more children. She nodded and said, "I didn't want this one."

Slowly, the vision started to disperse. I reached out my hand to see if I could touch the scene. This was a clearer vision than the one in the shower. It was more tangible and real. Grammy didn't need to know about this one. It was painful for me to watch, but she would probably take it twice as hard.

The door to the bedroom creaked open. A pair of bright, smiling blue eyes peeked around the door. I lifted my head and smiled, awaiting the rest of my grandpa to come into the room. He was smiling, holding a big sunflower in his hand. There are many kinds of sunflowers, but the one he was carrying was the kind that, if left to grow, would produce hundreds of sunflower seeds and weigh about five pounds.

"Happy birthday, Muriel," he said and put the sunflower on the bedside table.

We hugged and he was already warm from the morning sun. Gramps smelled of earth as he always did, and I breathed it in. It was one of my favorite smells.

I looked at the sunflower and back at Gramps. "Why did you cut that down?" I asked. "There would have been tons of seeds on that. We could have roasted them and feasted."

"Because this flower," he explained, "is like you right now. It's not quite ready to bear fruit, yet it can still share joy and beauty with this world."

"Wow, Gramps, very poetic of you," I responded with a grin. "So you killed it."

He nodded, and patted the bed before getting up to go. When he reached the door, he turned around and said, "Sometimes, it's nice to remember the flower before it gets too big for her britches." He winked and went back to his chores.

After showering and getting dressed, I went to the kitchen. Grammy was a busy little bee, flitting around stirring this and baking that. She sang "Happy Birthday" immediately after I came into the room. What was it with my family thinking they could sing? It's like punishment. The last stanza was finally approaching, but she added the "how old are you now" and the "you look like a monkey and smell like one too" verses. Apparently, I had been extra bad this year.

When the screeching was over, the hugging commenced. The hug was always worth the offenses my ears had to suffer. "Thank you, Grammy," I said, only thinking of the hug. The kitchen had many different work stations in each corner. "Would I be in your way if I made some toast?" I asked.

"Toast," she huffed. "Not on your birthday. Go sit down and I will get you some eggs and fruit."

There would be no need to argue with that. I was famished, and eggs were always welcome on my plate. As I waited for my breakfast, Gramps would pass by various windows as he busied himself in the yard and garden.

"Hey, Grammy, how often do the visions happen?" I asked.

Grammy looked around to see if Gramps was still outside. "It's different for everyone," she explained. "When Oris are young and there is much to learn, the visions are constant- sometimes all day. As we age, they no longer occur as often. Some people think it is because we have learned as much as we can from them."

"What do you mean by some people?" I asked confused.

"Uh, not sure why I said that," she waved off my question.

My suspicions were raised by her answer, but the eggs and fruit she placed before me distracted my train of thought and I quickly forgot any follow-up questions. "Thanks, Grammy, it looks so good," I complimented. It was a gorgeous day out, and I sat at the kitchen table watching Grammy cook and Gramps do chores outside while I ate.

Just as my breakfast was almost devoured, there were loud engine sounds that filled the air. Grammy went to the window to attempt to see who was here or what was going on, but the tree blocked her view. Gramps sounded like he was greeting someone so it mustn't be a stranger. Not being the slightest bit curious, I sat there drinking my juice and chalked their reactions up to small-town living.

Gramps came into the kitchen, "Look who I found, birthday girl!"

"Happy birthday, Muriel," my father said.

"Daddy!" I screamed and ran to him for a hug. "What are you doing here?"

"I'm sorry. I'll go," he joked and turned to pretend he was leaving. He turned back around, "I'm on a motorcycle run that just happened to pass very close to here. A little detour was nothing if it meant I could wish you a happy birthday. This is Hans," he said pointing to the guy behind him. "He's from Germany, but he is here doing business with the company I work for. We got to talking and he mentioned he liked motorcycles and wanted to see different parts of the state. So here we are."

We all exchanged greetings. It was so nice to see my dad. I had only been with my grandparents for two weeks, so for him to stop by this soon was a real treat. We spent a couple of hours together. When it got close to lunch time, Grammy asked them if they would like to stay. They declined, saying they should get back on the road. After waving goodbye and a tear or two, they were gone as quickly as they had come: the sound of their motorcycle engines still audible even after they were out of sight over the hill.

"That was nice that your dad stopped by," my grandfather said.

"It was good to see him," I agreed. "I wonder if that German dude really does like motorcycles. He looked green like he was going to throw up."

"Maybe American food doesn't agree with him," Grammy said, "but I have eaten German food and you would think our cuisine would be easier to digest."

After the commotion of visitors, we enjoyed a tasty lunch. I wished my dad and his friend would have stayed, but I was glad that he stopped to see me at all. Grammy started clearing the table, which was normally my job. Having a birthday came with certain perks.

The phone rang and Grammy's hands were in the sink. She sighed from the disappointment of not being able to answer it, and asked if Grandpa would get the phone. If Grammy could help it, she always answered the phone. She believed that grandpa's technique wasn't as etiquette-rich as it could have been.

"Yeah," Gramps yelled into the phone as he answered it.
He handed the receiver to me, "It's for you, birthday girl".

"Hello," I answered, dreading the response from the voice on the other end.

"Birthday girl?" the male voice questioned.

"Yes," I said wondering who this could be.

Grammy could sense the tension and knew it had to be my mother. She quickly wiped her hands and went to the living room. She thought leaving the room would put me at ease. Grandpa didn't budge. He sat back down at the table. Gramps was unaffected by most of life's happenings. It was an admirable quality.

"This is Douglas," the voice announced. "I went through my grandma's address book to find your grandparent's phone number. I had such a wonderful time yesterday. Can I drive out to see you tonight around 8?" he asked.

It took a minute to get my bearings as I had assumed this would be my mother calling. "Um, that would be nice," I responded, trying not to smile.

"There are other people close by," he guessed. "Watch for me out front because I don't want to honk. It might wake up your grandparents. I miss you, and it hasn't even been 24 hours. I think you should tell me your name tonight. It's only fair. You held out on me that your birthday was today."

"That's nice," I ad-libbed. "What did you say to Gramps when you called?"

"I asked if the beautiful young houseguest was available," he answered.

"You really know how to think on your feet," I joked.

"I'm sitting down, but thank you," he said. "Well, I don't want to interrupt any more of your celebration, so I will see you tonight."

"That sounds good. You take care of yourself," I finished the conversation. If Grammy was listening, that seemed like a plausible ending to a conversation with my mom. I hung up the receiver and unplugged the cord from the back of the phone and tucked it under the phone. Just in case my mother did decide to call this year, we wouldn't want Grammy questioning the earlier call.

Because she could eavesdrop just as easily in the other room, Grammy waltzed into the kitchen shortly after I hung up the receiver. She left the dishes to soak and started a solitaire game at the table. I picked up a piece of Gramps' newspaper but only pretended to read it while I thought about Douglas driving here.

"So how was your phone call?" Grammy asked.

"It was good," I said, relieved that I could answer honestly.

"Well, I am going to go clean some of my guns," Gramps announced. "Maybe load a couple."

"Why would you do that Wayne?" Grammy growled at her husband.

"We have a beautiful young houseguest in our midst," he winked at me and left.

"I will never understand your grandfather," she started. "He can use a word like 'midst' but continues to answer the phone like a Neanderthal."

"Pretty sure Neanderthals never used a phone," I kidded, choosing to side with Gramps after he covered for me with that phone call.

"You know what I mean," she said perturbed.

"Ah, ah, ah…no getting annoyed with the birthday girl," I reminded her. It was only one day of the year, so I needed to take full advantage of it.

Grammy got up to finish the sinkful of dishes. "Why aren't you telling me about any of your visions, Muriel," she inquired. "You must have had at least one or two since the one in the shower."

"I had one this morning about my birth," I said.

"Did you cry a lot when you were born?" Grammy asked.

"That is an interesting question," I commented. "I didn't cry at all. Why? Does that mean something?"

"It means you are an Oris with a bent for the Earth. You'll be more grounded than most," she smiled. "Well, as grounded as an Oris can be. You will appreciate nature. When and if you have children, you will probably stay."

"You know all that because I didn't cry when I was born?" I asked.

"Yes, the Book of Deidra records generations of births," she answered.

I shook my head and turned back toward the table. After living with the knowledge of being an Oris for only a few short days, I was already fed up. One of the dogs came by me and nudged my arm to be petted. "How about, for my birthday, we don't talk about Oris stuff," I said. My Grammy didn't answer, but she obliged me in my request for the remainder of the day.

Cake was served later that afternoon, and presents were opened. As much as I appreciated all they had done to make my day special, it was seeing Douglas that I couldn't help looking forward to. The secrecy added to the excitement, and I was practically giddy with nerves.

The 5 p.m. news halted everything in the household. As they watched, I looked around the house to make sure everything had been cleaned up. Grammy's small kitchen garbage was full from wrapping paper. I took it outside to dump and brought the dogs along so they could go potty before bed.

My motives were selfish. If everything was taken care of by the time the news was over, there would be nothing stopping them from getting ready for bed. Six may seem a little early, but an early bedtime was a prerequisite of country living. Grammy and Gramps would don their pajamas and have their teeth brushed by 6:30 p.m. They would then get into bed for reading. With any luck, both would be snoring by 7:30.

It all worked to plan, and I was sitting in the living room by 7 p.m., listening for sounds of sleep. There was some rustling, which put me on edge, but I realized it was the dogs. The dogs! Those two animals barked every time a leaf fell from a tree. Douglas' arrival would wake my grandparents for sure.

I walked into the kitchen where the dogs slept and tried to reason with them. "Now listen, there is going to be a car pulling up, but you can't bark," I explained. They just looked at me, and it was apparent this little talk wasn't going to change their canine nature. They would do what they've always done…bark. I paced the kitchen trying to come up with a plan.

It took fifteen minutes, but I had an idea. I grabbed an old blanket and took the dogs outside. They may still bark, but if they were already outside, the barking wouldn't be as loud and I could shush them at the gate. The gate was the farthest place on the property from the bedrooms. I laid out the old blanket on the other side of the well house (a small shelter for the ground water well). It was just big enough to hide us from view if my grandparents came looking.

Every car that drove by in the next 45 minutes made me jump, (which meant I jumped twice because there wasn't a lot of traffic on the road). The third car was Douglas. He slowed and came up the short lane of my grandparents' drive, the tires making noise with the dirt and gravel beneath them. The dogs briefly lost their minds, but they were easy to get under control. I nervously shushed them while looking back up at the house to see if any lights flickered on. The TV was left on, but I purposely shut off most other lights. If my grandparents did wake up, it would be easy to tell because lights would be turned on as they made their way to the back door.

Douglas got out of the car wearing that smile that did strange things to me. "C'mon, let's go," he waved for me.

"I can't," I refused. "You have to come in. If my grandparents wake up and I'm not anywhere to be found, they will freak."

This is the first time I had seen Douglas look frightened. It was not an attractive look for him. Even when he was "rescuing" me from the pool, he had a confident air about him. "Listen," I explained, "it's understandable if you don't want to come in, but I have it all planned out. We hang out behind the well house where we can't be seen. If my grandparents come out of the house, we'll know because the lights will come on. If they come out, I tell them the dogs wanted to go outside, which happens all the time."

After explaining my genius plan, I watched Douglas weigh the odds. His hesitation infuriated me. "Goodnight, Douglas, I'll see you later," I said as I turned to walk back to the house.

"Wait," he said a little too loudly and forcibly for the dog's liking. I shushed them from barking or growling at him. He lowered his voice and explained, "I just brought you a little cupcake for your birthday, and I wanted to sing "Happy Birthday" to you."

Not another singer. One more rendition of that song today might do me in, so I asked, "How about we skip the song and we share the cupcake?"

He grabbed a box out of the car and made his way to the gate, which I opened for him. The dogs knew that was a sign of a friend, but they still were required to do their due diligence as dogs and smell every inch of him. Once Douglas was accepted into the pack, we walked toward the blanket. The house was still black except for the TV scenes lighting up the living room area. Douglas put the box down when we reached the blanket and gave me a hug that erased all my irritation from earlier.

"Happy birthday, what's-your-face," he whispered.

"Muriel," I said, "my name is Muriel."

He stopped hugging me and looked into my eyes. It was uncomfortable and addicting all at the same time. "Muriel," he smiled, "is such an unusual name. I've never met anyone named Muriel before."

"Yes you have. My Grammy's name is Muriel," I told him.

He smiled as he started planting little kisses on my cheek. "Well," he remarked in between kisses, "I've never met anyone I wanted to kiss named Muriel."

The little kisses made their way to my neck, which was completely distracting. My eyes started to blink much slower until it was a job to keep them open. Douglas put his hand on the other side of my neck as the kisses were headed north to my ears. He barely breathed on them when the goosebumps covered my entire body. Abruptly, I pulled away and looked at him. He smiled with a twinkle in his eye that made me realize he knew exactly what those kisses were doing to me.

"Maybe we should celebrate your birthday now," he sat on the blanket and patted a spot close to himself.

While he patted the blanket, I could practically hear warning sirens going off in my head. The spot I chose was on the other side of the blanket where the box was between us. Douglas opened the box and took out a cupcake, some candles and a lighter. It was the sweetest thing. He lit the candle, "You need to make a wish, Muriel. I love saying your name…Muriel."

There was no need to think or spend too much time pondering a wish. It was an easy decision. I closed my eyes to blow out the candle. There are probably wishes made by people every year at their birthdays. No doubt, many were frivolous but mine were always serious. This year was no exception: I didn't want to be an Oris.

Douglas took the candle out of the cupcake. After removing the paper, he held it out for me to take a bite. He moved the box so he could scoot closer to me. He squinted at me and said, "I think you may have some icing on your lip. Let me help get that off." He leaned forward and kissed me. How could something I had only done once before feel so natural- so effortless? At first, my mind was thinking about the cupcake, thankful there were no remains of it still in my mouth. After a few more kisses, there was nothing going through my mind at all.

He smelled so good. His lips were softer than I remembered, but after a few minutes his hand wandered up my shirt. My reaction was to grab his hand and remove it. He looked a little surprised. He probably was used to getting his way.

"I'm sorry," he apologized. "Was I moving too fast?"

"Fast, why would you say that?" I questioned. "I mean, we've known each other for 48 hours and I'm still wondering when we're going to set a date for the wedding."

"Are you always sarcastic?" he asked.

"Yes. Is that a deal-breaker?" I wondered.

He smiled and shook his head no. He grabbed my hand, bringing it to his mouth. He kissed the back of my hand then traveled all the way up my arm until reaching my neck. This was all new, but it was safe to say that the neck/ear area was definitely a hotspot. So much so, that we had gone from a seating position to lying down on the blanket without me being aware. He had his arms around me, and mine were around him. We kissed for a long time until one of the dogs came over and started licking Douglas' face. Douglas rolled over, grabbed the cupcake and threw it for the dogs to chase down and eat. We laughed but tried to quiet ourselves.

We flopped back on the blanket, facing the stars. "Tell me something," he said. "I want to get to know you. Your name was a good start, but I sense there may be more to you than your name."

Gazing upwards, I answered, "There isn't much to know. Just a standard teenage girl, I guess."

"I don't hang out with standard teenage girls. Trust me, you are far from standard," he announced.

His statement was meant as a compliment, but it got my defenses up. "No, I suppose you don't," I sneered. "You didn't get that good at kissing all by yourself. Exactly how many girls have had the incredible honor of your company?"

"I don't know how many girls I've kissed," he told me seemingly annoyed. "I don't keep count."

"Yeah, that doesn't seem like the right answer," I concluded.

"What would you have me say?" he wondered.

I paused to think about that and spoke my thoughts out loud, "There really isn't a right answer to that question. If you say one girl, and you are that good at kissing, you must have really kissed the one girl a lot. And if you say fifteen or more, you seem like a playboy. But, in the end, who wants to deal with a bad kisser anyway?" I looked over at him to see that beautiful smile. I smiled back, "You'll be the last person I ever ask."

He turned back toward the stars. "Do you ever wonder if there is life on other planets?" he asked, pointing to the stars.

"I hope not," I answered. "Look at how beautiful they are, untouched and pure. If life existed in other places, there would be pain, broken relationships, illness, greed," I looked over to see Douglas concerned, "sorrow, disappointment…what?! Why are you looking at me like that?"

"You can be very dark," he observed. He rolled towards me. "I do want you to know something about me, though," he shared. "I've been with three girls. I mean, had sex with three girls."

I raised an eyebrow. "Okay. I am not sure how to respond to that," I said.

"You don't need to respond at all. But I feel like you should know. The thing is, I don't know if it was real," he stammered. "We would be making out, which led to clothing removal. Clothing removal led to sex. It all seemed like some sort of natural progression, but it was a physical progression, not an emotional one."

"Dude, that was deep," I responded. Douglas laughed out loud. I shushed him.

"You know if you kiss me that will keep me quiet for sure," he hinted.

So that is exactly what I did- over and over again.

My name cut through the air like a machete, "Muriel? Muriel, are you out here?" my grandfather's voiced beckoned.

Douglas and I missed everything. We didn't see the lights going on in the house or hear the door opening up in the back. My eyes grew wide. I put a finger over Douglas' lips so he didn't speak, and whispered in his ear, "I've got this. Just leave fifteen minutes after we go inside. Grab everything when you go so there is no sign we were out here." The dogs had been sleeping right beside the blanket. Once they stirred, I got up. Douglas grabbed me for one last hug.

The dogs and I came around the well house. "I'm by the well house, Gramps," I answered. "The dogs wanted to get out one last time for the night." I walked toward the back porch.

The dogs were not doing their best acting job. One was stretching and the other was yawning. My grandpa knew too much about animal behavior to believe my version of the chain of events. When one of the dogs lifted its leg to pee on the lilac bush, I figured the jig was up.

Gramps was only interested in going back to bed. He looked very fashionable under the glow of the porch light. He was in a plain white t-shirt and some plaid boxer shorts. His runway ensemble was completed by a ratty robe over the whole look. I noticed one of the pockets was weighed down with something.

"Alright," he said, "go to bed now, Muriel. It's late." He ushered the dogs and me inside. His robe pocket hit the door frame and the thud seemed very loud in the quiet of the evening. Gramps was packing heat. He wasn't joking earlier about loading his guns. We walked through the screened porch, which led to the back door.

When I glanced at the clock in the kitchen, it was almost 11 p.m. The last three hours felt like they sped by. I poured a glass of water for myself and told Gramps I would be going to bed soon. The dogs both got a couple of extra treats for their contribution in tonight's caper. I waited to hear Douglas' car start up, but it never did, even after fifteen minutes. If his car stalled or wasn't working, I would be in more trouble than I cared to think about.

After checking the door to the bedroom hallway, I saw that it was closed. Gramps was probably too exhausted to wait for me to get to bed. Quietly, I unlocked the back door and tiptoed through the back porch to the porch screen. My heart beat fast. Sometimes the screen door would make a terrible screeching noise when opened, but I hoped this wasn't one of those times. Not sure if the dogs had more bark in them, a couple of steps outside the porch were all I was willing to risk.

"Douglas," I faintly spoke into the night. "Are you still behind the well house?"

"No," I heard from behind and practically jumped through my skin. He put his hand over my mouth while saying no, which was good thinking. He then began kissing my neck and put his arms around my waist. It made my knees weak, so I leaned back on him.

He turned me around, "I had a great time tonight, Muriel. Just be gentle with me, because I've never felt like this before."

"You sound like a girl," I stated flatly and smiled.

He smiled back. "I assure you," he said as he pulled me close to him, "I'm not a girl." Off he went into the darkness. I heard his car start and saw his headlights come on when he got onto the main road. Just like that, he was gone.

And, just like that, I missed him already.

Chapter 12 Road Trip

Packing my suitcase for this adventure with Lorrah made me wonder how many times a year I would be separated from my family. Yesterday, I accepted this role like some sort of superhero, but today the doubts started to invade every thought. The questions that I thought were answered yesterday only spawned more questions, which left me feeling ill-prepared for the task ahead. Most of the women I would lead were probably better equipped for the job. I zipped the suitcase shut.

During the car ride, I would come clean with Lorrah. She needed to know that being an Oris was never something joyful for me. If living normally were a possibility, there would not be a second of contemplation. It had been years since I'd thought of saying a prayer, but the dread of the coming days brought me to my knees. With my hands clasped on the top of the bed and my heart weighed down by worry, I said "Lord…" and then fell to the floor.

This was different than any vision before because I had no awareness of my real surroundings. It consumed any spare senses. My Grammy flashed before me over and over again at different ages. She was praying for me, "Give her strength, heal the pain, guide, protect, may she know peace, take time for joy, growth, gain maturity, health, acquire wisdom…" My senses were alive during this Oris slideshow. Grammy's perfume was in the air. The different seasons of her home during the prayer were detectable: the burning stove of winter, the hum of the air conditioning in summer, the pitter patter of rain on the window in spring. It was the first time I wished for a vision to continue.

The motel room slowly came back into focus. It was incredibly humbling to know she prayed so much. I returned to the bedside on my knees so I could continue my own prayer. "Lord," I started, opening my eyes to a squint, making sure I was still upright, "it must be evident to you that this child of yours is completely clueless about the next couple of days. All I ask is that you allow me to honor Grammy's memory. She meant so much." The tears were flowing which made speaking out loud difficult, but there was one last thing that had to be said: "Thank you for giving her to me. Amen."

Even though it had been a while for a prayer to cross my lips, I could have easily stayed in that room for three days praying and still had more to say. That one would suffice for now. I stood up and straightened my outfit. Walking by the bathroom mirror, I could see that some of my makeup had smeared, so I fixed it. The toilet was right there and, because this was going to be a lengthy car ride, using it seemed the mandatory course of action.

I scanned the room to make sure nothing was left behind. The motel key was on the dresser, but that would be fine. It saved me a trip to the front desk to check out. The clock on the bedside table read that it was only 7:30 a.m., but I could get some coffee while waiting for Lorrah. This room felt stifling now because there was too much to be accomplished elsewhere. I grabbed the suitcase and left.

Right outside my door was a gorgeous car. The window rolled down to reveal Lorrah with coffee and croissants in hand. "C'mon Muriel, let's go!" she yelled.

She popped the trunk so I could throw my bags in. I got in on the passenger side and smiled, "Good morning."

"Good morning! We have a lot to do before the meeting tomorrow so I figured I would get coffee and breakfast for us," she explained. "It will save time."

"Are you early for everything?" I asked.

"Yes," she answered as we pulled out of the parking lot and turned toward our destination.

The trees that lined the road were just beautiful. I sipped the coffee and ate my breakfast while watching the landscape rush by. We drove in complete silence for a half hour. Between the quiet, the scenery and the prayer earlier this morning, I was calm. Now that my grandparents were gone, I wondered if there would ever be a reason to return to this town. Did this drive signify leaving behind a huge piece of my history?

A sharp turn shook me out of that train of thought. The more pressing question at the moment was: How is Lorrah not getting pulled over? She had been speeding ever since we left the parking lot. The speed limit ranged from 45-55, but when I glanced over at the speedometer we were traveling 60-70 miles per hour. This was mountainous territory which made those kinds of speeds dangerous.

"You need to slow down a little," I instructed. "Some of these turns are sharp and shouldn't be taken at breakneck speeds."

Lorrah looked down at the speedometer while removing her foot from the gas pedal. "I am so sorry," she said. "It's nerves. I'm a wreck…so worried about everything…not enough time for explanations."

"You're not even communicating in complete sentences," I giggled. "Pull over at the next turnout and let me drive. You're a basket case."

The next turnout came quickly. Lorrah pulled in so we could switch seats. I adjusted the mirrors and buckled in. I eased onto the road while getting accustomed to the car controls. It was such a beautiful automobile, which led me to ask, "Your insurance covers all drivers, right? This car may be worth more than my house."

Lorrah laughed, "The insurance covers everything. No worries."

"Exactly how does a young woman like you afford this car?" I blurted out. When I heard the question out loud, I realized that it sounded demeaning so I attempted to re-word it. "I apologize. That sounded wrong. It's just that you were a foster kid. Even if you went to college and made good, you can't be more than 27 or 28. The dealerships aren't just handing over cars like this to anybody."

"Don't be sorry for the way you initially asked the first question," Lorrah said. "You don't have to explain why you asked that question either. I'm an Oris just like you, and we prefer to deal in blunt communication. It's natural. You have been trying to communicate against your nature for so long."

Lorrah's response was said with such pity in her tone that this comment took a while to digest, but in the end, she was right. In my youth, I spoke with abandon, which felt more authentic. As I aged, my communication had become a watered-down version of truth to appease those around me. What a relief to be able to speak directly.

"So, how old are you and why can you afford this car?" I tried out my new freedom.

She laughed, "Now you're getting it. I'm 27 and I can afford this car thanks to you."

Once out of the turn we were in, I glanced over at her in disbelief. Her answer was partially satisfying. I knew her age, but there was no way this car had anything to do with me. It was annoying that Lorrah didn't think she needed to expound on that last statement so I told her, "I am going to need you to explain that, please."

"Well, I was born in the year..." Lorrah started as I slammed on the brakes.

"You know what I mean," I said. And then I teasingly suggested, "Maybe we should stop and chat. Didn't you say we have a lot of extra time before the meeting tomorrow?"

"Ha ha," she groaned. "Fine, but I will explain as you drive. We don't have enough time for stopping. The quick answer: you see the leprechauns." She pointed to the bag of pastries and asked, "Are you going to finish the last croissant?"

"The little green-suited men with pots of gold," I mocked. "I have never seen one in all my life. What are you talking about?!"

"Leprechauns are just a folk tale to explain away an Oris vision," she said. "They're not real."

"Oh! So, I was able to pay for your car because I see Leprechauns that aren't real," I recapped. "It is all so clear to me now. I'll just be getting out at the next stop."

"Let me try this again," she sighed. "I forget you have not read the Book of Deidra, and I fear that my explanations are a bit lacking."

I nodded in agreement, "Take your time to think it over. Explain everything as though you are dealing with a remedial Oris, because you are."

She took a few minutes to collect her thoughts. "Muriel, the leprechaun has been in Irish folklore for a long time. They are like this country's Tooth Fairy or Easter Bunny. Of course, none of them truly exist. The imagination of generations of Irish people gave the leprechaun life," Lorrah explained.

"The stories of these creatures were started by Oris women so they could communicate with each other about men who would be of great value," she explained. "In early Oris history, that meant many things: a prosperous farmer, a brave warrior, a leader. As time went on, the focus turned to wealth and the leprechaun was born with his pot of gold." She laughed, "I'm not sure whether it was the Irish fondness for drink or dreams of riches, but the leprechaun began showing up in Irish mythology."

"Okay, but I don't understand how I am connected to these little guys," I interrupted.

"It has been centuries since Oris women have been able to see a hint of green in a man or boy when they first meet," she went on, "but you can."

It was an absurd notion for Lorrah to think this was a gift I possessed. But then I remembered the first time it had happened- when my father brought Hans to my grandparents' house. He just looked sick to me, but Grammy knew better. In the years that followed, she would often jokingly ask if my dad was doing business with other men who couldn't handle American food or motorcycles. After a while, she didn't need to ask, because I would volunteer the information. It became a topic of conversation and a joke between the two of us. Apparently, the joke was on me.

"So my grandmother used me," I accused.

"Everything Ellowee did, she did for you and her Oris sisters," Lorrah answered.

"Apparently, she held back on the truth a bit. That wasn't for me," I said, hurt by Grammy's secrecy.

"She couldn't be honest about this small part of being an Oris when you wouldn't accept the whole of it," she explained.

The next 15 minutes we drove in silence while I marinated on the conversation thus far. What Lorrah said was true. I never fully accepted the Oris name or history. If it wasn't for my stubborn stance, maybe my Grammy and I could have been even closer. But there was no time to concentrate on my shortcomings as that would take up more time than we had.

"So, then, how did you know these men would make a lot of money?" I asked. "Maybe they would be good farmers or warriors instead."

"It only took a little research to determine if they were worthwhile investments," Lorrah told me. "Between the fact that your dad works in advertising and you saw the green hue, almost every decision was foolproof."

"So, I was wrong sometimes?" I wondered.

"No. Every person you told Ellowee about made money hand over fist," she informed me. "One of them lost big in a divorce settlement and had to sell his company. And there was a lawsuit once, but that had nothing to do with your choices. Overall, we did very well."

"What do you mean by 'we'," I asked.

"Anyone who is in the Oris Foundation receives paychecks just for being members," Lorrah smiled. "I made a little over $100,000 last year. So, thank you, Muriel. You support many individuals and families." She put her hand on my shoulder and told me, "We need to take you shopping so you look the part. They won't believe you are Ellowee if you arrive for the meeting looking like this."

"I'm mildly insulted," I announced.

"Your hair, too, we need to get that done," she decided.

"Do we have time for all of this?" I questioned. "Besides, shouldn't I be genuine and represent myself honestly: Middle class, mom-hair and boring?"

Lorrah giggled, "You really are utterly clueless. Your grandmother left you almost 27 million dollars. We are going to fix your mom hair, and you will *yearn* for boredom in the years to come," she looked over at me, and it was impossible to hide my confusion.

"My uncle read the will. That kind of money wasn't mentioned," I said slowly.

"Of course not, how would that have been explained?" Lorrah huffed. "Ellowee saved all of her Oris payouts. She invested well and put the money into an account for you. She used a bit for travel expenses, but not much more."

"But the shag carpeting…collecting aluminum cans…working after retirement…" I spoke out loud trying to understand. "Why would they live so modestly?"

"I don't know," Lorrah conceded, "but your grandmother was an intelligent woman. She must have had her reasons."

I turned the radio on to listen to music, the news…anything. At some point in the broadcast, the weatherman called for rain, but the skies were blue without a cloud to be seen.

There was one town in the area that would have expensive clothing, and the road signs informed me that we were only 45 miles away. By the time we got there, Lorrah had already envisioned the kind of outfit she wanted me to wear for the meeting. We arrived too early, so we waited outside for a half hour. We would have had to wait longer, but when the salesperson got there and saw Lorrah's car, she knew we had money to spend.

Once in the store, I tried on outfit after outfit until Lorrah decided which one she liked best. The one she picked for the meeting was my favorite, too- a navy pantsuit similar to one my Grammy had owned. Lorrah tried to tie a scarf around my neck, but I protested. The look was a little too airline stewardess or 50's era for my liking. I was also tired of being someone's dress-up doll.

I found a beautiful silver necklace that cost more than four months of our family's income. When showing it to Lorrah, she didn't even blink at the price. I went back for earrings. By the time we got out of the boutique, I had purchased a pantsuit, one blouse, two dresses, three pairs of shoes, a new handbag, a necklace, earrings and sunglasses. The total bill was a little more than 17 thousand dollars. I wanted to throw up. Spending that kind of money apparently had the opposite effect on Lorrah. She wasn't anxious like she had been earlier today.

As luck would have it, just three doors down from the boutique, we found a salon that could take me right away. Lorrah addressed the hair dresser after we all got situated, "Is there any way we can fix the style? I was also thinking of some red tones to accentuate her skin tone."

The hairdresser asked me if that all sounded good. "Can you give me and my friend a minute to chat things over?" I asked the hairdresser. She put her comb down and walked to the front of the salon.

I looked at Lorrah and snarled, "Firstly, I am not a kid, so don't talk to the hairdresser like I'm not in the room or able to decide things for myself. Second, color it with a little red? Is that truly for my skin or a little nod to the Irish contingent we will be meeting tomorrow?"

"Listen, every little bit helps," she said impatiently. "If you know what you want to do with your hair, go ahead and make the decisions, but we have very little time before the meeting."

The hairdresser came back. "So, how would you like your hair done?" she asked.

Turning from one side to another, I looked in the mirror while running my hands through the shoulder-length hair. It must have appeared that I was wrestling with a couple of grand ideas. Finally I announced, pointing to Lorrah, "Go ahead and do whatever she wants." Lorrah started to laugh which made me dislike her intensely for the next five minutes.

Two hours later, I emerged from the salon chair. My hair looked gorgeous, so I made sure to get a good look at it. Stylists are like magicians, and there would be no way I would be able to duplicate this feat on my own. The color was perfect and the length was just a bit above my shoulders. It felt so good.

Lorrah decided she was feeling better, so she drove the last leg of our trip. All total, we drove for three hours. Between the driving time and pit stops, we got into town a bit before 2 p.m. Lorrah had called ahead to reserve a two bedroom suite for us.

Upon checking in, she asked the clerk to place the dinner order she called in yesterday. He nodded, while staring at me for a few seconds until Lorrah blurted out, "Yes, she is a beautiful woman! About the dinner…" He blushed and told her that the meal would be delivered to our room within the hour.

"Oh, and can you please have these clothes dry cleaned and ready for tomorrow morning at 6 a.m.?" Lorrah asked as she set the clothes from the boutique on the counter. He looked wide-eyed at the clothes and then back at Lorrah. You could tell that getting them done that quickly was not normal procedure. However, Lorrah's tone made it apparent that she wasn't really asking, but telling him.

"Yes," he trailed off. Protocol may have been to say ma'am, but he was right not to call her ma'am. Lorrah was much too young for that.

"Thank you," she said before making her way to the elevator.

The room was gorgeous. First class digs all the way. If money was no issue, I didn't understand why we were sharing a room. I posed the question, "Why aren't we in separate rooms?"

"We have a lot to discuss." Lorrah answered. "We technically do have separate bedrooms, but this shared space will allow for more time to cover the material."

"Do you prefer one of the bedrooms over the other?" I wondered. Lorrah shook her head no. The bedrooms were practically identical so I just picked one and put my bags inside while Lorrah was setting up a workstation at the dining room table.

I walked over to the sliding glass door and opened it to let the most magnificent breeze come through the room. There was a balcony so I stepped out onto it. We were three floors up. The grounds of the hotel were well-kept, and the whole property was nestled into the side of a mountain.

"Do we meet in this hotel tomorrow?" I asked.

Lorrah didn't lift her head up from shuffling the papers and files. "No," she replied, "the meeting is about an hour from here. I probably didn't need to get a place so far out. No one will recognize you because this is the first time they will be meeting you. As Ellowee, you shouldn't stay very close to the meeting place. Picking different accommodations at each location every year might be wise."

"Should I be taking notes," I inquired sarcastically.

"That would be a good idea." She held up a notepad and asked, "Do you have a pen?"

I came in from the balcony to sit at the table. It was disappointing that all that good sarcasm seemed to be lost on Lorrah at the moment. She was all business. Since dinner was going to be delivered to the suite, it was safe to assume we wouldn't be going anywhere. I slipped my shoes off and made myself comfortable.

Lorrah watched me, "That's a good idea. I'm going to take my shoes off, too." She dragged all her luggage into her room and removed her shoes. She glanced at her watch as she returned to the table, "Okay, it is 2:30 and we have a lot to cover. We'll take a 30-minute break when dinner gets here, but we need to go over some guidelines and practice your speech."

"Ready," I announced after opening the notebook and grabbing a pen out of my purse.

"There are three important things that you need to accomplish tomorrow." She listed them off, "One, you will inform the Oris that Ellowee has died. Two, you will introduce yourself as her successor. Three, you will attempt to avoid answering every question they ask you."

"Why would I avoid every question?" I inquired.

"Because you won't know any answers," she quickly replied. "You can say you are grief-stricken over your loss."

"I am," I admitted, glad there was no lying necessary. "Why are people asking me questions anyway? What exactly happens at these meetings?"

"That is another topic we have to cover," she sighed. "I suppose we should review the flow of the meeting before anything else. First, the local Oris representative will bring the meeting to order. At this point, you will be introduced. The women will know right away that something is amiss when your grandmother is not present. You may have to raise your hand to quiet the crowd."

"Crowd!" I interrupted. "How many people typically attend?"

"This is one of the large chapters," she informed me. "Usually there are 50-75 Oris in attendance."

It was difficult to comprehend that there were so many women who shared this so-called gift. "How many meetings are there yearly?" I wondered. "The Oris foundation has how many members world-wide?"

"Muriel, those are questions that we don't have time to cover," she rushed. "Let's focus on tomorrow. When you are introduced, you give your Ellowee name only. You must not disclose any personal information. This is imperative. You don't mention your husband, where you live or that you have a daughter. You do not even hint at hobbies or use any descriptive speech that may give away where you live."

"What do you mean by descriptive speech?" I questioned.

She rifled through her papers and pulled out a thin book. She handed it to me, "Start with this. When people are from certain areas of the country, they often use words specific to that region. Luckily, your speech is a bit confusing. When you speak at these meetings, you need to use the most accepted terms nationwide."

"I have to read a manual to speak?" I said out loud in disbelief.

"Yes. I am the only person that can know where you live," she explained. "We will talk about why later. Where is your husband from in New England?"

"How do you know he's from New England?" I asked surprised. "He doesn't even have an accent."

"No, but when we were walking away from him yesterday on Main Street, I heard him ask your daughter if she wanted to dip her toes in the brook one last time," she explained. "Only people from New England use the term brook."

"Yeah, well, New England is a big place," I said, trying not to seem impressed.

"What does he call a submarine sandwich?" Lorrah pressed.

"A sub," I answered.

"That is the most accepted term for that sandwich. You need to call it that, too," she smiled. "What do his parents call the same type of sandwich?"

"A grinder," I answered.

"He's from Connecticut or Vermont," she announced. "And if we had time to chat about which stores he shopped at or brand names of common products like milk or bread, I would probably be able to pin it down to the state and area."

She was right. My husband was from Vermont. This made me uncomfortable. "Do you know where I'm from?" I wondered.

"Since your grandmother lived around here and I know your dad could drop in at her house by motorcycle, that's not really fair. It must be close by," she finished. "Although, you did say something that ensured you were raised on the Pacific coast instead of anywhere else in the country."

"What was that?" I asked genuinely amused.

"You ordered a bear claw at the coffee shop yesterday morning," she said. "People from the West Coast call it that most often." She paused and then went on, "Please, just read that booklet and try to use the most widely accepted terms or words- and the fewer words- the better."

There was a knock on the door, which made me jump about a foot off the seat. It was the dinner Lorrah had ordered. We hadn't eaten since early this morning so we both made quick work of our meals. The tenderloin steaks were cooked to perfection. The steak, baby asparagus tips and fresh salad were filling enough, but the waiter also put two slices of cheesecake in the mini fridge before leaving.

I was grateful we enjoyed our meals in silence with no talk of Oris nonsense. Lorrah had been sharing so much information with me, but it was the information she kept to herself that interested me most. I knew there was more to this position than she was letting on. The fact that my home location should never be disclosed was troubling.

After the last bite of dinner was enjoyed, I started scribbling on my pad. It was the announcement of my Grammy's death. When I handed it over to Lorrah, she marked through the phrase "car accident" and wrote "no details." She handed the pad back to me. We went on like this for a while. I wrote something down that she would approve or amend. After a couple of hours, we had completed a short announcement and introduction for tomorrow's meeting.

"After you get through the beginning of the meeting," Lorrah informed me, "then comes the time that information is exchanged or shared. You decide if the topics shared are worthy of filtering. I realize you may not understand what is being talked about, so look at me in the audience. I will be facing you. If I take a sip of water, approve the filter. Otherwise, deny it."

This was no longer feeling comfortable. "Maybe this was a mistake," I said. "How can I approve a filter when I don't even know what that is?"

"I wish I had time to explain everything in detail, but I don't," Lorrah said. "I promise I will answer all your questions eventually. Once you read the Book of Deidra that will help immensely." She handed me a page filled with my Grammy's writing, "Here is the information that you are to share with the room. Your grandmother had written down some info that had already been filtered. You read it and that is all."

"Can you at least sit by me during the meeting?" I asked.

"No," she said, "no one can know we are more than strangers. Your grandmother was given a guide when she became Ellowee because she was so young. And your grandmother knew you would need one because she never properly trained you. Your leadership will be questioned if they know you have a guide. You will appear weak."

"Wow, tough crowd," I nervously joked. "What makes you think I'm not weak? Perhaps you, yourself would benefit from a different leader."

"Maybe," she agreed. "But for your grandmother to say you would be our best leader yet was a bold statement. She led for 65 years with honor. If I'm being honest, I don't think anyone could lead better than her. Maybe I'm just curious to find out why her faith in you has never wavered."

I laughed and said, "Curiosity is an eager confession of ignorance."

"It's just that kind of treacherous remark that will endear me to you," Lorrah smiled.

The laughter and the smiles dissipated. We sat there with our thoughts. In the end, I hoped my Grammy's faith in me was not in vain.

Lorrah stood up and announced, "We need to get to bed because we're going to get up early. After tonight, I will no longer refer to you as Muriel. You are Ellowee or El, for short."

I picked up my shoes and walked to my room, "Good night, Lorrah."

After shutting the door behind me, I climbed into bed and read the book she gave me to help choose the right words. After the book had been read, I laid it on the bedside table and turned the light off. I whispered to myself in the darkness, "Well, Grammy, we're off like a herd of turtles…"

Chapter 13 Mirror, Mirror

After Douglas left, I got ready for bed. The excitement of the evening made me feel like it would be difficult to get any sleep. However, the comfort of my bed and all the day's events knocked me out immediately.

That evening was a restless one. Disturbing visions visited me while I slept. I saw my mother giving me a bath when I was little. She was thinking of how long it would take to dunk me under the water before I stopped breathing. Once she was rid of me, she would be free. The thought of her freedom delighted her. She was crying at the end of the vision while draining the bath water.

Douglas was a welcome sight that evening in my dreams. He was chasing me everywhere, but I wasn't the least bit interested in being caught. We were all over the globe in very remote locations. There was a frantic look on my face which made me think this wasn't a game.

The other vision was of my Grammy inside a doctor's waiting room. She was the only one there. The doctor came out to talk to her, but none of the conversation was audible. Then, my mother came into the waiting room from the back. She looked fine, as there were no bandages or other signs of injury. She was probably sixteen or seventeen.

For the second time in a few short hours, my name was an interruption. "Muriel," the faint voice chimed. "Muriel, you need to wake up," Grammy's voice was clear now. She was shaking me pretty good.

"What, what's the matter?" I asked groggily.

"It's almost 8," she informed me. "You were also loudly mumbling. I didn't want your grandpa to worry. Were you having visions?"

"It's not the visions, Gramps or the mumbling that has me concerned as much as the fact that it is 8 in the morning," I groaned, while putting the pillow over my head. I lifted the pillow back up to ask, "Why are you waking me up?"

"We have lunch in town with Lullabelle today," she chirped.

"Lunch," I questioned, "and you think it will take me four hours to get ready? You really need to give me a little credit. I have been dressing myself for years. It won't take me longer than 2 hours tops." I placed the pillow back over my head.

Grammy lifted the pillow. "Lou is my oldest friend and I want you to make a good impression," she explained, ignoring my sarcasm. "I know you have met her many times, but you are growing up so it would be nice if we could all have a conversation together."

"How about I go to the pool?" I suggested. "You and Lulu should have a nice lunch together." That was a self-serving suggestion because I thought Douglas may be lifeguarding again. It was a small town and they couldn't have that many qualified lifesavers, could they?

"No, you get ready. Wear something nice," she told me. "And lunch isn't at noon, it's at eleven." She left the bedroom.

"Of course it is," I said under my breath.

Douglas was on my mind instantaneously. It was a little frustrating that I was thinking of him so fondly, so soon. Realistically, nothing would come of it. The fact that we were going into town two days in a row hadn't happened in the last nine years I visited my grandparents during the summer. Also, there were so many girls checking him out at the pool! And he had already been intimate with three girls. Talking myself out of liking Douglas shouldn't be that difficult.

It would be a good visit with Lulu. She was one of the nicest people I had ever met. She was also an amazing cook, which meant lunch would be delicious. Listening to Grammy and Lulu share old stories was always entertaining, but I needed to remember not to compliment anything in Lulu's house. A couple of summers ago, I told her how cute her honey jar was with all the little bees on it. Lulu insisted we take it with us and I sat in the car on the way home with a honey jar in my hands and an irate Grammy in my ear!

That settles it, Douglas will be forgotten. The rest of this summer will be filled with…something. This was a big decision, so I will figure out what the "something" is later.

After 45 minutes of getting ready, I walked into Grammy's kitchen. I picked up a banana and got some yogurt out of the fridge. "Check it out Grammy," I remarked, "I'm ready with two hours to spare."

She patted the seat next to her at the four-person, round table and said, "Tell me about your visions last night while you slept."

There was some editing of what I would share with her. The drowning baby vision was definitely out because it was utterly depressing. She may be able to pick up that I have a crush on a boy if someone is chasing me around, so the Douglas vision was also not going to be mentioned. Before we talked about any of it, I had a question, "How do you tell the difference between visions and dreams? Couldn't some of these nighttime visions be harmless dreams?"

"Not anymore," she answered. "Once you go through your junction, if you do dream, you won't remember any of them."

"That seems fitting that being an Oris also takes dreams away," I said. The only vision to share was the one with Grammy in it. She wanted me to share my visions, but there was no doubt she wasn't keen on being in them. "I had a vision of you and Mom in a doctor's office. She was probably a little older than me at the time. You were talking to a doctor, but mom didn't look hurt," I finished. I looked at Grammy and waited.

"Well, I suppose you will find out soon enough," she spoke slowly. "Your mother has a mental disorder. Sometimes, Oris women are driven crazy by their visions, but your mom was never quite right. Your vision must have been on the day we got the diagnosis because she refused treatment of any kind after that and I couldn't drag her to a doctor's office."

"So, what is wrong with her? Does it run in our family? Will I get it?" I peppered her with questions.

"Calm down, Muriel. It does not run in the family. For you to know the name of the ailment doesn't bring understanding," she explained.

We sat at the table for a while. I ate my yogurt and banana while Grammy played a little solitaire. She had been dressed and ready to go when she woke me up at 8 a.m. Her perfume was assaulting my senses, which didn't make for an enjoyable breakfast. It wasn't even 10 when she suggested we go.

"We'll be so early," I argued.

"It will be fine. You and I can talk or pick up a couple of things at the store. We could use some fresh milk," she said.

That was all I needed to hear. Grammy used powdered milk, and she and I would often argue about the taste. It was awful, but Grammy insisted if you mix it right and it's really cold that you can't tell the difference between that and the real stuff: lies.

We went outside where we found Gramps and the dogs. Poor Gramps looked exhausted from last night's activities. He said he wanted to take a nap and I suspected he may take advantage of the peace and quiet as soon as we left.

The ride into town was uneventful. When we pulled up to Lullabelle's house, it was 10:20. We were 40 minutes early. Grammy started to get out the car, which made no sense to me.

"We can't go in there yet. It's too early. Let's go get that milk and come back," I suggested.

"I'm not going to knock on her door or bother her. I'll just sit in the swing until she's ready for us," Grammy responded.

Lullabelle's house was a picture-perfect country home. It was almost perfectly square, painted white with green trim and had a porch that encompassed 75% of the house. On that porch was a beautiful swing that did look rather inviting. Grammy walked up the steps at the front of the house to make her way toward the swing. She sat on the fluffy cushions and began swinging. She smiled, while waving at me. I waved back.

The front door of the house opened and Lullabelle emerged. Lullabelle was a plump woman with a smile that could put anyone at ease. She laughed at Grammy on the swing while shaking her head. I imagine she had come to expect such antics from her friend. Grammy and Lullabelle were each other's oldest friends. Lullabelle still had an apron on, which made me think she wasn't done making lunch.

Lullabelle waved me out of the car. "Hi, Lullabelle," I said walking up the stairs to the porch, "sorry we're so," I couldn't get the word "early" out before I was wrapped up in a hug.

"Look at how grown up you've become," she said wide-eyed. "I'm not sure I would have recognized you if you didn't look a lot like your grandmother when she was your age. You must have all the boys after you. Come in. Come in."

The aroma from inside her home was wafting out onto the porch. I cursed myself for eating anything so soon before we came. The inside of her home was just as soft, sweet and open as Lulu. A couple of big couches with huge cushions angled around a coffee table. There was a lazy boy chair at the other corner, which faced the TV. It was nice because you could see into the kitchen, dining room and the backyard all from the main sitting room. There was a stairway which led upstairs to two bedrooms and a bathroom. It was the kind of house I could picture myself in if it were somewhere other than out in the country.

Lulu had put out some appetizers for us. She called them pre-meal bites. I called them delicious. Deviled eggs, open-faced mini roast beef and blue cheese sandwiches, and a dip with veggies were all poised on the kitchen counter between the living room and kitchen. I had a couple of appetizers before they were offered to me. This earned me a glare from my Grammy that even Lulu couldn't miss.

"Oh, Muriel," Lulu scolded. "That is what they are there for!"

Lulu's dog, Blackie, wasn't around. I wasn't sure why she called him Blackie, because the dog was white with no trace of black on him anywhere. "Where is Blackie?" I asked. "It's so quiet. He usually barks at us for a good 10 minutes."

Lulu smiled and said, "This was the perfect day to send him to the groomer, don't you think? We can visit and eat in peace!"

Grammy and Lulu were chatting about something while I strolled along the walls of Lulu's house. There were so many pictures and interesting things hung up. I froze when I came upon one picture, looking at it in disbelief. There would be no need to ask Lulu about the picture, because right as I turned to ask, the back screen door opened and Douglas walked in.

"What are you doing here?" Lulu asked Douglas, appearing disappointed. "I thought you were working today."

"The schedules got changed. Nobody called to let me know," he said. With a deviled egg in my mouth, I stood very still as though that would render me invisible.

"Let me introduce you to my guests," Lullabelle told him. Once he turned to see my Grammy, his expression was a worried one. "You know Mrs. Chamberlain," she said. "She is one of my oldest and dearest friends." I began chewing frantically because there was no doubt my introduction was up next. Lulu continued, "This is her granddaughter, Muriel." Lulu motioned in my direction.

I only bumped into half the things in my path while walking toward him. Sticking out my arm to shake his hand, I said, "Douglas, you look familiar. Have we met before?" My attempt at playing it cool was an utter failure.

He shook my hand while smiling, "I hope so. My grandma hasn't even introduced me yet and you already know my name." Lulu and Grammy were far enough away that they couldn't hear him mocking me as he whispered, "Smooth."

"Where did you two meet?" Lulu asked.

Grammy interrupted, "Probably at the pool. All the kids go to that pool. Why don't you both go outside before lunch?"

We couldn't have gotten out of the house quick enough. Lulu's backyard was very lush and green. There was a little potting shed at the far end of the property. Douglas grabbed my hand so he could lead me there. He started kissing me as soon as we got behind the shed. In between kisses, he spoke, "I cannot believe you are here. This was meant to be. I can feel it."

As much as I was enjoying those lips, I pulled away. "I just got over you this morning," I giggled. "This is not helping me."

He seemed genuinely concerned, "What do you mean *got over* me? You are all I think about. It's maddening and intoxicating all at the same time." He tried to kiss me again, but I put my hand up to stop him. "Please, can I kiss you," he asked, "please?"

Manners go a long way. I dropped my hand, and he started kissing my neck because he knew it drove me crazy. We kissed each other for a few minutes before Lulu called us in for lunch. He smiled when he heard his grandma calling us and put his forehead to mine.

Walking in the back door, I saw Lulu setting a place for Douglas. She instructed us to wash up for lunch, so we did as we were told. All of us sat at the table where a beautiful casserole dish was unveiled. The casserole, fresh salad and French bread would no doubt be the best meal eaten by me all summer.

During lunch, there wasn't much chatter, which was becoming uncomfortable, so I spoke up, "Lulu this casserole is delicious. Thanks again for having us over." Lulu smiled while she chewed. "So, Douglas, do you like working at the pool?" I asked.

"It's something to do," he said. "I make a paycheck, but there is really no place to spend it around here. I'll have money for school clothes when I go home." He smiled at me for a little too long, and I think Lulu must have noticed.

"So many girls are after my grandson," Lulu exclaimed. "They call the house all the time. You would think he was the only boy in town. Who is it you have a date with tonight, Douglas?" she asked as she patted his hand.

Douglas almost spit out his salad as I waited calmly for the answer. "Her name is Trisha," he said very uncomfortably. I put my fork down, smiled at him and raised my eyebrows, then cocked my head a little hoping to hear more.

Douglas looked at Lulu, "Well, Grandma, to be fair, I made that date with Trisha last week, and since then someone so amazing has come into my life." He glanced around the table, "This girl is something special. Someone I could see myself with for a long time." It seemed that he was blushing.

Grammy chimed in, "You're sixteen, a long time for you could very well *be* a week." Everyone except for Douglas giggled.

It was how his chin jutted out that clued me in on the fact that he was angry. Anger wasn't an emotion I had seen in him yet, but the fact that no one was taking him seriously upset him. I knew what it was like to not be taken seriously, so my giggling stopped.

"I'm sorry, Douglas," I apologized. "We shouldn't laugh at you. Maybe you should concentrate on the date you have with Trisha," I advised. "You did make a commitment to her. And how much can this other girl really mean to you after a mere week?" He looked at me as though my words pained him.

He wiped his mouth then excused himself from the table. He went straight upstairs as I watched him go.

Lulu patted my hand, "Don't you worry about Douglas. He just needs to mope a little and he'll be fine. He has the pick of girls in this town, and there is no way one of them has stolen his heart. It was exactly this way last summer," she explained.

We all continued to eat our delicious lunch. Grammy and Lulu talked while I sat there feeling like a jerk for having laughed at Douglas. All of a sudden, the meal didn't taste as good as it had before. I thought about excusing myself to the restroom and knocking on his bedroom door, but maybe this would be a better end. He would go on a date with Trisha and that would be that.

After another hour, Lulu and Grammy had run out of things to talk about, so we said our goodbyes and started for home. It was a quiet ride full of regrets.

When we arrived at the house, a car was just pulling out of the drive. Grammy pulled up alongside the car and rolled her window down. It was Cassidy, a girl who worked up at the country store. There was a boy in the car with her.

The store was on the small side and only a quarter mile away, but Grammy never shopped there because the prices were too high. She would make me go to the country store every now and then if it was an emergency. Needless to say, there were rarely emergencies.

"Hi, Mrs. Chamberlain," she waved. "I was wondering if Muriel wanted to go into town with us tomorrow. We wanted to go swimming and hit up the frosty shop."

Grammy looked over at me and then at the boy in the car. "That would probably be O.K. Who is this?" Grammy pointed at the boy. "Will he be going with you girls tomorrow?"

"This is my boyfriend, Jeff. He might go. I'm not sure," she answered.

Not wanting Grammy to inquire any further, I asked, "What time should I be ready tomorrow, Cassidy?"

"I'll pick you up at 11. Eat before we go," she instructed. Then she drove off. Cassidy and I were friends a few summers ago, but we hadn't hung out in over two years. She was a couple of years older than me, and perhaps her affinity for dolls or girlish things passed when she was fourteen. It was easy to understand now that I was getting older, but it hurt my feelings back then.

When we pulled all the way up the drive, the dogs were glad to see us. After running into Cassidy, it made me appreciate their consistency that much more. We walked toward the back door where Gramps was just coming out of the screen door. It was apparent he had taken advantage of the quiet and napped. He looked refreshed.

"Wayne, did you talk to Cassidy and her boyfriend?" Grammy wondered.

"No Muriel," he answered. "I heard the door but didn't get it. Thought it may be someone tryin' to sell me something, and I got everything I need." He winked at me.

Yes, he definitely napped. Gramps and I would get in trouble if she knew how late we were up last night. Gramps had a crushed aluminum beer can in his hand because, once in a great while, Gramps enjoyed a beer. This was also classified information. I hugged him and, with great stealth, took the beer can out of his hand so I could put it in the can barrel. This was one of many secret agent missions.

Grandpa hugged Grammy after I did, and we all went inside. "So, how is Lullabelle?" Gramps asked.

"She is good. Just as sweet and gracious as ever," Grammy told him. Gramps was never interested in where or what Grammy had experienced on her other little excursions. Grammy knew exactly what he was fishing for.

"She didn't send me a little something or ask you to say hi?" Gramps hinted.

"Oh, yes," Grammy answered, "she did say hello." Grammy smiled, all the while enjoying his feigning interest. He was sniffing around for leftovers. Lullabelle would always send something for him. Grammy didn't make him suffer too long. She pulled out a few plastic containers. They were filled with all the treats we had for lunch.

"Yippee!" Gramps shouted as he took his food. "I love Lulu."

Grammy rolled her eyes as Grandpa rifled through his goodies. "You don't get that excited about my cooking," she mentioned.

Gramps was too smart to even acknowledge that remark, so he went about devouring the leftovers. The nap must have brought on his appetite, because usually he was a light eater.

I changed my clothes into something more casual and went to the living room to flop onto the couch. It didn't take long for me to succumb to an afternoon nap. In between awful visions of my mother, Douglas was chasing me again. One vision of my mother showed her giving birth to a baby boy. If making mental notes while sleeping was possible- note to self: ask Grammy about that one.

When I awoke, it was almost 4 in the afternoon. The nap lasted a little over an hour, but I didn't feel well-rested. Stretching out, my arm bumped in to something. It was Grammy. There was an L-shaped couch in the living room. I had slept on the long part while Grammy sat and knitted on the smaller part of the L.

"Hello, sleeping beauty," she smiled. "How was your nap?"

"Confusing," I answered. "How come I don't feel rested after seeing visions?"

"Muriel, you are lucky your grandfather is not here! You have got to be more careful about your surroundings when talking about this," she admonished.

"Where is Gramps?" I wondered.

"Vern's horse is foaling and he went to help," she explained.

Grandpa told me many times that horses and cows don't require any assistance when they are birthing their calf or foal. Occasionally, a person may need to intervene, but it was highly unlikely. He probably wanted to go see his brother and have another beer.

"I had a vision about your daughter," I mentioned. Grammy didn't seem to appreciate me choosing that wording. "So, did she have a son that I don't know about?"

Grammy immediately started tearing up. The answer must have been yes. It was shocking to learn family history in this way. I sat up in disbelief while shaking my head. Waiting for more information was painful, but it was obvious that Grammy needed a minute.

She grabbed a tissue and started to explain. "Your mother had a son three years before you were born. As a matter of fact, your father met and fell in love with your mother when she was pregnant."

"What happened to my brother?" I asked, finding it hard to believe we were having this conversation.

"He was adopted by a good family," she answered.

There were hundreds of other questions to ask: Who was the father? Do you know what his name was? Why didn't my mother consider keeping the baby? What did Grammy think when she heard about the pregnancy, etc. Those questions would have to be handed out in small doses over time or Grammy would shut down.

"Does it mean anything when someone is chasing you in a vision?" I changed the subject. I thought this would bring great relief to Grammy, but it seemed anything that escaped my lips today concerned her.

"Why would someone be chasing you?" she trailed off. She searched her memory while continuing with her knitting. "Do you know the person chasing you?"

"Never mind," I waved it off. "It's not important."

"It might be," Grammy said concerned.

"I'm going to go take another shower," I announced as I got off the couch and headed toward the bathroom. Grammy kept knitting.

The well water was their most valuable commodity and she would generally not allow two showers in one day during the height of summer. She didn't want to talk anymore. She practically pleaded to hear about my visions before today, but today's words were a vehicle of pain. Whether she was reliving the sadness herself or upset by my new knowledge of the truth, I do not know. It was painful for her all the same.

The shower was refreshing. I stood under the showerhead in a way that the water flowed from the top of my head down the rest of me in equal parts, my tears mingling with the water. "I have a brother. I have a brother," I repeated.

After stepping out of the shower and toweling off, I wiped the steam off the mirror. The person looking back was familiar, but not at all who I had once thought. She was unsure of who she was and what she would become. Her confidence had left. How can someone be confident in an ever-changing reality?

The thought of what I had learned so far this summer was not my biggest concern. My biggest concern was the sinking feeling that there was more to be discovered.

Chapter 14 The Meeting

The phone by my bed rang at exactly 6 a.m. It had a red light that lit up as the phone rang, making it easy to find in the darkness.

"Hello," I whispered after wrestling the handset to my ear.

"This is your 6 o'clock wake-up call," said the voice on the other end.

"Thank you," I trailed off.

The voice interrupted, "Please press 5 to turn off the alarm, or we will call back."

It was a recording. I smacked the phone with my hand a few times. The number five had to have been pushed at least once. It didn't take long for a feeling of dread to come over me. The day ahead would not be an easy one.

Lorrah could be heard humming outside in the main living area of the suite. She must have already brewed the coffee because the smell was enough to lure me out of bed. My beautiful new hairdo was now stuck to parts of my face and weaving in every direction. I laughed at the thought of showing up like this, fresh from the sheets. It wouldn't be pretty, but it would be closer to reality.

First stop of the day would be the bathroom. On my way there, I saw Lorrah, but it was too early for words so I didn't bother using any. The shower was a good start to waking me up, but the coffee would be the hero of the day. When I emerged from the bathroom, I only had my bra and undies on because the suit was being dry-cleaned.

Lorrah handed me a cup of coffee, and I sipped the life back into me. "Good morning, Lorrah. How did you sleep?" I asked.

"It was restless and short, but it was something," she answered. "The concierge dropped off your clothes while you were in the shower. I put them in your room."

I nodded and took my coffee with me to change. The blouse purchased at the boutique was a beautiful maroon silk that would go perfectly under the suit. After getting myself dressed, I changed over everything in my old purse to the new one.

The next order of business would be attempting to get my hair to do 50% of what the hairdresser did with it yesterday. Even though 50% didn't seem like a lofty goal, I'm not quite sure I achieved even that. Too bad this meeting didn't call for a ponytail.

Lorrah knocked on the door to let me know she was going to order breakfast to save us some time. She no doubt wanted to review for the meeting, and a restaurant would not be somewhere we could talk uninterrupted. It seemed that the same nervous energy she dealt with yesterday had returned.

Fiddling with my hair for another 15 minutes didn't help anything. I packed up all my toiletries and went to the bedroom to start filling my suitcase. It didn't take long as there were only pajamas and what I had worn yesterday. The dry-cleaned clothes could hang in the car.

When I came out into the suite's living space, Lorrah was letting the waiter in with our breakfast. He set the table for four and received a handsome tip from Lorrah on the way out. After he left, I placed my suitcase near the door and hung the clothes on the coat rack.

"Here is your booklet about regional speech," I said, looking at the table as I handed her the booklet. "Why did he set so many places?"

"I guess he thought we had other people with us because I ordered a lot of food," she explained.

"Are you that hungry?" I asked.

"No, I just didn't know what you liked to eat for breakfast, so I ordered a little of everything," she said as she looked at the food on the cart. "I may have gotten a little carried away."

I walked over and lifted all the domes off the platters. There *was* a little of everything: Pancakes, waffles, fruit, yogurt, scrambled eggs, toast, poached eggs, mini Danishes, bacon, sausage, eggs over medium, biscuits and gravy, hash browns and an omelet with ham and cheese. There was also a carafe of orange juice.

“We are never going to eat all of this,” I announced the obvious, while looking at her.

“I know,” she admitted, “but I wasn’t sure what to order!”

I looked around at all the food and couldn’t help myself, “Where are the bagels?”

“Oh no, I didn’t order any bagels! Let me call for some,” she said as she picked up the phone.

“I’m joking! Put that phone down,” I demanded. “Can you relax? Let’s eat.” I grabbed a plate to start enjoying the breakfast feast before us. It was like breakfast Thanksgiving. I only took a couple bites of each thing, but my plate was full.

“Are you ready for the meeting?” Lorrah asked.

“I think so,” I answered in between bites. “My notes are in my purse. I need to share the news that my grandmother has passed, introduce myself and watch you drink water so I know whether to approve or deny a filter. Oh! And the best plan is to say as little as possible. ”

“Perfect,” she announced.

“How is it you became my guide?” I asked Lorrah, out of the blue. “Are there certain requirements? Did my Grammy know you very well?”

Lorrah contemplated that question herself. “Hmm,” she started. “I would like to say that it was because I am the best Oris for the job, but I would venture to say Ellowee chose me due to the fact that I have no ties…no family to speak of.”

“What about your mother?” I questioned. “Have you ever thought about finding her?”

“I think she’s dead,” Lorrah sighed. “I had a vision of her going overboard on a yacht. It was storming pretty badly when someone wrestled her over the rail and into the drink.”

Lorrah told me the story like she was telling me about a walk in the park. There was no emotion and no need for me to gasp or feign my condolences. We both knew the inner workings of our mothers…thoughts that bordered criminal…actions that embarrassed. It was an unspoken similarity that brought me comfort.

"You are still young. What if you want to get married and acquire ties?" I wondered.

"Muriel, I am only going to need to be with you for a short time," she smiled. "You will get the hang of this in no time." She wiped her mouth with her napkin, and then put it over her plate.

I squinted at Lorrah, "I thought you weren't supposed to call me Muriel anymore," I reminded her. I got up and pushed my chair under the table.

"I'm not! Good to know neither one of us knows what we're doing. Very comforting," she said sarcastically. Lorrah grabbed her belongings and put them close to the door. She opened the door and looked down the corridor. She must have expected someone to come retrieve them.

"I don't mind carrying my own bag," I said, "and yours rolls. Do you think we can bring them down ourselves, princess?"

Lorrah frowned, "You just become accustomed to certain things."

"Oh, I know," I giggled. "It's called being spoiled."

Once the bags were loaded into the car, we drove toward the meeting. There wasn't a lot said during the drive. Lorrah was super nervous, and I was wishing I had drunk a second cup of coffee because sleep was summoning. All the fresh air was too much to take. Before a snore could escape my mouth, the car came to a stop. We were in a parking lot that was adjacent to a golf course and resort. The resort was up on a hill overlooking the small golf course. It looked like something out of the movies. The sign read: "Mt. Carmen Resort and Golf."

Lorrah pointed up the hill at the resort, "That is where the meeting will be held."

"It's beautiful," I observed in awe. "How is it that we can have a meeting there? Won't people hear what is going on?" The thought was a little troubling.

"Mt. Carmen Resort and Golf is an Oris property," she smiled. "I will go over our property holdings later, but when a meeting comes up, we simply don't take reservations for two days. Some Oris travel here and stay the night before the meeting. They check out the next day after the meeting, and the resort carries on normally. The resort still keeps up appearances while the employees get two days off."

"What time is the meeting?" I asked.

"Nine," she answered as I looked at my watch.

"It's a little after eight," I observed, after looking at my watch. "What gives with the constant earliness? I could have gotten another half hour of sleep!"

"Visions can come at any time so you need to make sure you allow for extra time. Just in case," she explained.

That made sense. I wonder if that was why Grammy was always early.

Lorrah informed me that I would be walking up to the resort alone. No one could know we were together. She gave me a special lanyard and explained that everyone had to have one to be in the meeting. The local representative was identified by wearing a silver lanyard. Once I found her, I was to whisper in her ear: *Behold, Ellowee.* The representative would then know the situation and introduce me.

Lorrah gave me the car keys and emphasized how important it was that when the meeting was over, I needed to leave first. The other Oris would remain behind for an hour or so because they were not supposed to know where Ellowee went. There was an offering left in five large bins outside the resort that I was to pick up. Lorrah instructed me to load the bins in the car and find a place to donate the contents. After that, I needed to change so I could pick her up right where we were now. Lorrah suggested wearing a baseball cap and sunglasses to help disguise my appearance.

All this new information made me nervous. Why Lorrah didn't share any of this with me before was beyond reasoning. But it was time to get up there, because I didn't want to be late. The car door slammed behind me and similar feelings to the ones when I first went off to college or walked down the aisle came to me. The kind of feelings that confirm nothing will ever be the same again. I also couldn't help wondering why I had never been to one of these meetings before.

The inside of the resort was not a disappointment. I followed some women into the meeting room. The windows were from floor to ceiling with a great view of all the greenery on the golf course and beyond. It almost made me forget that I needed to be looking for a silver lanyard. It was awkward to look at everyone in the breast area so I sat down at one of the tables and tried to find it from afar.

It was 8:35 a.m., which was making me antsy. Two women sat down at my table and said hello. They introduced themselves and then told me that they were mother and daughter.

"By mother and daughter, do you mean this is your birth mom?" I asked, immediately curious. "And you have a relationship?"

They laughed. The daughter said, "It is unusual, yes, but everyone has darkness to them. The fact that I can see my mother's doesn't mean that it should be held against her." The mom smiled at her daughter and patted her arm.

I looked at the mom. "And you stayed the whole time with your daughter?" I asked.

"Yes. I am an Earth Oris so, as you know, I tend to stay planted," she explained.

This woman has me confused with someone who has been living the Oris lifestyle for some time. The fact that this mother and daughter are even sharing a table confuses me. "How old are you?" I asked the daughter. "How is it you can get past the visions you have of your mother?"

She laughed, "I am 23, and what my mother has done or thought is not the issue. It is whether or not I choose to forgive. That is the key. I imagine my darkest thoughts can't be pretty either."

Ideally, there would have been plenty of time to interview them about their relationship. Glancing at my watch, I saw that it was 8:45, so I asked them if they knew where I could find the local representative. It was also a good way to elude any questions they had for me that could identify me as a fraud.

The mom spoke up, "Oh, Joanie is around here somewhere." She looked over the women that were in the room. "There she is," she announced, pointing to the woman near the door greeting others as they came in.

"Thank you so much," I said. "It was very nice to meet you both." I raced off toward Joanie.

Joanie must have recognized that I wasn't a normal attender because she said something to the security guard standing next to her while I approached. Before I could get near her, he stepped in front of me.

"Please state your business," the guard said. His voice was so deep that I felt it in my stomach.

"I need to speak with Joanie, please. It's very important," I added.

The guard asked if he could frisk me and I obliged. It seemed a bit much, but when in Rome... He looked at Joanie, "She's clean."

Joanie gave me a very suspicious look and asked, "Are you an Oris or a Zero?"

This was not the protocol that Lorrah covered, so I just stood there trying to get my bearings. Grammy had told me I was an Oris so that is how I answered: "I am an Oris."

The suspicious look did not leave Joanie. My answer was the right one, but perhaps it wasn't delivered soon enough for her liking. She nodded at the security guard and he walked only three steps away. I leaned over and whispered in Joanie's ear, "Behold, Ellowee." The look on her face became one of utter sorrow. She tried to control her weeping.

She bowed her head down slightly. "Please forgive my suspicion earlier," she said between tears. Joanie left the room quickly. I assumed she needed to get herself together before the meeting began.

Judging by my watch, the meeting would start in almost five minutes. When I turned around, it was evident that I was the only one that hadn't taken a seat. I scanned the room for Lorrah, making it seem that I was looking for a seat. She was exactly where she said she'd be.

I sat alone at a table farthest away from her. When 9 a.m. came, there was no sign of Joanie. This must have been unusual as the whole room started speaking in hushed tones. Eyes darted around trying to catch sight of Joanie or quite possibly my Grammy. No one would have been happier to see her here than I would be.

About five minutes passed before Joanie took the mini-stage in front of the big windows. I retrieved the notes from my purse, sighing away nerves the best I could.

Joanie addressed the group, "Good morning. I am so glad everyone could make it here safe and sound. There are only two people missing from the chapter. One was very ill while the other had a wedding to attend." She paused, "We have no new inductees this year." It was the next sentence that Joanie struggled to say: "Please, welcome Ellowee."

The women were looking around for my Grammy. I wanted to stay seated or slink out of that room. When I stood up to make my way to the stage, the room was silent. Lorrah had me expecting something quite different. Slowly, the room was filled with sobs and crying. By the time I finally got onto the stage, most women were blowing their nose or wiping tears from their cheek.

"My name is Ellowee," I started. "I am from the line of Enya, an Oris. My grandmother has passed away and named me to be her successor." The words were spoken with confidence as though I was groomed for the position. "She died quickly. Her death was not from natural causes, but it was peaceful. I imagine she would have lived to be a hundred if natural causes were to blame," I ad-libbed, as a small smile crossed my lips.

There were no questions, just more silence. This made me wonder if Lorrah had even been to one of these meetings! Peering down at my notes while hoping to rush this process along I asked, "Does anyone have any filters to discuss?"

A woman in the back of the room stood up and spoke, "Hello Ellowee. The Zero movement is growing. Is there any way to better monitor them? Could we find out if there is a level of organization involved or if they have an agenda? Thank you. Welcome to the ranks." She sat back down.

Appearing to be deep in thought, I looked around the room until I saw Lorrah taking a sip of her water. I looked back in the woman's direction and replied, "The filter is approved. Thank you for your input." After a couple minutes of silence I spoke again, "This is the first chapter I have visited to share the news of my grandmother's passing and, if it is all the same to you, I would prefer to adjourn early."

There were no complaints, so I declared the meeting adjourned and fled from the scene immediately. I grabbed my purse and left. Beads of sweat were formulating on my brow and upper lip as my nerves were getting to me. Once outside the front resort doors, I fumbled around for the keys to Lorrah's car. The large bins that I was supposed to take away were piled to the left, and I wasn't sure if all of them would fit in her car. They would be tied to the top of her car if it meant I didn't have to come back here again.

When I started off down toward the golf course, I noticed Lorrah's car had been moved to the upper lot. That would make sense that she would park here. Although, sharing that bit of information would have been helpful. I pressed the remote lock and sure enough, the little light came on inside. After pulling up to the front of the resort, I loaded the bins. They all fit in the trunk once I moved the suitcases into the back seat.

Lorrah told me I could look at the contents of the bins so I would know where to donate them. I began driving when, about two miles down the road, I spied a church. It seemed a safe place to stop and was ideal because it was on the same road as the resort, so finding my way back would be simple. I pulled into the parking lot and drove around the building where the car couldn't be seen from the road.

Peeling off the jacket of the pantsuit was mandatory. I threw it into the back seat on the way to the trunk. When the cool breeze hit me, I realized that I had sweat through the maroon shirt completely. After opening the trunk, the bins were hoisted out and placed behind the car. Feeling rushed, I quickly opened the bins to reveal their contents. The sooner I could get this over with, the better.

Inside the bins were packages of bagels, powdered milk, cheese, instant potatoes, canned fruit…all the things Grammy stocked in her pantry and freezer. But it was an instant devil's food cake mix that had me watering the ground with my tears. Gramps' birthday would have been in a couple of weeks. I wondered if the Oris women knew what all this was for. Did they think it was for charity or future meetings? Did they do this at all the meetings so it wouldn't look suspicious here? When Grammy brought it all home, it appeared that she had been shopping all day- nothing suspicious about that. Today, the bins *would* go to charity. I left them at the back door with a note on one of them: If anyone is in need of these, please distribute as you see fit.

I rifled through my suitcase and found a t-shirt and pair of jeans. Changing in the car was uncomfortable, but I needed to get back in time. I took my earrings off and put the sunglasses on. Lorrah said to wear a baseball cap, but neither of us packed one. I fashioned one of her scarves into a cover for my hair. In reality, the scarf was more suspicious looking and out of place than the baseball cap would have been. But now that my hair had the tint of red, it was probably a good idea to cover it up.

The drive back to the parking spot was quick. It appeared that an hour hadn't passed because the parking lot to the resort was still packed. I turned left before the entrance to the resort to make my way down to the small lot by the golf course. There was one other car there so I found a spot as far away from it as possible.

Lorrah came down the hill to the car only five minutes after I had parked. When she got close enough, I unlocked the doors. She plopped in and blew out a lot of air. She then rested her head back on the seat and glanced over at me. "Let's get out of here. You can stay at my house for a couple of days before you go home," she said. Observing the scarf on my head, she said, "Why didn't you wear a baseball cap?"

"Do you own a baseball cap?" I asked testily.

"I have a couple at home," Lorrah answered, "but I thought they handed them out at the hospital as part of your mommy kit." She laughed.

"Where to?" I asked, trying to ignore her attempt at a joke.

"Just go out to the main road we came in on and get onto the highway heading south," she looked over at the gas gauge. "We need to stop and get gas soon, so I will drive from there."

After we filled up the tank, I got settled in the passenger seat. The stress of the day's events and the early wake up were too much, so sleep came quick. It was only when we drove down the bumpy road leading to Lorrah's home that I stirred. "How long have I been asleep?" I asked surprised to see the huge body of water before me.

"A couple of hours," she answered.

Lorrah's house was absolutely gorgeous. It was three stories high with glass balconies peppered around the house. The house wasn't very big, but it was nestled on a low cliff with a small, private beach. From what I could tell, the closest home was a half mile away. I started hauling my luggage toward the stairway to the right of the garage. Lorrah opened the garage where there was an elevator. "C'mon in," she encouraged. "This is how I got my furniture inside, and it comes in handy when I am carrying a lot."

I did as she said. Lorrah pushed the 1st floor button and we started ascending. When the elevator doors opened, the view of the water was breathtaking. The décor and artwork choices were impeccable in her open, airy first floor. It was just like homes I'd seen in the movies. There was a small bar in the corner, a huge T.V. on the wall and a kitchen fit for a gourmet chef.

Lorrah interrupted my thoughts, "Through that door," she pointed to the left, "is a guest bedroom. It's small, but it should suffice. You can put your bags in there."

The guest bedroom was bigger than the master bedroom I shared with Rick back home. It was the entire length of the house and maybe 20 feet wide. There was also a personal balcony in the room overlooking the beach. I put my bags down when Lorrah popped her head into the room.

"Will this be O.K. for a couple of days?" she asked.

The room was heavenly, but it had become tiresome appreciating the beauty of everything. "It will be fine, thanks" I answered. "I'd really like to take a shower and clean up."

"Sure," Lorrah responded. "Towels are in the closet. Actually, anything you might need is in the bathroom closet in case you forgot something. I'm going for a swim."

I pointed toward the water, past the beach and asked, "Out there?"

"Yes," she giggled. "I am an Oris with a water bond, and it's hard to stay away."

"Can you explain some things to me tonight?" I asked. "Like, what is a Zero and why did Joanie ask me if I was one? What did that woman mean when she said, welcome to the ranks? And filters…"

"Whoa, slow down," Lorrah interrupted. "I'm going for a swim. There's some frozen pizza in the fridge. We'll pour a glass of wine and talk about everything this evening."

"Fair enough," I conceded.

Chapter 15 Reservoir Dog

Rays of sun were streaming through the window, slowly waking me up. Grammy had traded in her vacuum for raising the shades. The method may have changed, but the outcome was the same: I was awake and not happy about it. It was 8 a.m. and too early to be up, so I lay there wondering why on Earth she felt the need to interrupt my precious slumber this time! Maybe I had forgotten something. The curiosity was too much, so I drug myself out of bed to ask her.

She was on the back porch putting laundry into the washing machine. "Grammy," I startled her. Then I asked, "Why were my shades pulled up in the bedroom?"

"So you would wake up when the sun came up," was her response.

I waited patiently. Surely, there was other info to follow but, alas, she had nothing more to add.

"I see," I said unsatisfied with her explanation. "I'm going back to bed."

She shut the lid on the washing machine and informed me, "You have to eat and get ready to go."

Then I remembered that I was going with Cassidy to the pool. "Please tell me that you did not wake me up at 8 a.m. so I could get ready to go to the pool at 11," I raised my voice.

She looked at me blankly, "Well, technically, I didn't wake you up."

"AH!" I screamed in frustration and left the room.

After brushing my teeth, washing my face and throwing on my swimsuit, I walked back into the kitchen. At my place at the table sat a plate of breakfast: some toast, a soft boiled egg and fruit. This was the way Grammy said she was sorry. Not sorry enough to verbalize an apology, but sorry enough to do something kind. Her peace offering appeased my anger.

Grammy joined me at the table with her coffee while I ate breakfast. When I was finished, I place the napkin on the table and said, "Time, 8:35. It took me 35 minutes to get ready and there was no rushing. If you subtract the time we argued, it could have been done in less than half an hour." I went on continuing to prove my point, "If you subtract 30 minutes from 11, I could have slept until 10:30. Two and a half glorious hours of sleep ripped from my life. If you keep stealing this kind of time away, there could be adverse effects: stunted growth, underdeveloped brain function, premature aging..."

"Are you done?" she interrupted.

"I don't know," I feigned concern. "All this sleep deprivation may cause forgetfulness. How would I know if I am ever completely done?"

"You're done," she decided. I giggled because it was apparent that she was irritated. Grammy had a serious tone to her voice, "There are going to be so many things that happen or come about in life that you will not be ready for. I've always considered myself to be early or prepared, but regardless of how much I try, there are circumstances we can't control."

I thought about what she said before replying, "Why did you get me up so early when all I'll be doing is swimming with Cassidy?"

"Cassidy has not been around for a couple of years," she explained, "which probably hurt your feelings. You are going to spend time with someone you haven't seen in a while and because of your ages, may not even know anymore."

Grammy was absolutely right. I didn't want to go swimming with Cassidy in the first place. For all I knew, she could be a wretched person. Plus, if Douglas were on duty today, he wouldn't be that excited to see me after yesterday's events. Maybe this situation did require more thought. I excused myself from the table and went to the living room where, after a solid five minutes of thinking, I started having unwanted visions.

My mother was yelling in one vision over and over: "Who's my real dad, who's my real dad…" In another vision, she was slipping her wedding ring off to sleep with someone other than my father. As if that wasn't bad enough, it was my father's brother. I also saw flashes of her giving birth: The excitement when her son was born and the stark contrast of disappointment when I came along was obvious. And, yet again, Douglas was chasing me around the globe.

I shot up to find my Grammy in her chair looking at me. She looked frightened. She couldn't be blamed for that because these visions had already produced some unfortunate truths that brought her pain. I smiled at her.

"Tell me what you saw," she whispered.

I shook my head no and said, "It's not necessary."

"You don't know that," she corrected me. "Now, tell me everything because you have been trying to spare me and you need to know the truth. Whatever you see, I have already lived through. Go on," she urged, "there is nothing you will tell me that I don't know. However, there is much you'll see that you do not understand. Let me help you."

"Mom was yelling 'who is my real dad'," I said.

"Your mother was four when I married your grandfather," she explained, not missing a beat. "He is not your biological grandfather. She always thought that her life would be better if she knew the sperm donor. Her father came from a Greek family, and they didn't accept me even after they heard of my pregnancy. They wanted nothing to do with me, and your biological grandfather was apparently a weaker man than I thought because he agreed with his family."

I sat there confused, hurt, and reeling. Not because of a deep desire to know my biological grandfather- my Gramps was the only one I needed. But all this new information was too much. It was making me angry. "I see," I said. "Let's recap. I have a brother, Gramps isn't a biological relation, my mom slept with my uncle, my mother was happier to give birth to a son she would give up more than a daughter she would keep. Oh, and a boy keeps chasing me around."

"Tell me more about this boy," she said.

"Do you really think that should be our focus as we move forward with this conversation?" I asked sarcastically. I got up and announced, "I'm going outside to wait for Cassidy." I grabbed a towel and a couple of granola bars as I left. While making my way down to the gate, I saw Gramps puttering around the yard. I ran over to him, gave him a huge hug and told him that I loved him very much. He was one of the few relatives that made me feel grounded. The fact that we weren't blood relations would never concern me.

Cassidy pulled up just in time, because it appeared Grammy was coming out to continue our talk. I jumped into the passenger seat and buckled up. It was a relief that Cassidy's boyfriend wasn't with her. We started backing up, while Grammy retreated back into the house. Gramps waved.

"Thanks for the invite, Cassidy," I said. "It will be good to get out of here today."

"You're welcome," she smiled. "I'm helping out a friend."

"We haven't spoken in two years, why would you call me a friend," I wondered.

"Oh," she laughed, "I'm not talking about you."

I didn't even care what she meant. The window was rolled down, so I stuck my hand out and took in the sights. When we got into town, Cassidy took a left at the main road instead of a right to the pool. Maybe she was going to pick up her boyfriend. There was no way I was going to ask about her sense of direction, because if she gave me another bitchy response: I would hit her, then we'd get into a car accident…there would be blood everywhere. Better to just keep my mouth shut and avoid those events.

Cassidy turned off the main road and drove over cattle guards a quarter mile or so to the reservoir. No one was supposed to swim there, but the older high school kids drove out there all the time. She stopped the car and I looked at her. My door opened, which made me jump.

"Hello, miss," Douglas said. "May I help you out of the car?" He put his hand out for mine and helped me out of Cassidy's car.

Cassidy leaned over the front seat looking out the passenger door to tell Douglas, "Here she is safe and sound, so now we're even. You better get her back before dark though. Her grandmother will expect her to be home, and her grandfather is still a great shot."

Douglas shut the door. "Thanks Cass. You're the best," he said. She drove off, and it was a relief to know I wouldn't be spending time with her today.

It was all a little too much to believe. Douglas still had my hand, so he walked me closer to the water where a blanket was laid out. On the blanket was a picnic which Lulu must have prepared. It was hard not to be surprised by all that had gone on in the last five minutes. "Um," I started speaking, not sure what to say.

Douglas just smiled. "Are you surprised?" he asked.

"Did Cassidy just deliver me to you like a pizza? Is that what just happened here?" I wondered. "And why would you want to see me after I hurt your feelings yesterday?"

"My grandma went on about how she didn't want me talking to you because you were so young," he explained. "She thinks every girl who meets me falls for me. When you said something that could make me mad, I pretended it did."

"Didn't it? I was serious about you going out with Trisha," I confessed. "I can still get over you, and we can be friends this summer."

"Let's go for a swim," he said, as he took off his shirt.

"I do need to tell Grammy I went swimming, so I might as well," I said, while taking my shirt and shorts off. "Is Cassidy going to give me a ride home later?"

"No. I will," Douglas announced. He took my hand and we walked into the water. It was cold, so the walking got progressively slower as the water level rose on our bodies. He let go of my hand and dove in. When he came up for air, he was wearing that smile that is difficult to resist. "You might as well just jump in because it's not getting any warmer," he remarked.

This was not an invitation, but more of a dare. I dove in. When my head came above the surface of the water, I let out a little scream. Douglas came over and scooped me up in his arms.

"So, pretty girl, tell me how the last 24 hours have been since we've been apart?" he asked.

"Hmm," I thought, "it's all been a little confusing. You have an idea of who you are and where you come from then, in an instant, you find out there are things you didn't know." I continued my rambling, while barely taking a breath. "The person you thought you were is forever changed and now tomorrow can't be anything like yesterday because you are not the same."

"What?" Douglas exclaimed, not quite following my train of thought. He sat down in the shallow water still holding me.

"Let's just say that I am heartbroken. That about covers it," I answered while tearing up.

"Hey, hey," Douglas said concerned. "Are you O.K.?"

"I don't know," I responded.

"I'm sorry you are having a rough summer, but I can tell you that you have already made this summer special for me," he complimented, while looking into my eyes.

He kissed me. That kiss made me feel like everything was going to be O.K. All my troubles really did melt away. We looked at each other and smiled. I splashed him a little, which got me tossed out into the deeper water. We laughed and splashed each other for a while until we got closer and could kiss again. The splashing wasn't even a close second to the kissing.

"So, I have been thinking about this summer," he announced. "And because I have already had a 'first,' I want to do things with you that can be our firsts together." He reached down in the water for a minute and came back up with his swim trunks in his hand. "I have never gone skinny-dipping, so I thought that was one thing we could do first with each other."

I looked at him like he was crazy.

"C'mon. After we do this, you can pick a first the next time we're together," he reasoned. "It's just like swimming, but with no clothes."

"I do know what skinny-dipping means, Mr. Dictionary," I said, sarcastically. "This is crazy."

"Exactly," he smiled. "Crazy is not always a bad thing."

I went out into deeper water and took my bottoms off. I threw them toward the beach. "Listen," I said, "when I get out of the water, you have to promise you will turn around like a gentleman."

"I promise," he assured me.

I untied both bows on my bikini. When I threw the top, it didn't quite make it to the beach so Douglas kindly retrieved it and threw it all the way. We were skinny-dipping! There is nothing quite like the feeling of having nothing between you and the water out in the great outdoors. It was a wonderful freedom that I had not experienced before. I swam out into the deeper water, and Douglas came out farther, too.

As we treaded water, I was curious and asked, "How did you get Cassidy to do this for you? She said she owed you one."

"Last summer, I went out on a date with a friend of hers as a favor," he blushed.

"You are quite the gigolo," I smiled.

He was not happy with my assessment. "I wish you would stop saying things like that. You are all I think about," he explained. "There are times I wish that wasn't the case, but it's been you ever since we met in that drugstore parking lot. It's been you when I gave you that flower. It's been you at the pool…at your grandparents' house…at my grandma's house…right now. It is just you."

For the first time, I believed him. This made me immediately uncomfortable, so I changed the subject. "You know that flower you gave me might have saved my life," I announced. "My Grammy and I stopped at a stream to talk, and a bull came up behind us. The bull ate the flower while I made my escape."

"Did you hear what I said?" Douglas asked, seemingly annoyed with my attempt to change the subject.

"Yes. I just don't know what you want me to say. The idea of caring for you scares me," I admitted.

I swam back to shallower waters where I could touch the bottom. Douglas followed.

"Well, tell me how you do feel because I need to know if I even have a chance," he demanded. "Help me understand what you want or what you are feeling."

"I'm feeling overwhelmed and pressured. We have known each other less than a week," I tried to explain. "Hanging out with you has been fun, but I don't understand why we have to label whatever this is." He looked sad. "How would you want me to answer those questions?" I wondered.

"I want you to tell me that you love me and all you want is me," he pleaded. "I know it has only been a few days, but I care about you."

I paused before I said anything because he *had* to be joking. Yet, there was no sign of frivolity or attempts at comedy. "That is the sweetest thing anyone has ever said to me and probably ever will," I confessed. "Now turn around and let me give your back a hug…you know, 'cause we're naked and all."

He still seemed sad, but he turned around and I wrapped my arms around him and gave him a big hug.

"I'm turning back around," he announced.

"No you're not," I yelped.

"I am," he argued.

Douglas then started to turn his body. We were laughing and splashing until I finally had to jump on him piggyback style to ensure he couldn't turn around. When all the thrashing was over I whispered in his ear, "You promised." There was a kiss or two on his ear just to convince him.

"Fine, but let me carry you up to your suit," he compromised, "and I will let you get dressed without looking."

"Deal," I breathed into his ear.

"You keep that up and all bets are off," he told me.

After the suits were put on, Douglas and I enjoyed the picnic that Lulu had made. We talked about what we had experienced in our young lives so far. It hadn't been much, but it was ours regardless. Between the full bellies and the lapping water, we both fell asleep. When I opened my eyes, my head was resting on Douglas. I looked up at him trying not to wake him.

"Well hello, sleepyhead," he smiled.

I smiled back, "Have you been up long?"

"For a half hour or so," he answered. "I didn't want to wake you."

And just like that, at that very moment, I knew I loved him. All my internal arguments about knowing him for one week, his wild ways or the age difference went away. There was no way I was saying that out loud, but what a beautiful little secret to carry home.

"We better get going," I mentioned. "It must be around 3 or 4. I don't want Grammy to worry."

"Me, either," he said.

We stood up to pack things away. Once everything was loaded into the car, he took the opportunity to kiss me. And, as usual, he was good at it.

Hugging me, he said, "Today I did two new things that I have never done before. I skinny dipped and napped with someone. Two things in one day: I wonder what tomorrow has in store."

"Are we seeing each other tomorrow?" I asked confused.

"Yes, whatever it takes," he insisted. "If it's O.K. with you…"

"I would like that," I nodded and smiled.

He walked around the car and opened the door. The reservoir was in the rear view mirror in no time. While we were driving back, Douglas peeked over at me and asked, "What are you thinking?"

"Well," I giggled, "at this very moment I am thinking: Why am I so attracted to a boy who asks such girly questions?" I repeated

Douglas' question, "What am I thinking?" I shook my head in disbelief. "Who asks that?"

"Sometimes you can be a little mean," he smiled.

"Yeah, well, sometimes you can be a little girly. It all evens out," I concluded, as I waved my hand around.

He reached over to hold my hand while he drove. I was grateful that Douglas had to keep his eyes on the road because I couldn't stop smiling.

When we got to the beginning of my grandparents' lane, Douglas put the car in park so we could kiss. When he pulled away to look into my eyes, I smiled and traced his face with my hand. It was the first time there was no need to avert my eyes or feel uncomfortable.

"So, have I finally won you over?" he asked.

"I think you have," I leaned back on the seat, "but I am a little worried how my Grammy is going to take this. Maybe it will be O.K. If nothing else, I will try to sell the friends angle and see if that will allow us to spend more time together."

Douglas put the car in gear so he could drive all the way up the lane. I jumped out quickly in case my grandparents were viewing the events. I waved to Douglas and opened the gate. There was no need to look back as that may be suspicious, but I wanted to. It would have been nice if we talked more about doing something tomorrow. Now that there was no doubt how I felt about Douglas, it would be important to see him as much as possible.

I came in the back door to find Grammy at the table playing solitaire while a pot simmered on the stove. "Who just dropped you off?" she asked.

Grammy knew exactly who dropped me off. Otherwise, she would have just assumed it was Cassidy. This was some kind of test. I was determined to pass so my smile disappeared and I answered, "Lullabelle's grandson." Not using his name would hopefully give the illusion of indifference. "Cassidy is a huge jerk and she deserted me."

"This is a long way out for Douglas to drop you off," she sounded concerned, but was still testing me. "Why didn't you call me? I would have come and gotten you."

"I don't know, Grammy," I said, slightly irritated. "If it makes you feel better, you can give Lulu some money for gas or yell at Cassidy, but I am not responsible for other people's evils or kindnesses."

She just looked at me not sure how to respond. I mean, it had to happen sometime, right? The moment in time where I could defeat my genius grandmother and feel like I may be able to navigate through life with skill. This was that moment.

She slyly smiled as though she was proud of my response. Maybe it wasn't the victory that gave her the most pleasure, but the ability of her opponents to spar that fired her up.

"I have been thinking about your mother," she announced. "We need to go a little easier on her. Yes, she has done and thought some terrible things, but so have I and so will you. It is human nature."

The lightening-quick change of subject was like conversation whiplash. It didn't afford me much time to enjoy the recent victory.

"What? "Where is this coming from?" I asked, sitting down at the table with her. "Did she call you or something while I was gone?"

"Maybe you should try to get to know her better," she suggested. "She is your mother after all."

At this, I stood up. "Do you see her here?" I sarcastically asked while looking around for dramatic effect. "How am I supposed to get to know her? She left when I was three, and it is somehow my responsibility to pursue her? No!"

My Grammy was upset. Unfortunately, this topic would always fire me up. But, seeing the sadness come over her broke my heart. It was not right for me to be a further source of pain. She meant too much to me.

Softening my stance, I tried to express myself with a little more compassion. But, the truth was still evident in my words and it can be a difficult thing to swallow- no matter how it's delivered.

"I can understand that you still love her. She will always be your daughter, but she was never a mother to me," I explained. "You are my mother. End of conversation."

And it was.

Chapter 16 Q & A Time

After showering, I walked out onto the bedroom balcony of Lorrah's home and breathed in the fresh air coming off the water. I could see Lorrah swimming toward the shore. A half hour in the water was quite an impressive work out. As I watched her, I wondered if this was a life I would like: freedom, money, beautiful surroundings. Would this be enough to make me happy?

It was a difficult question because growing up I had people in my life that showed me the value of love, relationship and family. Nevertheless, different lifestyles beckoned me. It was the freedom I craved more than the money- the idea of a day being entirely mine. No longer trying to sneak in some time for myself, but owning all the minutes in the day. I had never lived this way so to think it is better may be a foolish hoax.

It reminded me of the time I told Rick how much I liked the look of a couple large, green hills off in the distance. He laughed at me and explained that they were mounds of garbage that had been covered with grass. Sometimes, things look good until you get up close.

As Ellowee, there can't be a life of selfishness anyway. Not if I am to lead a group of people. I am not sure how this will be accomplished, but there is no doubt that I have it in me to do it. What an unusual and sudden confidence to possess.

"Hey," Lorrah waved and yelled from the beach, "a penny for your thoughts."

"If only they were worth that much," I joked. "I'm going to call home. Hope your swim was good." Lorrah waved, as she continued to walk up to the house. I had only wrapped a towel around me after the shower, so I threw on a long t-shirt and underwear.

I picked up the phone, realizing just how homesick I had become. Knowing Rick and Deidra were going to be on the other side of a phone conversation was exciting. Just the sound of their voices would put me at ease.

The phone rang after I dialed, but there was no answer. The call went to the answering machine so I left a message. "Hi, it's me," I said. "Just wanted to call and tell you both how much I miss and love you! Training is going well, and I'll only be here for a couple more days. I will try to call later, big hugs." I returned the receiver to its home and realized all the money in the world couldn't be better than family.

Not being able to contact someone was disappointing, which made the wine Lorrah had talked about even more enticing. I went into the kitchen and poured a glass. I took the pizza out of the freezer and preheated the oven per the directions.

On the horizon, the colors of the sun started to morph into a deep red color while it appeared to be sinking down into the water. Lorrah entered the room and saw the beautiful sunset. "Red sky at night, sailor's delight," she chimed. "Red sky at morning, sailor's warning."

I poured another glass of wine and handed it to her. "Cheers," I said as we clinked the glasses together.

"I am not sure where that saying is from," Lorrah said, "but, I am glad the sailors will be delighted tomorrow."

"The Bible," I informed her.

"No, I don't think so. It's an old poem," she said.

Nothing annoyed me more than when I knew something to be true and was questioned about it, as though I would just be saying stuff for the hell of it. Afraid that I would glare at her, I concentrated on the view through the window.

"True," I countered, "but the oldest reference about red sky forecasting was penned in the Bible. The book of Matthew, I believe. Jesus was trying to make a point that the people could look for the signs of weather, but be blind to the sign of the times."

"How do you know that?" Lorrah asked.

The buzzer signaled that the stove was preheated. I unwrapped the pizza and put it into the oven. The directions said to cook it for 20-30 minutes, so I set the timer for 25 minutes, a good midway point. I walked to one of the couches and took a seat.

"My Grammy taught me that," I finally answered. "She was always telling me stories from all kinds of literature. It is amazing how much poetry, song lyrics and wording comes directly from the Bible." I changed the subject, "Question number one: what is a Zero?"

"A Zero is an Oris who doesn't wish to keep our lineage a secret," she frowned. "They may be trying to organize and form an agenda of their own. They are dangerous because they are motivated by personal gain and power. Your mother is a Zero."

I questioned her assessment, "My mother is an Oris, just like me."

"She is an Oris, but she is not like you, El," she explained. "She doesn't care about others. She has no allegiance to her own kind, only to the wealth that can come of it. Because they have goals opposed to ours, we started calling them Siro, which is Oris backwards. It sounds so much like Zero that the name just stuck."

The fact that my mother was out for herself was not a surprise. It was no different than any other day. "The woman in the meeting said that they may be organizing," I interjected. "Why would that be a concern?"

"Long ago, when an Oris didn't want to be a part of the fold, they would go off on their own. They were going rogue, as we would say," she explained. "There is nothing wrong with that. Your grandmother even feared that you might go rogue at one point. It is common to tire of this burden," she paused to take a sip of her wine. "However, there are some of these rogue Oris that wish to take advantage of information in visions or gifts."

I thought on this for a second, and asked, "Well, haven't you kind of done that: the nice car, the beautiful home and the travel?"

Lorrah smiled. "I suppose that is true, but the funds are acquired by and for the collective Oris Foundation," she said. "May I share some history with you that may help you better understand?"

"Yes, history is wonderful," I answered, a little surprised by my words.

"A long time ago in Irish culture, there were quite a few Druidesses," Lorrah began. "These women were young, beautiful and possessed an uncanny ability to lead or offer wise counsel. They were believed to be goddesses and were even worshipped in some cases. When the Romans came, they had very little patience for the female rulers or a 'mother goddess' society. The Romans believed that women were for bearing children and objects of pleasure alone."

"I think I remember my Grammy telling me a story like this when I turned sixteen," I added. "These Druidesses were most likely early ancestors of Oris women."

"Yes," Lorrah affirmed. "That is what many believe. When the Romans invaded, they marked these Druidesses for death because they were threats to the kind of society the Romans wished to impress upon the Celts. Druidesses were burnt on the stake and often raped or degraded beforehand," Lorrah continued, obviously upset by what she was sharing. "The Roman traditions did have one light at the end of the tunnel."

"The nunneries," I interjected. "It was a place for many Oris women to not only hide, but also escape the pressure of having children…more accurately, female births."

Lorrah was surprised, "You know more than I thought! When the Druidesses started to be seen as witch-like figures, they came up with the name Oris. There was a lot of Latin available to them in the nunnery. Some stayed while others left to have families."

"I'm not sure what this history has to do with the Zero movement," I interrupted.

"Even back then, there were Druidesses who thought they could do better on their own. They believed waging war was in their best interest," Lorrah shook her head. "The Oris in the nunneries, on the other hand, began learning and studying Scripture. They would secretly read the Bible that was placed in the sanctuary. Many dropped their Pagan beliefs and adhered to a life of Christianity."

The timer for the pizza sounded so I got up to turn off the oven. "Go on, I'm listening," I urged.

"There isn't much more to share. Many of the Oris were able to support Druidess women through the nunneries. The Oris tried to convince the Druidesses to join them, but they remained unpredictable, dangerous, with no foundation of good to draw from." Lorrah went on, "They believe that the world has taken from them so it is their turn to take from the world," Lorrah shared. "And if they are organizing, I shudder to think what they are capable of."

"The pizza is done," I announced. "Where do you keep your plates?" Lorrah pointed to a cabinet. "O.K., so what is stopping a Zero from coming to one of these meetings and just saying they are an Oris?"

"That would be hard for someone to do," she mused. "Let's say, for argument's sake, a Zero comes to a meeting. The local representative knows everyone because the groups are not that large. The meeting we just attended today is the second largest chapter. If there is a new member, they have to be inducted into the Oris Foundation and someone has to vouch for them. The process is intensive. Most Zeros have never even heard the word Oris because it is not to be spoken aloud by an Oris, unless necessary."

"So, let me get this straight, because this is confusing," I said. "If someone is from our lineage that is an Oris and wants to join the foundation- they are judged worthy before they can become a foundation member? That seems a little harsh."

"It's not," Lorrah explained. "There really is no other way for it to be done. Very rarely does someone waltz through the doors without a connection to someone already there or knowledge of their lineage."

I handed Lorrah a plate of pizza and sat down with my own. "Makes sense," I agreed. "So what is a filter?"

"That's an easy question," Lorrah said relieved. "It's just an idea, occurrence or suggestion that is up for placement in the Book of Deidra. It is your job to decide if a filter is important enough to be cited in the book."

"How do I do that?" I wondered.

"You use your judgement and intelligence like you would with any other decision," she stated. "It is actually ingrained in you- in all of us- to do well with decision making. It is even rare that Oris would disagree with each other on important matters."

Lorrah reminded me of the thing that I was most curious about, "When do I get to read the Book of Deidra?"

"I only have the copy that belonged to Ellowee, your grandmother. You are Ellowee now," she commented. "I have strict instructions to only give it to you after you've read the letter she left."

I had just taken a bite of pizza but began chewing as fast as possible, so I could yell at Lorrah. My eyebrows were furrowing and my expression was becoming hardened. Finally when the last crumb was swallowed, I blurted out: "You have a letter from my grandmother and haven't given it to me yet! What the hell is wrong with you? Let me see it!" I put out my hand, expecting immediate delivery.

Lorrah had the nerve to shake her head, "Until we have a particular discussion, I cannot give it to you."

"Well, go on then- discuss," I said as my patience was vanishing. I motioned my hand as giving her the floor to discuss with me whatever she'd like.

"It's not time yet. I don't know the contents of the letter only the topic in the Book of Deidra that needs to be broached, but it will come up soon," Lorrah said, trying to be encouraging. "We'll be talking a lot over the next couple of days."

"If I have never read the Book of Deidra, how am I supposed to be talking about something in it?" I asked, feeling the blood pounding on my temples.

"Because the subject is about you," she smiled. "Your grandmother never saw your mother as Oris material, so the book has all your history in hopes that you would be Ellowee."

"My grandmother never vouched for me," I reminded Lorrah.

"That's not public knowledge so no one needs to know. In all her writings, she vouched for you," Lorrah smiled. "She loved you dearly El. You were blessed to have her."

"Don't you get tired of this Oris business?" I wondered also wanting to change the subject. There was no doubt I was blessed to have had my grandmother, but wandering down that road would have brought me to tears.

"Normally, there isn't a lot of Oris *business* to do," she explained. "We socialize, travel, lead our own lives and go to a meeting once a year. This is the first time I have ever been stressed by it."

"Dogs, nursing, lemon cucumbers, daffodils, swimming, walks, flies, poetry, water shortages, bad cooking, cows, neighbors, shopping, birthdays…" I rattled off random memories of my Grammy and stuck my hand out. "Does any of that get me the letter?"

Lorrah giggled, "I am afraid not, but that was a valiant effort."

"Fine," I said, disgusted. "Just know if you ever leave me alone in this house that I will ransack the place looking for that letter." I topped off our wine glasses and accepted defeat for now. "So, do you have a special someone in your life?" I asked.

Lorrah laid her head back, "Hmm, what is the right way to answer that?" she thought out loud. "I have a special someone who comes in and out of my life. Does that count?"

"How should I know?" I said incredulous. "It's your life!"

"Well, let me put it this way. He is a wonderful man who I care deeply about," she explained, "but he has serious reservations about me because he says that I don't need him for anything." Lorrah drank half her wine after that comment and looked out the window. "The thing is, I don't need him, but I want him," she squinted. "I'm not sure why that doesn't mean more to him."

"Do you get lonely in this house when he isn't here?" I asked.

"I spend 95% of my life lonely, whether I am with someone or not," Lorrah answered. "I'm not lonely here with you because you know more about me than any man I've known. You know where my money comes from, why my mom left, what it means to be an Oris and why I don't want children. Shall I go on?"

"No need," I informed her. "I completely understand."

Lorrah got up to retrieve another bottle of wine. She glanced back at me and asked, "How is it being married to a man and having to hide what you are?"

That was an easy question. I told her, "Being an Oris has never really been a big part of who I am."

"Ha!" she exclaimed. "If an ostrich buries its head in the sand, it doesn't mean it's any less of an ostrich. Tell me there isn't a day that goes by when you don't wonder how you and your daughter will get along after her junction."

Lorrah's words were reeking of truth. Half-smiling, I said, "Shut up." She walked back to the couches and topped off our wine again. This was my third glass, which meant a headache was inevitable in the morning.

"You're right," I admitted. "But there is hope. My Grammy told me that some Oris get passed over. Maybe Deidra will be a lucky one." How I hoped that would be the case for my little girl…to have no knowledge of this nonsense.

Lorrah looked sad and informed me, "Getting passed over has been documented once in the case of Enya. We believe there are other instances, but none have been recorded. We are investigating one case now where we believe a woman is posing as an Oris. She was actually at the meeting this morning. She comes with her mother and they get along a little too well."

"I met them. Why on Earth would someone pretend to be an Oris?" I asked.

"There are a lot of monetary perks to being an Oris," she reminded me. "But, more than likely, she would hide getting passed over because their life would instantly be changed. Everyone would want to know how it happened, which would mean endless questions and medical testing." She paused before delivering the bad news, "Your gifts are too strong. I've read what you can do in the Book, so I wouldn't hold out hope for Deidra getting passed over."

"You make it sound like I'm a superhero," I laughed. "I assure you that apart from my kitchen apron, there are no capes in my closet." Our giggles gave way to silence. We sipped our wine as the room filled with deep thoughts, dark places and a little hope that struggled to remain.

"So, was Rick your first love?" Lorrah broke the silence.

"Let's just say that he is the only man I have been *in* love with," I mused. "There were a couple other men before Rick, but they weren't for me. My first love was probably a boy I had met when I was 14. I still think about him to this day and wonder how he is doing or what became of him."

"Why do you say *probably* your first love?" Lorrah wondered.

I sipped my wine and explained, "Well, we were so young. He was sixteen and just adorable. All the girls in town were after him. So, when he started seeking me out, I was flattered. He was my first kiss, too."

"But you're not sure you loved him?" Lorrah asked.

I tried to explain, "There was a moment in time where he was all I thought about when we were apart, and when we were together, nothing else mattered. Doesn't that sound like love?" I mused.

"It sounds amazing," she said. "I've never felt that way about anyone."

"I haven't either," I concluded, "not since Douglas. But I wonder if that has to do with being young and singularly focused."

Lorrah chuckled, "I think you mean passionate. Singularly focused just does not sound very hot!"

"True," I agreed. "I can't finish this wine. I've drunk too much already. Would you be terribly insulted if I hit the hay early?"

“Not at all,” Lorrah said. “Hold on.” She went upstairs to her bedroom. She came back down and handed me an envelope. I recognized my Grammy’s handwriting immediately. It said: “To Ellowee, My Dear Granddaughter.”

Chapter 17 Gone

It has been three long days without a peep from Douglas. No phone calls or impromptu visits- nothing.

A couple of days ago, I called Lullabelle's number and there was no answer. The fact that no one picked up the phone was very strange. I called around 6 p.m., knowing that Lulu would be in for the night. Sometimes during the day she would garden or grocery shop, but she was always in before dusk. Her eyes weren't what they used to be.

My moping around the house had not gone unnoticed. Grammy and Gramps had asked me about it, but I just told them that I am really engrossed in a book I am reading. For the past couple of days I have been carrying around a book about the Gold Rush. It has occurred to me that actually reading a book is much easier than pretending to do so. However, my mind is having a hard time focusing on anything but Douglas. Now that we are finally on the same page and want to spend time together, he pulls a Houdini.

It is almost Grammy and Gramps' bed time, which is a small comfort. The sun is on its way down, so I can comfortably cry in the darkness. The smart thing would be to go to bed, but I prefer to poke and prod at my wounded heart. I'll picture Douglas' smile and try to remember how his kisses made me feel. If there is no possibility of feeling his love, then I will suffocate myself in the absence of it.

My dark thoughts were interrupted by the phone ringing. Grammy said she would get it. I ran into the kitchen hoping it would be Douglas. When she lifted the receiver, it was obviously for her. Grammy's side of the conversation was: "Fine…calm down…tomorrow afternoon…yes…it will work…I understand…good night!"

She hung up the phone and told me to hit the hay early if I wanted to go to work with her in the morning. She kissed my forehead and went off to bed. Luckily, she was scheduled for an early shift tomorrow (7 a.m.-3 p.m.). She was taking me with her, and I would stay at the hospital until the pool opened. There would be some answers at the pool.

There was no telling what would be found out, but answers were better than questions at this point- even if the answers hurt. Nothing could be worse than what I imagined in my mind. I kept trying to prepare myself for what I would see at the pool. My mind conjured up Douglas surrounded by throngs of beautiful teenage girls.

Being alone now, the tears escaped. They had been pent up all day. I had to wonder if this whole thing was just a game. Did he want me to fall for him so he could break my heart? Was it only interesting for him when I wasn't convinced of my feelings? The tears continued to fall. When snoring could be heard from the back rooms, I tiptoed to the kitchen and dialed Lulu's number. It was the second attempt in the last three days. There was no answer.

Maybe something has happened to Lulu. It was selfish that I felt relief in that scenario, but it didn't stop me from considering that possibility. If Douglas' grandmother was ill or got injured, he would have a good reason for not contacting me. It was shameful that Lulu's lack of well-being made me hopeful, but it did. I hung up the phone and went back to the couch to see if there was anything worth watching on TV.

There was nothing that could hold my attention, and now that I had found comfort in Lulu having an illness, I went to brush my teeth for bed. Before leaving the bathroom, I said a little prayer: "Lord, please don't let anything be wrong with Lulu. Forgive me for thinking such a thing. Help me find answers tomorrow at the pool. Sorry I'm contacting you when I want or need something. We should chat more when I have time. It would be better to always have time for you, huh? I'm not very good at his, but you know that. You know everything. And, if you know everything, why is it we do need to talk like this? Never mind, I can't do any more deep thinking today. Goodnight…I mean, amen. Amen."

Sleep did not come quickly, not when thoughts of Douglas flooded my mind. After an hour or more, I finally dozed off. The visions started immediately because I was in a heightened state of emotion. Through all the visions, it seemed that I was conscious as I yearned to see Douglas chasing me around the world. He was nowhere to be found.

My mother was up to her usual antics, but tonight's highlight reel was some of her better lies. There seemed to be no end to my mother's imagination. She also delighted in delivering news that would cause pain or sorrow. I watched as she told my grandparents about her pregnancy with my older brother. They were brokenhearted, and she turned around smirking as though she was enjoying their disappointment.

She told them that the father's parents forbid them from getting married or being together. The truth was that she ran away and didn't even tell the father that she was pregnant in fear that he *would have* married her. Marriage would cramp her style.

When she was 5 months pregnant and beginning to show, she told my dad the same sob story after he had already fallen in love with her. He believed all of her rubbish and made it his mission to become her knight in shining armor. My father offered to raise the baby as his own, but not knowing if it would be a girl or a boy, she demanded it be put up for adoption. She told him she wanted to be with him, but that they needed to start with a "clean slate."

The lies went on during the night: her age, occupation, marital status…everything was up for grabs. It made me wonder if anything my mother had ever said was based in truth. One vision showed her lying to my Grammy about going to town with her girlfriends. Instead, she went to the reservoir with a group of kids, so she could see a boy. This vision bothered me because I had kind of done the same thing. To have any similarities to my mother was sobering and made me want to tell Grammy everything.

The urge to use the bathroom was slowly waking me up. I fumbled my way to and from the bathroom when I realized Grammy wasn't in her bed. The house was so small that it would be easy to hear her in the kitchen, but there were no noises coming from any part of the house. I moved the window shade to the side, and it was light outside. Oh no, I thought, this is all wrong. The clock read 8 a.m. and Grammy's shift started at seven.

I ran through the house but only found the dogs. When I went outside, I yelled for Gramps and he came out of his workshop.

"Good morning, Muriel," he smiled.

"Not really, Gramps," I answered on the brink of tears. "Grammy was supposed to take me into town with her!"

"She said she didn't have the heart to wake you up this morning. You were sleeping so soundly," he explained.

Of all the days that she decided to let me sleep, this was not the right one! There was a lump in my throat. I went into the kitchen to make some toast because it was the only thing that might stay down. I put a little peanut butter on it and brought it to the bathroom where I started the water for my shower. Food in the bathroom was something that always disgusted me, but today it was more important to multi-task.

I was going to take a shower, get dressed and walk to town, if need be. Town was about eleven miles, and the pool was another two miles. Three miles an hour was about right if I kept a decent pace and didn't need to stop for too many breaks. 13 divided by 3 was a bit more than 4 so I just figured it would take about 4 1/2 hours to see Douglas. Every step and drop of sweat would be worth it. Leaving at 9 a.m. would get me there at about 1:30 p.m. Grammy's shift ended at 3, so I could spend a couple of hours at the pool.

There was a knock on the bathroom door. "Are you O.K., Muriel?" Gramps asked.

"Yep," I answered. "Just getting myself ready before I walk to town."

"Well, now, you are *not* walking all the way to town," he insisted. "If you must go, I can take you, but call your Grammy to make sure she picks you up."

"Thank you, Gramps," I said delighted. "I'll call as soon as I get out of the shower. You should have knocked on the door sooner. It would have saved me from doing a lot of math."

"What?" he asked, sounding irritated.

"Nothing," I responded.

Now I had plenty of time to get ready. There was no need to rush. I was giddy with anticipation and just knew there was a good explanation for why Douglas hadn't called or visited.

Every time I took a shower, it reminded me of my first vision and the landslide of information that seemed to keep on coming. It was completely irrational to be angry with a tub for being the site where I started my junction, but I figured I was allowed a little irrationality.

There was makeup in the top drawer of my Grammy's dresser in the bathroom. Instead of a cabinet or closet, she had a tall dresser that held all the towels, toiletries and such. I had never worn any makeup, but I put a little on to try it out. After inspecting my handiwork in the mirror, I immediately washed it all off. Someone would need to show me how to apply it because that couldn't have been correct.

My swimsuit was in the bedroom, so I peeked out to make sure the coast was clear before darting into the bedroom. After getting dressed, I retrieved the peanut butter toast from the bathroom. I threw it away in the bathroom garbage, putting toilet paper over it so it wouldn't be discovered. Wasting food in this house would get me into a lot of trouble, enough trouble that a ride to town could be cancelled. A big bowl of cereal sounded much better anyway. And there was no need to rush.

Once in the kitchen, I dialed the nurse's desk in Grammy's wing. Doris answered and told me that Grammy was tending to a patient. I left a message with Doris to have Grammy pick me up at the pool after her shift. Doris said she would make sure Grammy got the message. Everything was coming up roses.

Gramps came onto the back porch hurriedly looking in the upright freezer. He usually didn't move quickly, so I was concerned…concerned that whatever he was up to might affect my trip into town.

Sticking my head out the kitchen door to the back porch, I asked, "What are you looking for in there?"

"I caught a mouse in one of my traps and hid it in here," he answered quickly.

At this point, I wasn't sure I should ask any further questions. But I couldn't help myself and inquired further, "Why did you put a mouse in the freezer? Does Grammy know about it?" He brought his head out of the freezer just long enough to scowl at me. That was a "no" to my latter question.

There would not be an answer to the other question because he was in the middle of something, and wasn't going to take the time to explain. I could respect that. He found the mouse, raced into the kitchen, unpacked the mouse from the plastic bag and put it in a bowl. I looked on in horror because he placed it in the same kind of bowl we used for cereal. My earlier craving for cereal had miraculously disappeared.

He added warm water to his mouse-filled bowl and waited for about 5 minutes. He poured the water out of the bowl, took the mouse, told me to stay put, and off he went toward his garden. I squirted soap in the bowl and ran scalding hot water over it. An apple would be a good breakfast since cereal was now out of the question.

My curiosity was getting the best of me, so I went to Grammy's bedroom window to check out what Gramps was doing. He was outside of his garden fence on his knees, looking under the plants. He lifted his head up and threw the mouse to the corner of his garden. He bent over again to look under the plants. After a while, he got up and dusted off his jeans to come inside. I thought to myself that maybe he had finally lost it. All this country living or our family had pushed him over the edge.

Gramps was washing his hands in the kitchen sink when I walked in. At least he hadn't lost all his sense and still appreciated occasional hygiene. I didn't know what to say, so I grabbed a yogurt out of the fridge and sat at the kitchen table. He joined me after drying his hands.

"Do you like snakes, Muriel?" he asked.

"Nope," my reply was effortless.

"Why?" he wondered.

"They can bite, they hide places and they are just creepy animals," I trailed off.

"Hmm," he mused, "and what are your thoughts on pesky gophers?"

"I don't know. They are cuter than snakes," I giggled. "As a rule, fur is better than scales."

Gramps smiled, "There was a king snake in my garden this morning and I haven't seen one for a while on my property." Gramps went on, "See, the king snake will eat rattlesnakes that no one wants around. It also eats gophers and other rodents."

"Gophers are rodents?" I asked.

"Oh yea, they often carry parasites, too," he informed me. "When I was a little boy, my uncle was riding a horse on his property and the horse's foot went into a gopher hole. The horse tossed my uncle and injured him so badly that he was no longer able to work the farm. Their family lost everything," Gramps shook his head. "I had a gopher injure a couple of my dogs, too, because they bite. They eat plant roots in my garden which kills all the crops. Sometimes they even pluck the vegetables right off the plants."

"Don't snakes live in holes, too," I pointed out.

"Yes," Gramps nodded, "but the holes are smaller and usually hidden."

"What was the mouse for?" I wondered.

Gramps explained further, "I saved a mouse in the freezer because neighbors have been talking about seeing more king snakes this year. It would be quite a coup if I could convince one to take up residence here."

Gramps was a genius, not crazy after all. He was trying to show the snake there was food here.

"Did the snake eat the mouse?" I asked excitedly.

"I'll check when I get back from town," he said. "You can't spook them with too much noise or movement. It might be a good idea to keep this between us," he winked. "Grammy doesn't care for most reptiles, but they don't hurt anything. The king snake will be a priceless resident if it rids us of the gophers and rattlesnakes."

"It will be our secret, but I may have to share with her that you used the word 'coup' today," I said, and shot him a raised-eyebrow glance. "She will not be happy." We laughed.

"So, tell me about this boy," he inquired, changing the subject.

I was taken aback, not sure at all how to navigate the request. I sat still for a moment, searching his face to try and figure out just how much he knew.

"Walk to town?" he questioned, more like a statement. "Nobody in their right mind would walk that far in the heat unless it was for money or love. And because of the phone call on your birthday, I've ruled out money."

It was funny to me that Gramps and I both spent time this morning questioning each other's sanity. There were still no words coming forth.

"Muriel, I know he was here that night," he revealed. "I saw him jog around the front of the house when I went back to bed. Luckily, I heard you come to bed not long after that. I'm too cute for prison. Don't make me shoot a boy."

It figured that Gramps knew so much. He was so much smarter and observant than anyone gave him credit for. He was also loyal and must not have said anything to Grammy. Had he mentioned it to her, I would have been handcuffed to her wrist for the remainder of the summer.

"He works at the pool, and I met him in town right after I got here," I confessed. "He was my first kiss."

Gramps wasn't pleased with that last bit of information. After the words left my mouth, I had to question why I mentioned the kiss. What is wrong with me?!

"Well, a gentleman doesn't meet with you under the cover of darkness," he lectured.

"Even if he did everything right, do you really think Grammy would allow him to see me at all?" I countered.

He knew there was truth in that statement. If Grammy thought a boy was interested in me, asked for permission to take me out and brought a big bouquet of flowers…the answer would still be no. It wouldn't matter if it was high noon and he wore a three-piece suit. No dice.

"Your Grammy can be a bit protective," he said, as though it wasn't the understatement of the year. "He just better be good to you. I am still a great shot."

I smiled, "Well, I haven't heard from him in three days so it may not be an issue." The smile faded as the reality of my own words saddened me.

"And you are going to the pool to see what is going on?" he guessed.

"Yep," I said, "looking for answers. He finally has me thinking about him all the time and I just want to know if we are going to try to spend the summer together."

"What if he has changed his mind?" Gramps asked.

The thought of that was not very appealing. But I answered truthfully, "There isn't much I can do about that, but at least I'll know. Why would I want to spend time with someone who didn't want to spend time with me?" I shook my head and said, "It is just so hard to believe that he would pour his heart out one minute and then ignore me the next. Boys are so confusing!"

To this, Gramps slapped his knee and exclaimed, "Ha! Oh, honey, we are a lot simpler than you think. Once you figure boys out, they won't stand a chance." He smiled, "Why don't we go a little early? Maybe you can talk to him before the pool opens. That way, if he is there and you don't like what he has to say, we can come back home."

"O.K.," I agreed. I grabbed my stuff and we left.

The car ride was silent, but I couldn't help thinking that my grandpa was just about the best person I knew to help me out like this. We got to the pool almost an hour before it opened. It felt like we were on some kind of stakeout. We watched as a couple of cars pulled up, but there was no sign of Douglas.

"You know that he is working today?" Gramps asked.

"No, I don't, but I can ask his supervisor when he is scheduled if I don't see him," I answered.

"You were going to walk all the way here without knowing if he was working or not?" Gramps verbalized the facts. "I'm afraid you might like this kid more than you let on."

I nodded to confirm his statement. My eyes stayed on the pool entrance. His supervisor got there a half hour before the pool opened. Douglas should arrive soon because the lifeguards were supposed to test their equipment before the shift started. My heart sank when the pool opened and Douglas was nowhere to be seen.

"Gramps," I said, "would you wait here for five minutes? I'm not sure I will be in the mood to swim." Walking to the pool, my heart was beating very loudly. I checked behind me just to make sure it wasn't Douglas with a basketball.

The line to get into the pool moved fast. I saw a sign in the cashier's window that said: *Lifeguard Wanted: apply within.*

"You're looking for a lifeguard?" I asked.

The young girl replied, "No offense, but I think they are looking to fill the position with a boy." She looked at me and said, "But I can get you an application. We always have girls that want to work here because the head lifeguard was just dreamy. He had to go home a couple of days ago, totally our loss." She looked past me and said to the next kid in line, "Four dollars, please."

As others came to the window, I stepped backward until I turned and walked slowly to Gramps, who waited in the car. There was no doubt in my mind that she must have been talking about Douglas. He was dreamy and, now more than ever, it all seemed like it could have been a dream. He was gone without even a word. Do you do that to people you claim to love!?

Gramps kindly drove me home in silence. "When we get home," I announced, "I am going to take a nap." Sleep rescued me from my sadness after an hour of tears.

Gramps must have called to tell Grammy not to pick me up. At 3:30 she was shaking me awake, "I need you to get up, Muriel! You need to do something for me without asking any of your questions. Muriel, do you hear me? Rise and shine!"

"What do you want?" I yelled. "Leave me alone!"

"No, get up right now," she demanded. "Splash off your face if it will help you wake up. On the kitchen table is a lovely meal from the hospital. It was chicken parmesan day. Upsy-daisy."

There was no reason to fight the force that is my Grammy. Far too many battles were waged in our history to think I stood a chance, especially after just waking up. I imagined a cemetery full of tombstones that read: here lies Muriel's argument with her Grammy. The dates and times were listed on the stones. Their lifespans were all short.

The mention of food had my stomach growling, so I did as I was told. At least the chicken parmesan did not disappoint. It occurred to me that all I had to eat today was an apple and some yogurt, so further sustenance was necessary. Grammy sat at the table playing solitaire, while her eyes darted between me and the clock. She had never acted this strangely.

"So, what do I need to do with no questions asked?" I wondered.

"Around four that phone is going to ring," she announced. "I need you to pick it up, say 'Conchobar' into the phone and hang up immediately."

"Why?" I asked.

"That is a question!" Grammy shouted at the top of her lungs. "Damn it, Muriel, just do this one thing for me because I asked. This is very important. Can you do that?"

Grammy didn't swear like that, so I shook my head up and down in agreement- then started crying. Gramps came in when he heard me crying and started reprimanding his wife for her tone. They were talking loudly at one another while I sniveled.

When the phone rang, the room went quiet. Grammy looked at me with worry, as though I had forgotten her simple instructions. I slid the chair back to make my way toward the phone. I picked up the receiver, said "Conchobar," and hung up. If nothing else, doing this for Grammy should redeem my question of *why*. She had never gotten that angry at me.

"Thank you," she said. "I'm going to take a shower. Sorry I lost my temper." She grabbed her purse, a glass of water and left the kitchen.

Gramps retired to his chair in the living room to read the paper. His chair was wide enough for both of us to sit in, so I joined him and laid my head on his shoulder.

"Did your snake eat the mouse?" I wondered.

"Well, I'm not sure, but the mouse was gone, so that's a good sign," he answered. He shifted gears, "I know your grandmother can seem a bit testy, but she doesn't know what you went through today."

"Do you think I should tell her?" I asked, honestly looking for advice.

"God no, child," he blurted out. "Just try not to judge her too harshly. She is a good woman and loves you more than you know." He put the paper down and wrapped his arm around my shoulder. "Sometimes we have bad days, and those days can turn into weeks, months or even years," he shared. "But bad times often have a moral to the story, some bit of wisdom that can point you to a solution or help end rough patches. I truly believe that."

"Well, today was an awful day for me, but I don't see any moral," I concluded.

"That's because this is new for you," he explained. "You only need some practice."

"You know a lot of what happened today and over the last week," I said. "Go ahead and give me a moral to the story. Or, better yet, help me figure out a lesson in it all."

"O.K.," he accepted the challenge. He thought for a couple of minutes and said, "The moral of this story is- be careful, because even a small hole can sink a big ship." He looked at me seeming very pleased with his assessment.

I simply responded, "I don't get it."

"Well," he started, "this boy has left a small hole in that big 'ole heart of yours. The trick is to not concentrate on the little hole because that can ruin the rest. When you look at all the good, you won't even know how or when that little hole has healed. But it will. And it won't sink future relationships."

"That moral kind of works for your uncle, too," I observed. "If his horse hadn't fallen in that little hole, it wouldn't have sunk the farm."

Gramps slapped his chair. "See, you are good at this already!" he complimented.

I didn't have the energy to be the bigger person right now. Douglas' disappearance had hurt me, and the situation called for some good, old fashioned name-calling to numb the pain.

"For right now, I think the moral of the story is that all boys are snakes," I decided. "That just makes me feel better." I nodded my head up and down.

"Well, whatever gets you through, Aesop," he relented, and pat my shoulder. "Try and find yourself a king snake then, they are preferable. I'll save you some mice." He raised his paper back up to continue his reading. I kissed him on the forehead.

Grammy came through the door to the living room fresh from her shower. I got up and grabbed a book off the shelf to read in the bedroom. Normally I enjoyed Grammy's company, but after the way she treated me, I wasn't in the mood to talk.

Whether it was Gramps' wisdom or just having someone to talk to, I felt so much better. Thoughts of Douglas still crossed my mind every now and then, but a tear in his honor was never shed again.

Chapter 18 The Letter

After Lorrah handed me the letter, she said goodnight and went upstairs to her bedroom. I just stared at it as though I had never seen one of these newfangled contraptions called a letter. It was an envelope for standard, letter-size paper. I needed to find the best spot to read it because everything needed to be just right. It was the last time I would spend time with the most important woman in my life.

I grabbed the small blanket on the back of the couch and took the elevator to the ground floor so the letter could be read on the beach. I grabbed one of the lounge chairs and moved it off the patio and onto the sand, being careful not to get too far from the lights. There was a refreshing breeze in the air, which lifted the scent of Grammy's perfume off the envelope.

I sat and ran my fingers over Grammy's writing: *To Ellowee, My Dear Granddaughter*. The envelope did not give away where it would like to be opened. There were no rips anywhere or areas where the seal was weak. I picked a side and pried it open. The letter was about five pages long and looked as if both sides had writing on them. I took a deep breath, made sure I was on page one and began reading.

Dearest Muriel,

If you are reading this letter, I left this mortal coil before sharing the legacy of Ellowee with you. For that, I am deeply sorry. I failed you in regard to properly preparing you for this position, but I did so in the hopes that you would have a taste of a normal life- something you always wanted. It is still a mystery to me if that was the correct choice, but everything I ever did or didn't do was done in an attempt to protect you. You were my world.

At this point, the tears were flowing steadily. Grammy was right. I only ever wanted to be normal. But, it seemed not accepting my Oris history may have been a mistake. It could have been another thing we shared.

By now, you must have an idea of what is expected of you. Lorrah will be a good guide. Be patient with her as she can be a little excitable and anxious. You will be good for her and vice versa.

You no doubt have many questions, and it would be foolish of me to think I can answer all of them with a letter, but there are some things that you need to know going forward. It occurs to me that this may be the first time I have ever communicated with you where you did not interrupt or ask questions. Death does have its advantages. (I hope you are laughing.)

I am sure you did not expect such a large amount of money to be given to you. Grandpa and I did not live like millionaires, but we had it in the bank. Or, more accurately, I had it in the bank. Perhaps he is still alive and I have gone before him. If that is the case, please give him a hug and mention to him that I always thought he was a wonderful man.

He desired a simple life, and when I traveled, those were the times I indulged myself. You can do what you want with the money. It was a way to help support people in the Oris Foundation, but everyone has more than they need at this point. You know the value of hard work, which will serve you better than money.

You must still have the gift to see the green hue. However, I told people it left you after your marriage. There was no need to continue amassing money. If everyone avoids spending foolishly, they should be set for life and also be able to support future generations. You do not want people depending on your gifts for their gain.

You are special, Muriel. Those words are not being spoken because I love you or you are my granddaughter. Please hear me when I say you are gifted beyond any Oris I have known. The green hue has not been visible to anyone for a few centuries. I recognized the gift during the first summer when you came into your junction and only because the story of the gift was handed down for generations.

Your visions are also unlike those of other Oris. Your visions are more tangible. No one else's visions contain sound or scent. I have never had a vision where my mother wasn't the sole character. However, you have visions of other Oris women and historical images of our lineage. It is amazing! It seems you even receive warnings or helpful visions when decisions need to be made.

Speaking of decisions, it is time you know about one that you were not a part of, but were affected by nonetheless. It involved a boy named Douglas. Maybe that name means nothing to you. It is possible you did not reciprocate his feelings, but it would have done us no good to discuss him at the time. You were fourteen and action needed to be taken.

I adjusted myself in the chair to get a better stream of light for reading. The letter up to this point was interesting, but I couldn't imagine why Douglas' name was coming into all of this. I never told him that I was an Oris. We spent a week together, he was my first kiss and then he was gone.

Douglas came home to Lulu's one night after dropping you off at our house. Apparently, you two had been spending time together without my knowledge. He told Lulu how much he loved you. He hoped she and I would accept the relationship and even alluded to the fact that he wanted you to be his wife one day. Lulu knew immediately that something was wrong.

Douglas had girlfriends before, but never spoke so seriously about someone in such a short period of time.

Lullabelle called her son that night to pick Douglas up. Lulu told her son that she was feeling miserable and needed to see the doctor. What you don't know is that Lullabelle was my guide just like Lorrah is yours. She was my best friend, God rest her soul. She knew that you had gone through your junction and was gifted with the green hue vision. Lulu thought if you had that special gift, perhaps you had others we didn't know about.

Douglas' father came that next morning to pick him up. Douglas was crying and yelling, telling his father that he had to say goodbye to you...see you one last time. Lullabelle gave him a fake phone number and told him that it was your number at home. She told him to call once school started. Lulu also told her son that Douglas should not be allowed use of a car for at least a week. She was convinced that he would try to travel back to see you.

After Lulu had pored over Oris history for a couple of days and contacted people who may have some information, she came back to me with her findings. Back in the day of the Druidesses, when they were worshipped, they had a power over men. It guaranteed the men's allegiance and ensured they would serve the Druidesses. This was why many people believed they were witches.

It was originally thought their power was in a kiss. It could have been a kiss on the hand, cheek, lips- wherever. And not all Oris women were gifted in this way. Strangely, a Druidess' kiss rarely affected men in the winter. It turns out that the power didn't lie in the kiss at all, but in her sweat.

The day you met Douglas, you were a nervous wreck in the drug store. It was a hot day. When he helped you pick up your feminine supplies, he must have brushed your sweating arm. He went to play basketball but probably couldn't get you off of his mind. It was no mistake you saw him outside the restaurant. He was already under your spell.

Lullabelle was hysterical when telling me the news. She said that she couldn't have her grandson worshipping a girl he barely knew. She believed he was too young for this kind of emotion or pain. There were only two ways that he could be released from your hold over him. Either the Druidess died or, as you have probably guessed, she spoke the word "Conchobar" to release him.

Douglas was on the other end of the phone call that day. He had been trying to get in touch with you constantly after he left. I would unplug the phone during the day and then plug it in right before we got ready for bed. Lullabelle told him to try the number at 4 p.m. the day he called.

My arms were getting tired, so I let them fall into my lap. I was caught somewhere between a scream of frustration and a tear of despair. This information was overwhelming. There were quite a few pages of the letter left, and I couldn't imagine there was more to be shared or revealed. Watching the waves and breathing in the sea air helped calm me down so I could continue with the letter. It felt like it weighed 20 pounds as I lifted it to the light once again.

All of this information concerned me. Between your visions, the green hue and now this power in your sweat- you were considerably more gifted than anyone I had known or heard about. And if you had all these gifts, why didn't your mother and I possess them? We had the same lineage. Or did we? The only wild card was your father. I studied his lineage over the next couple of days and called in some favors from friends in Europe. There was no reason to believe he had anything to do with it. Your dad is Hungarian, German and Polish.

My friends in Poland and Hungary were having the same luck I was. We couldn't find anything. But an Oris friend of mine in Germany called and was able to explain some things. Your father's German lineage went through the house of Hess. The farthest she could trace it back was to a man named Reinhold Warin Hess who was born in 1308.

It didn't seem like this information was very helpful until I received the records she overnighted to me from Germany. While looking through some of Reinhold's marriage records, my blood ran cold. The first woman Reinhold had married passed away in childbirth, but the second woman he married when he was 30 years of age had an interesting name. Her name was Ada Deidra born in 1321. The name Deidra stuck out to me like a beacon. That was not a German name by any stretch and one that our people were quite attached to.

Ada did not have a last named associated with the marriage certificate, but I knew in my bones that it was "Stoffel." This must have been one of Enya's (Anna's) daughters! The dates worked out. Ada would have been around 17 when they married. Ada and Reinhold only had one child. Reinhold had passed away during the pregnancy. When their son was born, he was named Warin Gilfin Hess. Yet another nod to our Irish roots.

When Enya passed away at 61, she wanted to be buried in her homeland. Back in that time, this was a very difficult request. Ada, escorted by her son Warin, made the journey back to Ireland. The ceremony was quick and without a lot of fanfare. Ada and Warin returned to Germany, but not alone. Warin had met a young maiden in Gilfin that he couldn't seem to live without- after only knowing her for two short days.

Warin and that maiden, my dear Muriel, is the line your father descends from. Your dad's paternal line is very connected to your maternal line. You are probably thinking: so what?! And I would not blame you. When I told you the story of

Enya, it was history. Centuries of our ancestry handed down for generations. But, I have lived too long to not question some things. (Maybe that's where you get your incessant questioning.)

As I write this to you, I sense deep in my heart that Enya lied when she returned to Ireland in 1351. When she stood up and told all who would hear how her children were passed over. After that announcement, her lineage would no longer be recorded in the Book of Deidra, and she hoped her family would be free of the Oris life. It was also suspicious that when we looked into the Stoffel lineage, many of the records had been burnt during the great pestilence. How could that be when so many other records survived? She was trying to hide her family tree.

I never questioned the history of Enya until I aged and found that lying has offered my family protection as well. No one knows of your many gifts or that you have a daughter. The Oris life is something you have always run from, but I am afraid it has finally caught up with you, sweetheart. How I wish I could have spoken to you in person about all of this.

You should not tell anyone about your gifts. What you possess can be easily exploited. Your mother is the only Oris, for obvious reasons, that knows about your daughter. She will tell others. It may be wise to fake Deidra's death. She will have amazing gifts, too. I have studied Rick's lineage, and there is Oris blood on both sides. Deidra will be sought after. When your back is against the wall, you will do what it takes to protect your family.

Lorrah is also the only one who knows about all the money I left you. Whatever you do, do not tell your mother. She will be at your doorstep for all the wrong reasons. Did I even need to mention that? No, of course not. I can forget how intelligent you have become.

When we discussed your relationship with your mother, and you told me that I was your mother, it touched me deeply. I was humbled by the fact that you felt that way, and I finally knew what it meant to be loved as a mother. Being your mother brought me more joy than I could have imagined.

In closing...

I knew the end was coming as I held the last page of the letter, but I wasn't ready for a goodbye. It was too final. There were still so many questions. Don't leave me.

...you should burn this letter because it could be very dangerous to keep.

Random information and things to think about:

Douglas did stop obsessing over you but never entirely forgot you. He is an artist in San Diego and is doing quite well. His last name is VanMeter, in case you forgot.

To whom much is given, much is required. -Luke 12:48

I know you do not believe in God. I have always given you space to formulate your own opinions, but I want you to know that my faith was the only thing that got me through some days. If it were not for my faith, there would have been no strength to become Ellowee. I would have been too self-absorbed to love you or anyone else. There would have been no patience to have you visit over the summers. Gramps and I would not have stayed together, maybe not even been married in the first place. The simple life would have repulsed me.

It was the parts of me that God changed or touched that you loved most. Just take some time to think about that.

Well, my dear little lassie, you have quite a wild ride ahead of you. Don't forget to enjoy it.

I love you, my treasure.

Grammy

I closed my eyes and listened to the waves. They weren't crashing on the beach, as much as lapping the shore. The breeze reminded me of being in Ireland with Grammy and the scent on the envelope made it seem like a possibility.

It was just like Grammy to trigger so many emotions. This letter wasn't going to be set ablaze just yet. It would need to be read at least three or four more times before my head stopped spinning. It also wasn't in my nature to follow directions.

Opening my eyes, I folded the letter and put it back into the envelope. There were too many things to think on, so I escaped into the sound of the waves and thought about nothing except how much I missed her. It was hard to remember what her hugs felt like or how contagious her laughter could be. I sat there and tried anyway.

When my fingers and ears were sufficiently numb from the cold, I went back into the house to get ready for bed. Lorrah was in the kitchen getting some water. She asked if I needed to talk, but I shook my head and went directly to the bedroom.

I opened the door to the balcony in hopes that the breeze would visit me while I slept. Brush teeth, wash face, turn off lights- I went through the motions just like any other night. The coolness of the sheets was a bit surprising, as I climbed into bed.

The phone on the bedside table beckoned me. It was a strange time to make a call, but I needed to take care of something. My conscience was not clear and that fact would mean a restless night of sleep if this call wasn't made.

Laying there in the dark, my heart was heavy with one question above all others. As much as I tried to ignore it or evade thinking about it, it was relentless: If I had that kind of effect on Douglas, was Rick also under some kind of spell?

Did he love me for who I was or did he stay with me because he had no choice? All the arguments about having more children…the times when I thought he trusted my judgement. Was he just giving me my way because he couldn't go *against* my wishes?

My life with him couldn't all be a lie. Deidra wasn't a lie. I pulled the covers over me as though they would serve as a barrier to all these possibilities.

There was only one way to find out, but what a high cost for the truth. As the sound of the waves lapped the shore, I whispered into the darkness, "Conchobar."

Chapter 19 *Family Ties*

The next few weeks passed with the same hot and still normality of all the summers before. The only big news was that Gramps did convince a king snake to lurk in his garden. No gophers would eat his plant roots for the rest of the summer and fall months.

At dusk one day, Gramps asked me to help him pick some tomatoes. I moved the tomato vine and there, on the garden post, was the king snake. The snake wasn't the least bit concerned with the sight of me, but I freaked out. It may be possible I took flight after the snake discovery. Until I grabbed hold of Grammy in the living room, there was no telling how I got there.

Gramps was right about the small hole in my heart, too. After a few short weeks, I began to think less about Douglas and more about the excitement of starting high school. Between my killer tan and a shopping trip planned with Grammy next week, the important things were covered. My dad would often tell me how high school was a stepping stone into the world. That statement both excited and terrified me.

There were still a few weeks of summer to enjoy, but the arrival of the county fair this weekend was a sure sign that the last days of summer were upon us. The county fair was, without a doubt, the biggest event in the area. Livestock, cooked goods, garden vegetables, crafts and other categories were judged and awarded coveted blue ribbons. It was four days of rides, live bands, carnival games and the highly anticipated demolition derbies.

We would generally go for two out of the four days. The carnival games were my favorite part of the fair. The prizes became treasured keepsakes, except for the goldfish. For some reason, they didn't live very long. We started keeping track of their life span. The record was twelve days. Gramps said they must be stocking sick fish, because he could care for any animal.

At home today, everyone was giddy about the weekend. Grammy and I chatted as we watched Gramps working around the yard. Grammy started getting a little anxious when she saw the long extension cord being rolled out near the drive. That was for Gramps' brother, Jed. Grammy was not a big fan.

"Oh, yes, let's get ready for the idiot brigade," she said under her breath.

Jed would park in the driveway during the fair. It was usually just the three of them: Jed, Jed Jr. and little Jed. Three generations of country charm except without the charm. Grammy used to say they kept naming their sons Jed because they didn't know of any other names to use. When Gramps was tired of hearing that, he told her to stop.

"So, I was thinking about entering my zucchini casserole at the fair this year," she looked over her glasses to see my reaction. "What do you think?"

Her zucchini casserole was the best dish she made. However, her best dish, for comparison's sake, was Lullabelle's worst dish. Everyone in this town could bake or cook circles around her. Maybe it was her city upbringing or that she had never really learned how to finesse a recipe. Whatever the reason, it was important that I tread lightly.

"I really like that casserole," I said.

She squinted. "Do you really like it?" she questioned.

"Yes!" I said emphatically.

She was suspiciously watching me, waiting for me to crack. It wasn't going to happen because I was telling the truth.

She got up from the table and started opening cabinets and checking the pantry. If Gramps were here, one of us would say DOTI, and try not to laugh. DOTI was the acronym for Grammy's routine before cooking. Gramps called it: The Dance of the Ingredients. She would flit around taking inventory of what she needed and what she had.

The casserole entries needed to be turned in on Friday for judging, so she had a couple of days to gather supplies. She retrieved the garden basket and went outside. Gramps came in a couple minutes later. "Where is your grandmother?" he asked.

"She's probably checking on the zucchini in the garden," I answered. "She is entering her zucchini casserole at the fair."

"It will be nice to get another 'thank you for participating' ribbon," Gramps laughed while placing his hands on his hips. "You can never have too many of those."

"Hey, Gramps," I wondered, "Grammy won't see the king snake, will she?"

The snake completely slipped his mind. His eyes widened. "Oh crap, there is more than one out there now. I better go check on her," he said.

He was dashing out of the kitchen when a shrill scream broke the silence. Gramps and I peeked out the screen windows on the back porch to see her running toward us. She wasn't carrying a basket and didn't have one zucchini in hand. Grammy and the king snake had a run-in. We stepped back into the kitchen to brace ourselves for the unpredictable fit to come.

Gramps looked at me, winked and announced, "I've got this one."

"Do you know what I found out in the garden?" Grammy asked excitedly, through the screened-in porch. She hadn't made it to the door yet, but it appeared we were going to encounter the "I'm-trying-to-be-calm-but-I-may-explode-at-any-minute" Grammy. This could go either way.

"I suspect you found some fine-looking vegetables grown by the most handsome man in the county," Gramps smiled, but knew exactly what she was talking about.

She fought to not let a smile cross her lips and she won. "A snake, Wayne," she informed him. "A slithering, evil beast right near the zucchini plants!" She waited for an appropriate response, but wasn't pleased with the lack of reaction he had to this statement. She blinked for a while before yelling, "Go kill it! I want it shot, decapitated with a shovel or impaled with a garden stake. The only good snake is a dead one!"

Gramps left for the garden with his marching orders. The fact that Grammy wanted the snake gone is understandable, but the colorful ways she envisioned the snake dying freaked me out. Grammy got a glass of water and sat down at the table. After fifteen minutes, Gramps was outside the window with a decapitated snake dangling from his hands.

"I got him, Muriel," he informed her, "but I would stay out of the garden for the rest of the year just in case there are more family members taking up residence."

"Oh, thank you, honey! My hero!" she smiled and blew him a kiss.

I squinted at the snake Gramps was holding. Even though I was a city girl like Grammy, I had spent too many summers here to be fooled. It wasn't hard to decipher that the snake he held was a rattlesnake. It made me wonder just how many dead animals were being kept around here! Grammy was thrilled so I kept quiet, not wanting to ruin her joy.

The timely *honk! honk!* of Jed's RV in the driveway did it instead. Gramps waved at the incoming guests, still holding the snake in his hand. Grammy rolled her eyes at the sight of the RV. I watched Grammy to see how we would react. We didn't move from the kitchen table. Grammy taught me a certain protocol when welcoming expected guests, but it never seemed to apply to Gramps' family.

Over the next couple of hours, the men talked and got their site squared away. They unrolled the awning on the RV then set up a table and chairs underneath. The car they were towing was taken off the trailer so it was ready for trips to the fair. Once the electricity was hooked up, they loaded the fridge on the RV with food and beer they had brought in coolers.

The sun was starting to set when Gramps moved the big metal drum onto the hill. He filled it with kindling and firewood. Grammy was not happy about this sight and huffed in disgust, "They look like hobos."

It was true. They did look like hobos, but no one could see them. Grammy went into the living room to watch the nightly news and knit. The men put a grill top over the drum fire and placed aluminum-foiled packages onto the grill. Every year they would say they brought their own food so Grammy didn't have to be inconvenienced, but we all knew no one wanted to eat her cooking.

Their stay was really no trouble. They came inside to shower and use the restroom, and that wasn't very often. Grammy was convinced they were "watering" her flowers. If she had caught one of them, they may have ended up like the snake.

As the sun continued its descent, the fire spitting out of the drum became mesmerizing. I watched it through the kitchen window until the men started making their way inside. I hugged Jed and Jed Jr. It was nice to see them. Despite how Grammy felt, they were both very nice men. Little Jed, however, was a different story.

He only got the moniker "little" because Jed Jr. wanted to make sure people had a way to address all of them differently. Little Jed could be described in many ways but, being over 6 feet tall, little didn't seem the right adjective to use. He was only a couple of years older than me. However, he acted like a two-year-old.

He and I had a long history of pulling pranks, fighting or getting each other into trouble every summer. Had we been keeping score over the years, he was surely winning, and that motivated me to be extra evil this summer.

When Little Jed walked through the door, he looked surprised. There was no hug, which was consistent with all the other years. "You are beautiful," he blurted out.

My grandfather, Jed and Jed Jr. had walked into the kitchen ahead of Little Jed. This comment caused them all to stop and turn to look at Little Jed. Jed Jr spit some chew into the cup he was holding while Gramps furrowed his brow. They just stared at Little Jed, and it made for a very uncomfortable couple of seconds.

"I didn't mean anything by it," Little Jed explained. "She has just grown up a lot and turned out beautiful."

That comment didn't help his case. It earned him a swat from his dad, and it was apparent everyone wanted to hit him, but his dad was closest.

"What is the matter with you, boy?" Jed said pointing at me. "That is your cousin you are complimentin' in a backwoods kinda way." Little Jed was the boy that used to pull my hair, get me in trouble or scare the life out of me. This is the first time I had *ever* felt sorry for him.

"Grammy," I yelled, "come out to greet everyone." The men started straightening themselves up and getting ready for her to enter the room. This was a sure way to bring the attention away from Little Jed. I looked in his direction to grin at him briefly. He was red-faced but quickly grinned back.

"Muriel!" Jed exclaimed. "It's so good to see you!"

"Nice to see all of you," she spoke her first lie. "I hope you all are set up with your RV so we can enjoy the fair together." That was lie number two. Gramps' family wouldn't be enjoying the same things at the fair that Grammy would. The beer gardens or demolition derby were not stops on Grammy's fair agenda. "How is Deena?" Grammy inquired about Jed's wife. "She is a wonderful lady," she interjected before Jed had a chance to answer the question. This was probably a truthful statement. Grammy would respect Deena just for putting up with Jed.

While everyone exchanged dishonest pleasantries, Little Jed stared at me. I could see him out of the corner of my eye. His gaze made me uncomfortable, so I excused myself to the restroom. By the time I returned, all the men were back outside. They were standing around the fire sipping beer…no doubt sharing stories because of all the laughter.

Gramps stayed up around 10 p.m. when his family was visiting which was quite a change from 7:30. The women-folk retired to the back of the house early for reading or chatting. I never felt closer to

Grammy than days before the fair. I was close to Gramps, but he hardly spent any time with me when his family was in town. They did "manly" stuff together.

Grammy and I brushed our teeth and put our pajamas on before getting situated with our books in bed. No matter what book was selected, it magically got heavier as the pages were turned. I let it fall on my chest when I was tired of holding it up. Grammy was diligently reading, while I stared at her. She peeked over at me and dropped her book. We smiled at each other.

"Do you think you would have enjoyed your life more if you were normal?" I asked.

She grinned and responded, "There is no standard that makes a life normal. You learn that as you age because it's a life lesson that only time can teach."

"Well, then, let me ask you this way- has being an Oris made your life harder or less enjoyable?" I asked, getting annoyed.

"Sweet girl," she started. "How can I answer that question? I only know what it is like to be an Oris. Let me ask *you* something. What is your definition of a normal life?"

I had thought about this for a while so the answer came easy, "For starters: growing up with a mom and dad, having a brother or sister, big family holidays, family vacations, going to college, graduating, working, getting married and then starting the cycle over again."

"You live with your father, have no siblings and have a small family," she pointed out the obvious. "So by your definition, normal is not in the cards for you. The second part of your life can be normal starting with going to college."

"Can it?" I raised my voice, irritated with my circumstance. "Sometimes I can see my mother weighing the pros and cons of drowning me in the tub. That doesn't seem normal." Grammy shushed me. "I'm sorry," I apologized. "This is just not what I want my life to be."

"Being an Oris is not easy," she became solemn. "I would never tell you that, but hear this, miss- life is not easy. Everyone has visions they can't get out of their head," she said, as tears were filling her eyes. "People walk around feeling hurt, angry, betrayed or abused with nothing but pictures in their mind of the pain."

"You really know how to cheer a girl up, Grammy," I said.

"This should encourage you," she pointed out. "Your life will be filled with pictures." She flung the covers off and went to the closet. After a couple of minutes, she emerged with a picture of a man, which she handed to me. She sat on the side of the bed and said, "That man is your biological grandfather. When I told him the news of my pregnancy, he wanted nothing more to do with me. I remember holding that picture for hours, crying."

I sat up in bed wanting to get a good look at this man. Grammy gave me some time to inspect the picture before continuing.

"As time passed, that picture no longer made me cry," she explained.

"Did you love him?" I wondered.

"Wouldn't it be nice if I could tell you the tale of a great love story," she answered. "The truth is that he was the first man to tell me he loved me. I couldn't get my panties off fast enough." She shook her head.

"Nobody uses the word 'panties' anymore," I politely informed her.

"Yes, honey, that's what you should concentrate on," she said sarcastically, "my vocabulary. The point I am *trying* to make is that I don't look at that picture anymore. Pictures of your Grandpa Wayne, friends, family, travel, and my career have filled my life and mind."

"Why do you still have this picture?" I asked while handing it back to her. "How long has it been since you've looked at it?"

"It's part of our history and you know how I feel about history," she smiled. "The last time I looked at it was the day you were born. It's the first time I was thankful for meeting that man," she said as she put it back into the closet.

"I'm going to go get some water. Would you like some?" I asked.

"No, thank you, honey," she answered.

After pouring a glass of water from the pitcher in the fridge, the back door opened and Little Jed started to walk in. When he saw me, he didn't know what to do, so he stood there frozen in the doorway. His indecision was mildly entertaining. A low growl came from one of the dogs as Jed was interrupting his sleep after a busy day of guests.

"Hi," he said. "I am really sorry about my comment earlier," he apologized. "I didn't mean it."

"No problem," I said. "You think I'm ugly. Is that what you mean?" I teased.

"No! You are stunning," he answered, getting red in the face again. He looked at me but couldn't keep eye contact. "I just want you to know that I'm not a pervert or anything," he explained. "We're not even related. We're not really cousins."

He wasn't watching me, but tears started to fall. Did everyone know more about my life than I did? He looked up to see me silently crying. "I am so sorry!" he exclaimed, visibly upset by my reaction. "Didn't you know?" He handed me some napkins.

"Don't be sorry," I said. "It's just kinda fresh information, and it bothers me that parts of my life are common knowledge to everyone but me." I started crying louder once the words were spoken.

Little Jed stepped forward and wrapped his arms around me. I cried on his chest while he stroked my hair. He smelled like the fire burning outside. After a few moments, I was able to get myself together and take a step backwards. Little Jed had always been my enemy, which made tonight's whole scenario very confusing. He combed his hands through his wavy brown hair and rested them on the top of his head.

"Listen, please forgive me," he said, as he closed his eyes. "I'm an idiot who needs to keep my big mouth shut."

I shook my head. “No, you were very sweet. Thank you,” I said. “Maybe you should just stop running around calling people beautiful.”

He smiled and said, “You are the first person I’ve ever called beautiful.” He put his hands on his hips and laughed, “It seemed to go over well, especially with the audience. The funny thing is that I don’t talk much, but when I do- I usually say something stupid.”

I poured him a glass of water. “It’s good that you can laugh at yourself,” I admired. “That is an important quality to have.”

“There is a lot of material to laugh at,” he said. “My name, for starters, is a tad overused in my family. I’m not sure if you noticed,” he sighed. “Sometimes I want to be my own person with my own name. Sharing is highly overrated,” he explained.

“Makes perfect sense to me,” I agreed. I looked him up and down for the first time as a boy and not an irritation. “There are a lot of things about you to be proud of,” I noticed. “You are tall, good looking and have a great sense of humor. The girls must love this country-boy thing you have going on.”

He shook his head. “I am extremely shy around girls,” he confessed. “I’ve never had a girlfriend, a date or a first kiss for that matter.” He thought about what I had said for a moment and asked, “Do girls like the country-boy thing?”

“I’m sure some girls do,” I said in a high-pitched voice trying to encourage him. My response raised his eyebrows. “And you don’t really have an issue talking to girls,” I pointed out. “You are doing quite well right now.”

“I’ve known you for years,” he said. “You don’t really count.”

I gasped and smiled, “Ouch. That hurt. I’ve never been so offended!”

Little Jed rolled his eyes and said, “Over the years, I’m sure you’ve been more offended by other things I’ve said or done!”

“You are right about that, but only two or three hundred things!” I responded. We both laughed. “Thanks again for being so sweet to me tonight,” I said.

He shook his head and turned a little red again. He mumbled, "No problem."

"Goodnight," I said as I walked toward the entrance to the living room.

There is no telling what came over me, but I turned around, walked right up to Little Jed, put my hands on the side of his head and looked him in the eyes for a moment. He looked a little surprised, while I smiled. We met half way, me on my tiptoes and him bending over a little. His lips were so soft, and it was better than all the kisses with Douglas. I'm not sure if it had something to do with it being the excitement of a first kiss with someone or the fact that I initiated it, but it was sweet and without expectation.

"First kiss, check," I said, walking away. "Good night, beautiful."

It was hard not to laugh the whole way to the bedroom. I didn't want Little Jed to hear me and think it wasn't a perfect kiss or I was laughing at him. The kiss was amazing, but what made me laugh is that I couldn't believe I did that! Before entering the bedroom, I got my giggling under control. Grammy and I were having a serious conversation earlier and it would seem strange to be laughing.

"Are you O.K.?" Grammy asked when I came in the room. "That took a while."

"Yep, I'm fine," I got into bed.

We both got settled with our books again. Grammy started reading her book while I pretended to read mine, sneaking glances at her. It wouldn't be long before she turned the light out. Her blinking was slower and she was adjusting her glasses a lot. Even though I was rarely in bed as early as Grammy, this scenario had been witnessed by me for years.

It was easy to forget that she was my age once. She had experienced and gone through many of the same things. She had a history before we met and was known by many other names than Grammy. She was a daughter, sister, wife, aunt, mother, friend, nurse, etc. She had boyfriends and probably had to try and figure them out too.

"I'm having trouble keeping my eyes open," she said. "Can I turn the light off?"

I closed my book and smiled. She reached for the switch on the light above her head. A couple of clicks and it was pitch dark.

Lying there in the dark was the first time I realized that my Grammy was truly fascinating…that she was so much more than just my grandmother.

"Good night, Grammy. I love you," I whispered.

"I love you too, honey," she whispered back.

Chapter 20 Catching Up

The information in my grandmother's letter produced psychedelic-like visions and night sweats that couldn't be escaped. I would wake up in a fog during the night struggling to stay awake, but exhaustion mocked me as it lured me back to sleep. A man's face came into view repeatedly. The face was that of a man, but the eyes belonged to a boy I once knew.

The history of my people played like a movie. Private moments lay bare for me to witness: Deidra being raped by the men she hated most and Enya suffering beatings at the hand of her prince because their daughters would not behave.

It was now evident that Enya did lie about being passed over; Grammy was onto something. Enya's husband was sick in bed and very ill at one point. He may have recovered. However, I watched as Enya placed a pillow over her husband's face. He struggled briefly but was too weak to fend her off. The pillow stopped his breathing and her beatings.

The daughters saw that murder in their visions and one of them threatened to tell people what her mother had done, but the daughter soon became very ill. While going in and out of consciousness, she rambled on about a pillow and a dress. The maiden caring for her decided the illness had affected her brain, so the mutterings fell on deaf ears.

But I knew what she was trying to communicate. Enya had paid a very sick, contagious woman to wear a new dress for a couple of days before wrapping it up as a gift for her daughter. A daughter she felt would betray her and bring disgrace to the family. The daughter loved the dress because she thought it was from her favorite suitor. She wore it three days in a row, plenty of time for the disease to take hold.

Enya's son would have lost his princely title if people knew she killed her husband. Enya may have thought she was protecting herself and the family name but, in the end, she had committed two murders to do so.

After the visions of Enya left me, I watched as Deidra was raped by King Conchobar. The king did not feel victorious in his physical dominance of Deidra. She just lay there with a far-away look in her eyes. She didn't struggle or fight…at least not in this vision. It was evident that the king wanted what Deidra couldn't give him: an embrace, a passionate kiss or to hear the words "I love you."

Deidra's warmth and passion had died with the man she loved- the man that was killed on the king's orders. She could never feel anything but malice toward him. The king thought so highly of himself that he expected Deidra to come around over time. She would surely start to appreciate the jewels, the lifestyle and the king himself.

The king's patience had run out, and he told Deidra that she was to be a wife again. She would marry Egan, the man who killed her husband. That was it for Deidra. She planned to escape during the wedding and get as far away as possible.

Deidra had a vision the night before her third wedding. It was the story of her real mother, an Oris, freely and happily handing her over to the king's men when she was born. After everything Deidra had been through in her life, this is what broke her. She would no longer fight. If her own mother believed she had no worth, it must be true.

Of all the visions I witnessed through the night, the sight of Deidra throwing herself out of the carriage was the one that troubled me the most. The vision ended before her head injury, but not before I felt the void of all emotion she carried to her death. So much had been taken from her that she was rendered empty. Deidra lacked the only thing that could have made a difference: hope.

Coming out of my slumber, I saw the light shining through the window and it felt like being lifted from the depths of hell. But once the information of the last 24 hours was realized- this morning became a different type of hell. My head was throbbing from all the wine I consumed the night before.

I lay motionless on the bed, realizing that the fate of my Deidra was sealed. All the years of hoping were senseless because no one truly gets passed over. When my mind shifted to Rick, the heartbreak was intensified. Did a spell of sorts keep him with me? We had so many arguments about wanting more children. During a few, I thought he may leave me, but he never did. Was he staying with me merely because he *couldn't* walk away?

Slowly, I lifted myself up into a sitting position on the bed. It was very apparent that last night was a restless one as the sheets on the bed were twisted and the pillows were strewn about. The smell of coffee was in the air, so I followed it to the kitchen.

"Good morning, Muriel," Lorrah said.

I smiled at her. Speech was not available to me yet. After pouring a cup of coffee to wake myself up and some water to rehydrate, I went back into the bedroom and mindlessly prepared for the day. Once I showered, dressed and applied makeup, I returned to the kitchen to get another cup of coffee, but the pot was empty.

"What happened to the coffee?" I yelled up to Lorrah's room.

"I drank it," she yelled back. Her answer was confirmation that my first words of the day were foolish ones.

"Can I take the car to that little café up the road?" I asked Lorrah.

"Sure," she answered. "Would you go to the supermarket, too, and pick up some groceries for the next couple of days?"

"Yes. I'll be back soon," I said as I grabbed the car keys.

"Don't forget to get coffee," she added.

In the elevator, on my way down to the garage, I tried to formulate a grocery list in my head. How would I shop for Lorrah when we had known each other only a couple of days? Did she have food allergies or dislike anything? I would just do what my dad always told me to do in situations like this: punt. I smiled thinking of him saying: "There are just times you have done all you can do or you are too tired to go any further." He would pause for a proper dramatic delivery and then finish, "It is then that you punt." He used to say it like he was a great philosopher or scholar. I hadn't talked to him for a couple of weeks, so I made a mental note to call him soon.

The remote for the garage door was on the keyring. I pressed it after the elevator opened. As the door rose, I could see a small truck blocking the car in, but no one was in the truck. When I looked up the stairs outside, Lorrah was talking to the driver.

"El," Lorrah said, "you are going to need to sign for this. He says this package is worth 32,000 dollars. Is that right?"

"Oh yeah, it was a long night last night and I forgot about this," I explained. "It was definitely a spur of the moment purchase." I started climbing the stairs. "I made the call to my new financial manager right before I went to bed. I asked him to buy a painting. The artist was someone I knew a long time ago."

When I got to the top of the stairs Lorrah handed me the signature form while asking, "Where did you know him from?"

"When I was a stupid kid," I giggled. "I don't even know if he's any good, but my curiosity got the best of me."

"He is good," the driver said, "and you were never a stupid kid." The driver lifted his head up and under the visor of the baseball cap was the same face I had seen in my visions the night before.

I stared in disbelief until finally saying, "Douglas, is that you?"

He smiled, which was all the confirmation I needed. We hugged, laughing about the reunion.

"What are you doing here?!" I asked excitedly.

"Well, I have been hoping for quite some time that someone named Muriel would order a painting of mine," he explained. "Thankfully, your name is not that common, so I decided to deliver this one myself. It was a long shot but worth the drive. Were you on your way out?"

My train of thought was lost for a second looking at him. "Uh, yes, I was going to the café down the road," I answered. "We ran out of coffee."

"Can I buy you a cup of joe?" he offered.

Lorrah took the keys from my hand and was already holding my package. "There is nothing more I would like to do today than grocery shop," Lorrah said, being very sarcastic. "You crazy kids have a wonderful time catching up." She shut the front door.

"Thanks, Lorrah, it's not like I planned this!" I raised my voice so she could hear through the door.

Douglas and I walked down the stairs to the truck. He opened the passenger side door for me. It was good to know he was still keeping up his gentlemanly ways. He got into the car, which briefly brought me back to when we were kids. The sight of his wedding ring and the weight of mine snapped me out of that very quickly.

He looked over at me and smiled. The ride to the café was silent. It seemed we were both trying to evaluate the situation, understand basic topics of conversation and wonder how or if we were going to explain this meal to our spouses.

Douglas opened the door to the café for me. Rick would always open doors for me, too, but I seemed to appreciate this more. He asked for a table outside where it was deserted, 10:30 a.m. being a strange time for people to dine. There was a slight breeze outside which didn't bother us. He pulled out a chair for me at the table.

"So, tell me about your life, Muriel," he said. It was the first time in a while I had heard a man speak my name with such adoration.

"Well, I got married in my early twenties to my college sweetheart, my grandparents passed away a few days ago and I just paid way too much for a painting by some hack," I laughed.

"Your grandparents," he repeated. "I am so sorry. I know how much they meant to you."

My eyes started to water. "Yes, they were the best part of my world," I choked back tears. "What have you been up to?" I wondered, trying to change the subject.

"I've been married since my early twenties as well," he explained, "to a woman I met at an art exhibit. I started painting when

I was sixteen and haven't stopped. Sometimes heartbreak can lead to things you never expected."

When the waitress interrupted our conversation, Douglas quickly ordered coffee and a muffin for both of us. He watched me while speaking to the waitress in case I had any objections. There were none.

"I did not break your heart," I whispered.

"Yes. You did," he argued. "It was my heart. I think I am better suited to make that determination."

"If I could only explain things to you," I hinted. "Help you to see that you never really cared for me at all."

Douglas sipped his water then put it down onto the table. "Your beauty is still undeniable," he casually mentioned. "I still see that beauty mark near your eye when I dream."

"No," I corrected him. "You don't understand."

"Because I'm not an Oris?" he smirked.

It was impossible to hide my shock. I didn't say anything because there was no way to know how much he knew or if he was mocking me. The waitress brought our coffee and muffins. We drank our beverages quietly, but my curiosity got the best of me.

"What do you know about being an Oris?" I asked.

"My grandma Lullabelle told me all about it before I went off to college," he said. "There were times I still thought of you. I felt bad because I was so skeptical at first. When she explained the visions and why she had a bad relationship with her mother, she sounded crazy." He sat back, resting his arms on his chair. He continued, "But when she told me about your power over me, I knew that it had to be true."

"In my defense," I explained, "I had no idea what was happening." I put my muffin down and wiped my mouth. "Would you accept an apology?" I offered.

"There is no apology needed," he answered. He smiled, "The funny thing is that the moment I came under your spell, I caught myself doing and saying things out of character, but I couldn't help myself."

"If you hadn't helped me at the drug store," I informed him, "none of this would have happened."

He looked confused, "It was when we kissed at the hospital that I felt the change."

Surprised, I asked, "Wasn't it when you were helping me at the drug store that it started?"

"No," he said flatly, "the drug store, restaurant, pool…that was all my own doing. I had never looked into anyone's eyes and felt so connected. Of course, at 16, it was probably just because you were hot," he laughed. "Do you remember when I kissed you in the hospital parking lot?"

"Yes. That would be hard to forget since it was my first kiss," I answered.

"After I kissed you, I apologized for not asking to kiss you and said 'I just had to see if I was right'," he shook his head, remembering the scene. "It was a terrible line I liked to use. Originally, I was going to say that I wanted to check and make sure those lips were as soft as they looked."

"Instead," I remembered, "you said you wanted to see if love at first sight was possible. And then I ran into the hospital thinking I just kissed a crazy person." We laughed.

"It was after that kiss that I was constantly wrestling with myself," he went on. "The only way to explain it is that I was saying and doing things from a purely emotional side of me while the logical part of my brain was shut off."

"Was it horrible?" I wondered.

He raised his eyebrows, "No, it wasn't. After I heard you say Conchobar over the phone, I stopped obsessing over you, which was a relief. But I think everyone should have at least one emotional experience like that: a pure, uninhibited love. It makes so many other things possible."

"I had no idea until last night that I was even capable of such a thing. My first reaction was to feel guilt. I bought your painting hoping that I could repay you in some way," I said tearing up. "It has me worried that my husband is only with me because he has no other choice."

"I'll get the check and we can walk back," he decided. "The fresh air will do us both good." He got up to pull out my chair. We walked down the road and arrived at Lorrah's.

"Thank you for everything," I said. "It was kind of you to deliver the painting and take me out. It was good to catch up."

He grabbed both of my hands. "I came here secretly hoping you were single," he admitted. "I would have offered you the world and asked you to run away with me."

"Conchobar," I said.

"No, no," he smiled. "Apparently, first loves die hard. May I kiss you goodbye?" he asked.

"Would that really be a good idea?" I winced. "I wouldn't want my husband kissing someone else."

"See, you are a better person than I," he shared. "Enjoy your painting. There is a card in there for you. My business card is included in case you ever change your mind about that kiss or anything else." He kissed my hand and began walking back to the café.

Douglas walked out of sight. What he didn't know was that I was not a better person than him. Losing my grandparents had made me an emotional wreck. The expectations of my new position as Ellowee were daunting. My relationship with Rick may not even be real. It was all pressing down on me.

What I wanted to do was throw all logic to the wind and spend the next 24 hours with Douglas under the stars, in the water, between the sheets...everywhere. Wanting to forget my present circumstances made Douglas an attractive escape from my current life situation, if just for a day. I almost called after Douglas, but Deidra would see.

On the other end of the so-called "escape," there would be ramifications that were unknown. The little kid in me selfishly squealed "do what you want" while the adult reminded: "you've made promises." Even through pain and uncertainty, logic had a way of winning out.

I walked slowly to the upstairs door to Lorrah's place. The door was unlocked, but Lorrah must have still been out shopping. I fell onto the couch the painting was leaning against, plucked the card off the package and read it.

Dearest Muriel,

It's been a long time, but you are not the kind of girl that is easily forgotten. Enjoy this painting. A critic once described my work as "painfully beautiful," which perfectly described the time we spent together.

Lovingly, D

As I opened the package, it occurred to me that I may not even like this painting. My grandmother trusted me with a lot of money, and my first purchase could very well have been a foolish one. Apprehensive, I turned the canvas around. It was a long stem daisy just like the one Douglas had given me that day outside of the restaurant. The colors were darker than they should have been which gave the flower a deeper dimension to appreciate.

Something occurred to me. I went and got a pen from the kitchen and wrote on the back of the card then held it up. It read: Dear Deidra, yes, there were some very unsavory thoughts that ran through my head recently, but I didn't act on any of them. That has to count for something. Please be forgiving. I love you.

I tossed the note in with the wrapping paper that the painting came in and threw it all away. Douglas' business card that he included got tucked away safely with the letter that Grammy had written. There were now two things in my possession that shouldn't be.

I went to the living room to sit down, just as the elevator opened. Lorrah was bogged down with grocery bags. She made her way to the counter as I watched and didn't lift a finger to help. "No, no," she said, "I have them. Please don't lend a hand."

"O.K.," I agreed, "you did say how much you wanted to grocery shop and I don't want to steal any part of the experience from you."

Lorrah started putting the groceries away, so I did get up and help her with the refrigerated goods. There really weren't that many groceries. Maybe shopping for just one extra person was daunting for her, but she was an amateur. I could have carried in twice the bags without straining.

"You must have only purchased enough for a few days," I said as we put the haul away. "Your cupboards are bare. Do you not like to stock up on stuff?"

"Only the essentials," she said as she unloaded a few bottles of wine and lots of chocolate. "Coffee, wine and chocolate are the foundation of any diet worth having. Yogurt and fruit are nice to have around, but frozen meals or dining out is where I get most of my sustenance. I don't do a lot of cooking," she explained.

She didn't need to tell me that last fact. Her kitchen had no spices, measuring cups or pans. The toaster, microwave and coffee maker were the only appliances. It was obvious she was not a cook. Groceries and cooking were not what was on the forefront of my mind. The close call I just had with Douglas was a sobering moment.

"These last couple of days have been very interesting, but isn't it time for the Book of Deidra now?" I asked. "Truth be told, I'd like to go home soon."

Lorrah slammed one of the cabinets shut. "That is what I was forgetting!" she snapped. She looked at her watch, "C'mon, El, we still have time to get it out of the safe deposit box."

Lorrah and I hurried to a bank about five miles from her house. She really was a terrible driver, not paying very close attention to her surroundings. It made me nervous.

When we arrived at the bank, everyone knew her by name. She was doted on from the minute we got there until we left: five-star treatment all the way. I could only assume that this is where she did most of her banking.

While riding back to the house, the book rested in my lap. It was a big book, at around four inches thick and just a bit bigger than a standard letter. The cover was made of dark maroon leather that was textured with little divots. There was no lettering on the outside at all. I was getting a little car sick from simply looking down at it, so any reading would have to wait. I ran my hand over it while looking out the window. Grammy used to flip through the pages of this book.

After we got into the house, I asked Lorrah if it would be OK to look at the book privately. "That copy of the Book of Deidra is yours now," Lorrah explained. "You don't need permission from me to do anything. If any filters are deemed worthy, they need to be added and then eventually put into the original book. It's in Ireland."

"My Grammy took me there once," I informed her. "The summer I turned sixteen we took a trip there. It was beautiful."

"Ellowee never recorded that trip," she said curiously. "I guess nothing of importance went on."

I nodded. Grammy probably didn't want to share what happened on the trip. Someday I would tell Lorrah. Once there were no doubts she could be trusted, I would tell her every nook and cranny of my life. To be able to have a friend like that has been a long time coming.

"If it's alright with you," I began, "it might be nice to order a pizza and stay in tonight. This is a lot of reading material." I held up the hefty book that hadn't left my possession since retrieving it from the safe deposit box. "Would you order the pizza?" I asked. "And can I get a schedule of all the yearly meetings that I need to attend?"

"Anything else?" Lorrah asked, a little put out.

"Not that I can think of," I smiled. "You make coffee and swim during your waking hours," I joked. "You should be able to fit in a phone call and copy a schedule." Lorrah seemed insulted by my statement, but the lack of responsibility in her life was hard to deny. "I know I am cramping your style," I mentioned. "If you want, you can hand me over to someone else."

“It’s not that easy, Ellowee,” she responded, with a serious tone. “There is a lot to be done and I took an oath.”

“Then I guess we are stuck with each other for a while, “I surmised. “I’ll see you later. I’ve got some reading to do.”

I walked to the bedroom and shut the door behind me. I wouldn’t be disturbed by anything…except the book I was about to read.

Chapter 21 County Fair

Little Jed and I were both sitting at the kitchen table waiting for Grammy's next zucchini casserole to come out of the oven. This had to be the sixth dish we had taste tested in the last two days. Gramps had been very pro-active in supplying Grammy with zucchini from the garden. No one wanted another snake incident.

Little Jed could not get out of taste testing. Grammy wanted a man's opinion, but Gramps and the other Jeds were hunting, fishing or going to see friends. If they didn't have plans when Grammy asked-they made some. She wasn't frustrated by their absence because Little Jed would stay behind with me to taste her creations. He learned quickly to lead with compliments and hold back on most criticism.

We sat at the table playing UNO while we waited. Our relationship was not like it had been in years past. Little Jed would play a Draw Four card and practically apologize to me for doing it. This behavior was not reminiscent of the time he pushed me down a rocky path then laughed because my knee was bleeding. The other day when we were walking to the RV to get a soda, he accidentally bumped me. He grabbed my arm to balance me and asked if I was O.K.

This politer, sweeter version of Little Jed would take some getting used to. If it wasn't sincere, I was in a lot of trouble. My guard was down, leaving me vulnerable to some grand attack. Glancing across the table at him gave me confidence he had mellowed, that there was nothing to be afraid of.

Grammy spoke from the other end of the country kitchen, "The zucchini casserole will be done soon, kids. Maybe another 10 minutes just to be sure."

My back was to Grammy, so I shot Little Jed a sarcastic look of excitement and we smiled at each other, trying not to laugh. I was glad the casserole would be done soon, because this game of UNO was getting boring. I couldn't prove it, but it seemed that the game was being thrown. I found it highly annoying that this win couldn't be chalked up to my UNO skills alone.

We tasted the casserole when it came out of the oven. There wasn't much difference between any of the casseroles, and it was getting harder to appease Grammy with our dwindling list of adjectives.

"This one is good, Grammy," I said.

"Is it better than the one you ate yesterday?" she started to ask questions. "Do you like the cheese combination in this one the best? Should I put more peppers in the dish or do you like it like this?"

"I liked the casserole from yesterday afternoon the best," Little Jed bravely started. "The egg and cheese ratio made for a denser dish, and the texture was better. It all depends on the judge's preference I guess, but I don't like it overly moist. And you cut up the peppers smaller yesterday. That was nice."

I just stared at Jed, amazed by his comments as Grammy announced, "Then that is the one I am going to submit to the judges. Thank you so much, Jed. That was my favorite too."

Feeling like I needed to add something, I said, "When the casserole is a day or two old and I reheat it, it tastes a lot better." Grammy was not giving me a pleasant look so I meekly added, "Um, and I like a little salt on top."

"That is very helpful, Muriel, since the casserole has to be turned in tonight at the fairgrounds. There is no going back now," she announced. Grammy dug through her purse and pulled out her wallet. She handed me some money, "Why don't you guys go up to the store and get an early lunch? I don't have time to cook because I have to get that casserole in the oven pronto." Grammy looked out the windows to see if she could spy the other Jeds, "And I don't know where everyone went off to."

Little Jed and I did as we were told and walked up to the store. There were a few sandwiches already made, so we chose those and got a drink. We sat at the picnic table outside the store to eat.

Over the last couple of days, Jed and I spent a lot of time together. It was comfortable. There were long stretches of silence where we respected each other's time to ponder. "Your casserole assessment was impressive," I commented. "You are quite the connoisseur!"

Little Jed smiled, "Don't be too impressed. I couldn't get to sleep last night trying to think of something to say about the casserole. He opened the twist-top on my soda and added, "Being around you makes it very difficult to concentrate, and I wanted to be prepared."

We ate the rest of our lunch quietly, while my face was flush from his compliment. The strangest thing happened or, at least, it felt strange to me. I started comparing Little Jed to Douglas. Maybe this was normal, but there was no way to know. A couple of months ago, there wasn't one boy- much less two. Either way, it gave me an odd feeling.

Douglas was much smoother than Jed. He always knew the right thing to say, but it could seem cheesy or contrived. Jed was a quieter boy. When he said something, you had no doubt that he meant it and put thought into his word choice. Douglas was more fun than Jed. He had better ideas of how to spend time together, but it was more comfortable spending time with Jed.

Jed and I had only kissed the one time. There had been plenty of other opportunities, but he didn't take any of them. It didn't seem right for me to initiate our second kiss, if there would even be one. And what was I thinking? *Should* there be one?! He was my cousin until I found out differently this summer. Oh, how a year can change things.

As I was spending time in my own little world, I hadn't noticed that Jed had gotten up. He picked a small wildflower and was heading back to the table. He reached out his hand in order to help me up. Without saying a word; he put the wildflower in my hair, looked into my eyes and kissed me in such a way that made my knees go weak.

The short walk back to the house was done holding hands until a honk of a passing car made Little Jed release my hand. It was his father. The fear on his face was unmistakable.

"I'm sorry," Little Jed apologized, "I should have never kissed you back there. My dad is going to…" He trailed off, not finishing his sentence.

Once we got back to the house, we went our separate ways. I was worried for Little Jed, which confused me. Just a week ago, I was practically planning his demise. This was to be: *The Summer of Muriel's Revenge*, but there were these new feelings floating around. Feelings must ruin everything. I was perfectly happy loathing him until he called me beautiful. Hmm, maybe words ruin everything.

"What are you thinking about, Muriel?" Grammy asked. The timer was going off for her casserole. She was entering the kitchen through the living room the same time I was entering through the porch.

"Why do you assume I'm thinking?" I asked.

"You were walking really slowly on the porch," she explained. "You always slow down and look like you're in pain when deep in thought."

"Oh," I said surprised, not realizing this about myself. "Well, I was trying to decide if feelings or words can ruin life more."

Grammy put on her oven mitts to remove the casserole. She was pondering what I said while placing the casserole on a trivet. "That is a tough one," she mused. "I would venture to say that both words and feelings have an equal opportunity to ruin life, but nothing is more dangerous than thinking too much or not thinking enough."

Grammy had a way with conversation. It sounded like she was done with the topic and had put her two cents in. I needed more than two cents on this one, maybe even a whole quarter.

"Please elaborate," I pushed.

"Well, let's use your two examples," she began. "Inherently, there is nothing wrong with feelings or words. They can both be part of a healthy life without ruining anything," She smiled at me and continued, "However, when you don't think before you speak, it can be bad. Conversely, if you think so much about what you want to say and never find the words to say it- not good either."

"And feelings," I asked, "kinda the same thing for those?"

"Not even close," she said slowly. "Feelings are WAY more confusing. There is no way to control those little boogers. If you are doing something because it *feels* good or it *feels* right, Lord have mercy! To sum it all up," she announced, "whether you are dealing with emotions or words, one needs to think before they act."

The way Grammy explained that made me giggle. She was very loud.

"Laugh it up, little girl. You'll see," she scolded. Grammy put the pot holders down and took her apron off. "I will be ready to go into town in about an hour," she informed me. "You need to get ready, too, because this will be our first night at the fair."

She was so excited. This casserole was good, but there was another participation ribbon on the horizon. We all knew it except for Grammy. Even if it tasted just as good as one of the front-runners, Grammy refused to do the required politicking to win. Schmoozing was not her strong suit.

Changing into a cuter outfit and running a brush through my hair was all that was needed to get ready for the fair. Hopefully, Little Jed would be going to the fair tonight. I skipped down to the RV to ask. When he came out of the RV, it was obvious that he had been slapped or hit in the face. His cheek was red and his lip a bit swollen.

"What happened?" I asked concerned.

"Nothing," he said as he turned away. He was embarrassed, so I pretended there was absolutely nothing wrong.

"Oh good," I exclaimed. "Do you want to ride with us to the fair? We are leaving soon."

"Sure," he said, "let's go."

Grammy insisted that the casserole ride in the front seat and even secured it down with the seat belt. That was fine with me because Little Jed and I had a chance to talk.

Little Jed told me, "I am going to the fair with you tonight because Uncle Wayne and my dad think you need a chaperone. They said you are too pretty to be wandering around on your own."

This irritated me. "So you wouldn't want to go with me otherwise, but only under strict orders?" I asked.

"Don't be dense," he retorted and slapped my leg. "But my Dad did see us holding hands, and I am lucky to be alive to tell about it. He was mad!"

Grammy must have heard Little Jed's last sentence because she asked, "Who was mad?"

"No one, Aunt Muriel," he fibbed.

"So, what do you kids want to do when you get to the fair?" Grammy asked. Little Jed and I spoke at the same time. He said rides and I blurted out games.

"Well, I will give you money," Grammy said, "and you can both go your separate ways."

Little Jed spoke up immediately, "I have instructions to stick with Muriel while we are at the fair. Uncle Wayne and my dad insisted that she be escorted."

"That's ridiculous," she remarked. "What if you want to meet a nice young lady there? You can't very well do that when they see you walking around with a girl already."

Little Jed looked at me and smiled. Grammy had been so entrenched with her zucchini casserole that it rendered her oblivious.

When we arrived at the fairgrounds, Grammy suggested, "How about you both go with me to drop off the casserole? You did help me decide which one to bring."

Putting the casserole into the competition wasn't why we followed Grammy into the building. The buildings were air-conditioned. It was 3 p.m. and the temperature was hovering around 100 degrees. While Grammy waited in line to submit her dish, Little Jed and I hung back.

"Oh no," I said.

"What?" Little Jed asked.

“The man accepting the contest entries doesn’t like Grammy much,” I explained. “He is wearing a judge badge too. This will not end well.”

“What did she do?” Little Jed asked.

I looked at him sideways because it was interesting that he would assume Grammy had done something. Gramps’ family didn’t like her very much. Little Jed must have thought Grammy was as bad as he had heard.

“I don’t know much about him,” I explained. “His name is Richard and his family has lived in this town as long as your family.” Little Jed was paying strict attention to me and even leaned in a little when I lowered my voice. It was very distracting.

I went on, “Richard was at the hospital for the arrival of his first grandchild. After the baby was born, he excitedly paraded the child around. Grammy was on duty at the hospital, and when he got to Grammy’s ward, he showed her the baby. He asked her if his grandchild was the most beautiful baby she ever laid eyes on.

“What did she say?” Little Jed cautiously wondered.

“She told him that she had seen a lot of babies in her day, that all babies are precious, but not all of them could be the cutest child she has ever seen,” I finished.

“Well, that’s not so bad,” Jed decided.

“Grammy says given it was one of the most unattractive newborns she had ever seen, she handled it pretty well. She was honest but considerate of his feelings,” I said. “Richard never saw it that way. He has been rude to her ever since.”

“How long ago was that?” Jed asked.

“Well, that girl over there was the baby.” I pointed to a woman in her 20s. “So, it’s been a while,” I giggled.

Grammy delivered her casserole to Richard. She smiled while chatting with him, but Richard didn’t seem to be enjoying the conversation.

Grammy walked to where we were standing and gave us some money. She seemed a little defeated.

"Thanks Grammy," I said cheerily. "Would you like to join us for a corn dog?"

"No, thank you," she said. "You kids go have fun and meet me back here at 8 p.m. The vegetable casseroles are going to be judged at 6."

Little Jed and I walked out of the building into the noise and chaos that was the county fair. Music sounded on the rides while the game bosses barked at those who passed by. The smell of the different food offerings wafted through the air.

"Did you really want a corn dog?" Jed asked.

"No," I answered, "I wanted to cheer her up. I'm still full from lunch, although fresh-squeezed lemonade will sound pretty good after being in this heat for a while."

He waited for me to make a move. It appeared he *was* going to follow me around today. Beyond the first couple of games, I spied my favorite. The object of the game was to spray water into a clown's mouth, which blew up a balloon. The first person to pop the balloon won. There was an empty seat, so I rushed over to play.

Little Jed dutifully stood by as I went from game to game until I got my fill of carnival games. "Well, what would you like to do Jed? I'm done playing games," I announced.

Nothing," he answered. "Between the noise and the heat, I'm starting to get a headache."

The booth that sold fresh lemonade was nearby, so I purchased two large lemonades, gave one to Jed and told him to follow me. We got our hands stamped as we left the fairgrounds and walked about a half mile to a little creek. The loudness of the fair was hardly even background noise by the time we arrived. I sat down on a rock then patted a spot next to me.

"You seemed like you were enjoying yourself," he observed as he took a seat. "You didn't have to leave. The ruckus was making my head hurt. My life is pretty quiet most of the time."

"Maybe your head hurts because someone smacked you," I hinted, while sipping on the lemonade. "Ruckus is a great word, by the way. I would have used the more poetic *din*, but they both work."

"Where did you get such a good vocabulary?" Jed wondered. "You use some pretty impressive words."

"My dad," I explained. "He always makes me look up words in the dictionary. Whenever I ask him what a word means, he tells me to look it up. I have to give him the definition, use the word in a sentence and list all the synonyms for the word." I continued, "I love my father, but that has got to be one of the most annoying things he makes me do. There are times he knows a definition, but wants me to read it so I will remember. There is a lot of stink-eye coming his way when he does that."

"He may be doing you a huge favor," Jed smiled. "Maybe you will be a writer one day: speeches for the President, manuals for space exploration or the next great novel. You never know."

"All I know is that it exacerbates me," I said.

Jed laughed, "You are younger than me, and I don't even know what that word means!"

"It means aggravate or annoy," I laughed with him.

"Thanks for bringing me here," Jed said as he bumped my shoulder with his. "My headache is nearly gone."

"We can stay here as long as you like," I told him. "And, I am sorry for not noticing you weren't feeling well. I get a little caught up in the games."

"Muriel, would you marry me?" he said.

"What?" I yelled. "No!"

He casually sipped his lemonade, trying to hold back laughter. I pushed him a bit and asked, "Why did you ask me that?"

Jed shrugged his shoulders, "I just wanted everything to be even."

"Even?" I wondered.

"You were my first kiss," he said. "I will remember that my whole life." He picked up a small stone and tossed it into the creek. "I bet no one has ever proposed to you before so I will be the first man that has ever proposed to you." He added, "I think that makes us even."

"That is very clever," I decided, "but what if I would have said yes?"

He laughed and said, "I have no idea. I didn't really think it through very well." There were a couple of silent moments where only the creek could be heard. Then, Jed spoke up. "It's a shame we weren't friends before this summer," he shared, as he squeezed my hand. "I kinda like hanging out with you."

"It's alright," I smiled.

He brushed the hair off my cheek and slowly leaned forward to kiss me on the cheek. When he sat upright again, he said, "It's a good thing I won't be here much longer. You would get me in all kinds of trouble."

We didn't stay by the creek for too long. Jed and I both knew that as dusk approached, some snakes came out at night to hunt. Getting back into the fair was no problem since our hands were stamped. Grammy was right where she said she would be, but it was only a little after seven so I was surprised that she was there already. When she spotted us, she waved us over.

"Hi, kids," she started. "If you want to stay longer, you can go home with the men. They got here a half hour ago and headed straight to the demolition derby. I would like to leave now." It didn't take a genius to conclude that the casserole judging did not go very well.

I turned toward Jed to offer a suggestion, "Why don't you go to the derby so you can have some fun at this fair. I'm not really enjoying this," I winked. "I'll go home with Grammy."

Grammy walked off toward the car. Jed gave me a hug after she passed while whispering that he would miss me in my ear. His sweet gesture made me want to stay with him, but I knew Grammy was upset and my company would help.

Smiling, I took two steps back until running into a woman. I apologized and turned around looking for Grammy. The car ride back was quiet which helped me appreciate the scent of the woods as the sun fell beneath the trees.

The men made it back home a few hours later, all of them except Little Jed. He was invited to a party that Uncle Jed allowed him to go to…especially because it was with a friend of mine, named Cassidy. Cassidy had a reputation for a reason, so whatever flirtation Little Jed and I had was most likely over. Avoiding him over the next couple of days was not difficult as he didn't want to see me either.

Grammy and I spent some time licking our wounds. Her participation ribbon was burned in the fire and so was anything Douglas or Little Jed had given me. Even things that reminded me of them got torched.

It wasn't long before my dad arrived to take me home. When the day came to leave my grandparents' house, it was always difficult. On one hand leaving them was sad, but on the other hand it meant a new school year, seeing my friends again, spending time with my dad…a fresh start.

The bags were loaded in the trunk of my dad's car. He tried every year to give my grandparent's money to offset the cost of food and buying me school clothes. It was never accepted, but he tried nonetheless. After goodbyes and hugs were exchanged, my father and I drove out of sight.

This summer made my head spin. It was the first summer that it was a bit of relief to be going back to my city life. I incorrectly thought that the drive home signified leaving all the Oris history and visions behind. Usually tears would flow for a while during the drive home, but this summer was so different. I was different.

After I had been home for a while, attending high school and playing sports consumed all of my time. When Grammy's monthly letter arrived it seemed like only a week had passed. The letter included the standard fare: weather report, Gramps' shenanigans, dog update, working at the hospital, etc.

At the end of the letter she wrote that Cassidy had been by the house last week. She wanted Little Jed's phone number and address so she could tell him the good news. He was going to be a father. After the summer I had, this did not surprise me.

It was a perfect reminder that snakes come in both genders. And no matter the type or usefulness, I don't think I'd ever learn to like them.

Chapter 22 Homeward

The Book of Deidra was a bit disappointing given that my visions had discounted a lot of what the book contained. There was one name in particular that I had hoped to find as the pages were turned, but Matilde was nowhere to be found. Matilde was the one person in my visions that it was easy to identify with. She valued truth. Although being willing to die for it was where the similarities ended. That was a kind of bravery that had never been tested in me.

The pizza must have arrived, because the smell started my stomach rumbling. When I came out of the bedroom, the sun was already hovering over the water. Being immersed in the book had erased hours of the day.

Lorrah was eating her pizza. "I am sorry I started without you," she apologized, "but I didn't know how long you were going to be. There is pizza and wine on the counter." She pointed to my guest room and asked, "So, did you enjoy your reading?"

If Grammy were here, I would have spilled my guts. So much of the book wasn't true from what I had seen in my visions. Bits and pieces were left out about my gifts, so there could easily be other things missing. I would have explained how Matilde died being brave and true to who she was. I would have erased false hope of anyone being passed over.

However, given the painful learning process I had endured my whole life; I would spare upending the Oris history recorded in the Book of Deidra- at least for now. Wisdom can be a frightening thing. It has a way of reminding us of how little we know. Besides, who is to say anyone would believe this new "Ellowee?" My extra gifts would be found out, endangering my family.

For now, I needed to observe. Find out if others doubt the book. Eventually, I imagined an inner circle of Oris women that could be trusted to discuss such things.

So many choices lay before me, but the fact remained that Grammy *wasn't* here, and telling anyone else this landslide of information was out of the question.

Lorrah's inquiry still loomed. Did I enjoy my reading? Not really, but there were other honest answers available to me. I finally said, "Well, I haven't finished it completely, but so far it has made me feel a little exposed."

Lorrah was confused. "Why?" she asked.

I put some pizza on a plate and elaborated, "Well, a lot of my childhood was in the book which makes me feel exposed. It is funny how so many people knew things about me that I didn't know. That isn't the right word," I corrected myself. "It's irritating how so many people knew." I took a bite of pizza that was far too big.

There were many facts that Grammy left out, but Lorrah didn't need to know what they were yet. I also needed to figure out why Grammy wouldn't include some things about me in the book. Lorrah was too new to my life to trust her implicitly. I poured a glass of wine, grabbed the pizza and sat in the living room with her.

"Don't worry," she said. "Most people know very little about you. The copy of the book is always with Ellowee. The original is in Ireland, and not everyone goes to see it." Lorrah laughed, "The only reason I know so much about you is that your grandmother left me a letter about you with my instructions."

"Really, what did it say?" I asked with pizza still in my mouth.

"Just the basics," she rattled off. "You used to have the gift of the green hue, a relationship with your mother didn't exist, being an Oris made you angry, you ask a lot of questions and she loved you more than anything in her life."

"Excuse me," I said and went to my bedroom to cry. After pulling myself together, I had come to a conclusion. It was time to return to my family. Lorrah could meet up with me later to set up our regional office and further educate me on the life of an Oris. It was time to pack up.

I needed to be in the presence of my family and the comfort of my own surroundings. Even though Deidra may very well reject me when she gets older, and Rick could be under a spell- it was home. One day, the word Conchobar will be spoken to Rick. It was the right thing to do. And when Deidra comes to me with questions about my life and the Oris heritage, they will be answered.

A soft knock on the bedroom door interrupted my train of thought but not the packing. "Come in," I said.

Lorrah saw me throwing stuff into my suitcase. "When are you going?" she asked.

"Probably tomorrow if I can get a flight out," I answered.

"I can call and get you a flight out tonight if you would like to leave soon," Lorrah offered.

It took a second before I realized that the cost of a last minute ticket wasn't a factor. Then I replied, "I would love to go home tonight! Thanks." Lorrah disappeared to accomplish her third task of the day.

Rick's voice was on the other end of the phone when I called home. The richness of his voice was like a calming force. I informed him I would probably be getting in late, so I'd catch a cab. When I told him that I loved him before hanging up, it was the most honest, heartfelt "I love you" I had ever spoken.

Holding the Book of Deidra, I walked into the living room and asked Lorrah, "How exactly does traveling with this book work?"

"Your grandmother always left the book in one place," Lorrah answered. "It seems a bit cumbersome to lug around. I wouldn't trust checking it in your luggage. It is far too valuable. But, if you carry it on, you don't want a lot of questions." Lorrah stated the obvious, "It's not normal-looking reading material."

"True," I agreed. "Then, how will we get it back to my house?"

"I am driving out," Lorrah informed me. "Would you like me to take it? I rented an apartment for six months, so driving out with a few things makes more sense."

I was a little shocked by the length of time Lorrah would be staying, so I neglected to answer her question except by handing her the book. It was nice to hand it over…to be rid of its disappointing pages.

"Your flight leaves in two hours," Lorrah informed me, "so when you are done packing, we should head out."

"It shouldn't take me more than a few minutes," I said, giddy with excitement. I scarfed down a couple more bites of pizza then went back to the bedroom to finish up. When the bags were packed, I went out onto the bedroom balcony to take one last look at the water and the chair where Grammy's letter was read. It would be nice if my family could visit here one day.

"Ellowee," Lorrah interrupted my train of thought.

"Yes," I answered.

"Did you want some more pizza?" Lorrah asked. "You haven't had a lot to eat today."

"I can just grab something at the airport if I need to, but thank you," I smiled.

Lorrah took my bags and put them by the door. She placed a folder on top of the bags and said, "This is the schedule of the next few Oris meetings that I have labeled as sales meetings for curious eyes. Your plane reservation number is in there, so you should be all set for the airport!"

Lorrah put her shoes on and grabbed the car keys. It didn't take long to understand that she was getting ready to leave immediately. I fumbled to get shoes on then grabbed my own purse. It took only a couple of minutes before we were on the road. I was daydreaming about my family when Lorrah started a conversation.

"It was odd that you read the Book of Deidra," Lorrah observed, "and didn't ask me one question afterward. Not one."

"You said that the book is always with Ellowee," I remembered, "so, I figured you couldn't answer my questions. Besides, there will probably be questions when I finish."

"Not buying it," Lorrah said suspicious. "I read that book front to back after your grandmother died, and I have hundreds of questions."

Following Lorrah's statement, there was an uncomfortable silence during which I could feel myself getting angry. She sounded accusatory, but there was no need for me to respond as she didn't ask a question. So I gazed out the window trying to calm down, hoping the airport would come into view.

Lorrah didn't push the issue, and we arrived at the airport without further discussion. After pulling up to the curb, we both got out of the car. Lorrah popped the trunk and we each grabbed a bag. When I tried to get the bag from her that she was holding, she wouldn't let go.

"Why didn't you ask any questions?" she stared at me.

"You've told me that Oris have very good judgement, and I'm not certain you can be trusted," I said, speaking more honestly than I had planned.

Lorrah let go of the bag. She didn't seem hurt, but concerned, like she had been found out. This reaction didn't help increase my confidence in her.

"Thank you for having me these last couple of days. It's apparent you don't entertain a lot of guests," I snarled. The airport doors automatically opened as I walked closer.

"See you soon," Lorrah yelled after me, still on the sidewalk. "We can continue this conversation!" Raising my hand with the smaller bag, I didn't even bother turning around. This whole interaction had infuriated me.

Once the doors shut, I breathed in and decided to leave my anger here before going forward. The ticket agent transferred my reservation into a gate ticket. What a pleasant surprise to realize, as boarding started, that the ticket was first class. After getting comfortable in the seat, I waited to see who would be sitting next to me, secretly hoping that no one would. When the doors on the plane closed, it was a relief to have the seat next to me empty.

The seats were amazingly comfortable. The food was delicious. Everyone should fly first class once in their lives. It wasn't long before a nap was in order. A smile must have been on my face before I fell asleep, being so excited to go home.

The visions started immediately. They were of Grammy at all stages of her life. Her beautiful history played before me to enjoy. It was like spending time with her: seeing her smile, smelling her perfume, hearing her voice. Near the end of the visions, I saw Grammy reading the letter she had written to me.

But, as my view of the vision panned out, it was Lorrah who was reading the letter. She was sitting in the coffee shop. Seeing this made me angry! How dare she betray my grandmother's trust! It must have been the day we met there because she was wearing the same outfit. She looked up from the letter when the coffee shop's door opened. It was me coming in to get some coffee.

I snapped out of the vision immediately, breathing heavily. That was the first time I had seen myself in a vision. Was it possible I could see my own life played out in these visions? Was I having trouble catching my breath because that shouldn't be happening, or was the reaction merely anger?

Ding! The bell sounded on the overhead speaker, "This is your captain speaking. Please return to your seat, fasten your seat belts and return your chairs to the upright position. We will be landing within the half hour."

It was difficult to believe that so much time had been lost. This was a four hour flight. Could I have been asleep for such a long time? Looking out the window didn't offer any clues. It must have been overcast, because no lights were visible on the ground. The slow decent eventually broke the cloud cover and made home easier to recognize. My grandparents were always home to me, but now they were gone.

I wanted to cry in anticipation of seeing Deidra and Rick. It wouldn't take me long to get home. There was no reason to wait for baggage claim as I told the ticket agent that my smaller bag was a purse. She didn't believe me for a second, but they must be more forgiving with the first class passengers.

When the plane stopped at the gate, I retrieved my larger bag from the overhead compartment. The flight took a few minutes to be cleared before the doors were opened. The stewardesses politely said goodbye and thanked us for flying with their airline.

Walking quickly, I reached the line of cabs waiting outside to drive passengers to their destinations. It was just before midnight, so the airport was pretty quiet in comparison to all the hustle and bustle of the daytime hours. The first cab saw me coming. He got out and opened his trunk for my bags. I reached in the smaller bag to retrieve my wallet and keys. In a matter of minutes, we were heading toward home. The cab driver wasn't talkative, but there would be no complaints from me.

When he pulled up to my house, I just stared at it. For someone who was excited to get home, I wasn't moving very quickly. It felt as though going into my house would mean leaving everything about my grandparents behind. The house looked so peaceful from the outside. The cab driver snapped me out of my thinking when he opened my car door.

"Thank you," I smiled. I got out of the cab to pay him. He had already retrieved my bags from the trunk, so after he was paid, he quietly left.

It was well-lit near the front door, which made it easy to use my key. The house was so quiet. I set all my stuff down but retrieved a clean pair of pajamas from my bag. In the downstairs bathroom, I took a quick shower to wash away the airplane trip.

Tiptoeing upstairs seemed necessary so the silence in the house wouldn't be disturbed. Deidra's door was open a crack. I peeked in at my baby girl who wasn't a baby anymore. As I reached the doorway of my bedroom, the sight of my bed comforted me. I ran to get under the covers with Rick. The warmth and smell was so lovely. My arms wrapped around him before sleep arrived.

When my eyes opened the next morning, the clock read 8:25 a.m. Deidra must not be up yet because she would have jumped up on my bed while giving me a play-by-play of everything that happened while I'd been away. This was the longest we had ever been apart.

I walked barefoot down the stairs. Rick picked me up in his arms and gave me a bear hug.

"You are never allowed to be away again," he said and then kissed me like we were newlyweds. "We should sneak back upstairs before…"

"Mommy!" Deidra shouted from the top of the stairs.

Lowering my voice, I told Rick, "Hold onto that thought. It won't be long." I turned around right before Deidra almost knocked me over with her enthusiastic hug.

"Oh, how I missed you, my sweet girl," I told her while squeezing her and kissing her face all over.

"Let's all sit and have breakfast," Rick said. "I made a frittata."

"Fancy," I said. I didn't even think Rick knew what a frittata was.

"Well, I have been cooking a lot over the last couple of days," he smiled, proud of himself.

Deidra crinkled her nose and said, "That's another reason why I'm glad you're home, Mommy!"

Rick stuck up for himself, "Hey! It wasn't that bad."

We went on autopilot. I got the orange juice out, while Deidra set the table. Usually Rick would just wait to be called, but he was involved now and took the frittata out of the oven. Once we got everything ready, we sat.

"May I say grace?" Deidra asked.

"Why would you ask that?" I wondered. We had never said prayers before a meal. As a matter of fact, prayers were scarce under our roof, so it was a curious request.

"Grandma Muriel used to pray all the time," she explained. "It will be a way to honor her memory." Deidra's whole face lit up with a precious smile.

Fighting back tears, I nodded my permission.

Deidra bowed her head and I watched her start to pray, "Thank you, Lord that Mommy could get home safely. Please help her friend get here safe, too. It's a long drive. Take care of Great Grammy in heaven. We are thankful for this food that Daddy made. He tries very hard. Amen." We lifted our heads and my eyes met Deidra's. She shot me a knowing wink, which took me by surprise.

Rick's frittata was not an ordinary dish. Because he didn't have a lot of ingredients in the recipe, he improvised. He explained how potatoes are a root vegetable, so he thought it perfectly acceptable to put carrots and beets in place of potatoes since they are also root vegetables. Deidra and I ate a lot of toast for breakfast.

"I have to get going," Rick announced, wiping his mouth. Most of the frittata was left on his plate, too. He probably wanted to pick up some breakfast before work.

Rick went into the downstairs bathroom and brushed his teeth, leaving Deidra and me alone at the table. I smiled at my beautiful daughter, and then a chill ran through my body.

"Deidra," I asked concerned, "how did you know my friend was coming out here, and why would you assume she was driving here instead of flying? We never talked about that." It also occurred to me that Grammy didn't pray in the presence of others. "And how do you know that Grammy prayed? I've only seen it in…" I trailed off.

"I saw it all," she calmly explained and smiled. "A lot has happened over the last few days." Then, using the same words my Grammy had spoken to me years earlier, and in a strangely authoritative manner, Deidra said, "When Daddy leaves for work, I think you and I should have a talk."

Made in the USA
Monee, IL
07 April 2024

56050868R00146